SHADOWBOXER
TRICIA SULLIVAN

First published 2014 by Ravenstone
an imprint of Rebellion Publishing Ltd,
Riverside House, Osney Mead,
Oxford, OX2 0ES, UK

www.ravenstone.com

ISBN: 978 1 78108 282 9

10 9 8 7 6 5 4 3 2 1

A CIP catalogue record for this book is available from the British Library.

Designed & typeset by Rebellion Publishing
Cover art by Eric Mohr

Printed in the US

In memory of my father
Denis J. Sullivan
who was in my corner from Day One
and who will always be in my heart

Tornado Weather

SOME DAYS I can feel the tornado weather in my bones before I even get out of bed. I just know I'm going to have a fight. It's out of my control.

The first time I remember it happening was in seventh grade. I woke up with my angry bones on, and when Angel O'Donnell told me that my psycho dad was watching our school playground from a parked car my ears filled with a roaring. My dad wasn't supposed to know where me and my mom were. We were supposed to be safe.

I just stood there, my mind playing out the last time I saw my dad, down on the floor beside my mom, crying, 'I didn't mean it, I didn't mean it.' Me calling 911 from the bathroom, whispering into the phone.

When I found out Angel was playing with me, I rammed her head into a row of lockers. She got five stitches and I got suspended. 'Why you so scared of him?' she sobbed, bleeding all over her friends. 'You're just like him. *He* should be scared of *you*.'

I don't want to be like my dad. Believe me, I try hard not to be like him. But some days when I get this weather inside me it seems no matter how I want to be good, sooner or later I'm going to let off on somebody.

This morning I was hung over from the beer and a half Malu had pushed on me for medicinal purposes (she said) after I'd messed up last night's qualifier match. I'd been crying most of the night, and I had a black eye. My reflection in the bathroom mirror looked like a koala minus the cute. I grabbed Malu's biggest, darkest pair of sunglasses, threw my gym bag over my shoulder, and went out.

It was pouring rain. The glasses fogged up and blurred with beaded water. A passing dude said, 'Nice shades,' and checked me out. I clamped down on myself. Not today. Besides, he had a point. I looked like an idiot.

Tommy Zhang, on the other hand, can make shades work even in the rain. That's because he's a movie star.

Tommy was getting out of his limo when I crossed the street from the bus stop to Mr. Big's Combat Sports Emporium. There were actually two limos parked in the disabled spaces plus a black van for the camera crew. Tommy Zhang was so beautiful, I could see his cheekbones from here. He was wearing his trademark dark suit and he had a whole bunch of WWE-style bodyguards. Posterboys for nandralone.

I'd forgotten Tommy would be here today. There would be pictures, and I'd have to hide in the locker room if I didn't want to be in them. I thought about turning around and going home, but I don't do running away.

I shifted my bag on my shoulder and limped towards the gym door. I put on the limp for show. It was a trick my dad taught me. 'You carry yourself like you no big deal,' he'd say. 'Let people underestimate you. Then, when they don't expect it—bang!' And he'd mime an uppercut.

It's pretty hard not to underestimate somebody my size, since I'm outweighed by your average Twinkie-eating grade-schooler, but I walk like I'm hurting anyway. Whatever else I might think about my dad, I respect what he knows about the street.

Today I was limping a little extra because I had a mango-sized lump on the lower part of my right shin where it had connected to Kristi Lombardi's skull in last night's qualifier fight for *Battle of the Bitches 3*. The kick had knocked Kristi out, and everything would have been sweet and fine, except for my 'problem'. After I kicked her in the head I followed her where she fell and stomped her with the same foot, just to be safe.

The judges didn't like that. I was out.

It was my own fault, which pretty much just made it worse. Now all I wanted was to get in the gym, sweat, and refocus. I didn't want to think about how *Battle* would be getting international coverage, or the big fight at the end of it, or the prize money, or other fighters sailing through the qualifying rounds because they had a grip on the concept of rules.

I didn't want to think what my mom would say when she found out I'd stomped a girl's head into the mat.

I just wanted to train.

But of course on the days you really want people to leave you alone, they get all up in your face. Tommy Zhang's bodyguards stood in front of the entrance to the gym and when I got closer, one of them blocked me off.

'Excuse me,' I said, head down, addressing the guy's belt buckle. 'I train here.'

'ID?' I could feel the bass of his voice in the bottom of my spine. He held out a hand. His fingers were about the size of my wrist.

I snorted. 'Do I look like I'm here to drink?'

'What? You got ID or not?'

I guess you don't need a sense of humor to make it in the bodyguard profession. I sighed. Just inside the glass door, Tommy Zhang was on the phone speaking Cantonese. His voice was soft, and he was talking so fast I wondered whether they had to slow down his dialog scenes. I already knew they speeded up his fight sequences.

'No, I don't got no ID. I'm Jade Barrera. I train here. Who the fuck are you?'

'Hey. Watch the language. You can't come in without ID. I have to shield my client from unwanteds.'

Tommy was laughing. He kept sniffing and throwing his head back. Must have been doing coke in the limo.

I said, 'Did I miss something? Last I heard, this was Mr. B's fight club, not Tommy Zhang's beauty salon.'

The guard showed a white half-smile.

'With that attitude, the only place you'll be getting into this morning is a police cell,' he said. 'You don't want me to be calling to complain about harassment, do you?'

I swallowed a laugh. I was already in Mr B's doghouse because of the disqualification. Through the dull beating noise in my head I reminded myself that I needed to not screw up again. No wise-ass comments allowed.

'Sorry, man,' I said, with an effort. 'No offense. I'm just a little surprised. I train here every day. We get champions from Thailand and Russia and Brazil, but I never needed no ID to get in. I know Mr. Zhang is a real important star, but couldn't you just ask Mr B? He knows me.'

There. How much nicer could you get?

The perfect teeth reappeared. 'I would've been glad to do that if you made a respectful request in the first place. Now I need you to wait while Chip checks the contents of your bag.'

A giant stepped forward. He had blond hair in two braids like a frigging Viking.

'Oh, give me a break,' I said. Just then Khari's Corvette pulled up and parked. Khari got out first, then Eva. Her red hair was all done out in perfect ringlets and she had five-inch platforms on. Khari had to wait for her to get out the car, then wait again while she adjusted her hot pants and checked her hair. They came up to the door together, ring girl and MMA god. He put a possessive hand on her little bitty waist as they approached the Testosterone Wall.

Khari they recognized with a 'How you doing, sir,' but Eva fumbled for her green card or whatever. A faintly panicked look came over her face; maybe she wasn't legal, after all.

Nandralone Man waved them through and Eva rushed inside nervously. Khari hung back.

'Hey, Jade, everything OK?'

'Man, I don't got no driver's license and Bruce Lee's bodyguards have taken over the joint.'

My heart was racing now. Khari always makes me act all stupid.

'I'll tell the boss,' Khari said over his shoulder as he went in. 'Don't sweat it, baby.'

He called me baby.

Tommy Zhang lowered the phone from his ear. 'Let her through,' he snapped, waving a bossy hand to reinforce his words. 'I know who she is.'

That would have been all right, but then he added something else in Chinese. I couldn't understand all of it, but a few words were familiar and not in a good way. I'd heard Hong Kong girls use them in school. I wasn't sure of the exact translation, but I knew I was being called some kind of ugly.

Chip the Viking moved aside and I walked in. Tommy Zhang was even better-looking in person than he was on camera. What else can I say about him? He's supposed to be the next Bruce Lee but he's about as dangerous as Steven Seagal—by which I mean, a twelve-year-old could probably take care of the both of them put together. He's acrobatic and moves like a dancer, and when he looked my way he was so beautiful that a part of me wanted to go, *That's OK, be as rude as you want, let me kiss your perfect ass,* but the minute you start doing shit like that it's all over. You can never get your credibility back.

'How ya doin',' I said to Tommy, smiling sweetly as I moved past him. 'You were real good in *Cloud Master*.' I didn't glance at him to get his reaction, but I knew it wouldn't be good. *Cloud Master* had starred Tommy Zhang's big Hong Kong cinema rival, Lo Kuk Leung.

I limped into the gym, smiling.

The front end of Combat Sports Emporium looks like one of those fancy West Coast operations where they shot the first two *Battle of the Bitches* shows. It has a shiny new reception area decked out with trophies and a smoothie machine. On the training floor there are new weights and cardio equipment, a big mirror and clean mats. Monika and Eva were standing nervously in reception, waiting to have their Tommy Zhang DVDs autographed. On the main floor, a boxercise class made idiots of themselves to the sound of Jay-Z. Eva's perfect butt jagged to the beat.

I wondered if a ring girl had ever gotten knocked out in the line of duty. Like, what if somebody accidentally-on-purpose dropped her with a left hook? Hmm. There was a thought.

I probably needed to hit something.

Keeping my sunglasses on, I headed straight to the back room. It was always kind of dark and smelled of old sweat and leather. This was where the pros trained. We had an ancient ring and an alley of heavy bags that had been pounded so hard you couldn't see the logos anymore. There was an open matted area for pad work and ground fighting. The boxercise music was muffled. I could hear the whipping sound of Cake jumping rope like a grasshopper on meth.

Khari was standing outside the locker room with Jamie Bell, a journalist from *The Cage* who was always hanging around. They were watching Cake train for his K-1 match in Holland next month. The look on Khari's face said, *Hell, I'm glad I'm not in the same weight class as him.*

Khari took in the state of me, whistled softly, and shrugged.

'You better keep those shades on, Jay-D,' Khari said, following me toward the locker rooms. 'Jamie just told me there's gonna be three camera crews coming later on.'

He shook his head like it was all just too decadent for him. In many ways Khari is an old-fashioned kind of guy. He can't understand why reality shows like *Battle of the Bitches* get so much attention these days. He can't understand why people like to see girls hitting each other, especially when some of the girls aren't very good fighters.

I guess that's why he dates a ring girl. She doesn't challenge his assumptions.

'You can have my photographers if I can have your paycheck,' I said.

'You're OK. You're the real deal,' Khari said.

'I screwed up bad last night,' I said.

'Hey,' Khari said, 'At least you were the one who done the stomping. At least it wasn't your head on the mat. Now get to work.'

Here's the truth. I'm happy in the gym. When I'm slippery as an eel with sweat, and my heart's going *boom-boom-power* in my ears. When Cake is my pad man, chasing me around the ring and I got incoming blows to deal with and I'm struggling to counter-time him and he's laughing at me, but I keep going anyway like my life depends on it. That's when I'm happy. Something wakes up inside me, opens its eyes, takes a deep breath. Something says *yes. Give me some more.*

It was a good workout. I only puked once. I even got it in the bucket. Khari offered me a towel to wipe my face, which was sweet, but then Eva came over to keep her claws in her man. I reeked of puke and she reeked of Estée Lauder. Who you think Khari be picking?

When I look back on it, I know this right here is the critical moment.

It's like, every so often, on a given day, you do something really small. Don't mean nothing—or so you think at the time. But later on when you think about it, this tiny decision leads to everything changing. If only you'd known about this one little thing, maybe you would have done things differently.

And maybe you wouldn't.

So, I could have held my ground and showed my confidence to Khari. Let him know I wasn't just a kid, but a woman to be reckoned with, you know what I'm saying? But I didn't. I let Eva spook me. I backed away from the two of them, went outside for some fresh air.

Bang. That was it, right there. Going outside just then was my Gwyneth Paltrow *Sliding Doors* moment—or it would have been if I'd been a white girl looking for the perfect man instead of a Latina looking for the perfect takedown defense.

It was still raining. I put a stick of gum in my mouth to kill the taste of vomit and looked around. Tommy Zhang's limo was pulled up around the side of the gym. The engine was running but I couldn't see anybody inside except the driver, who was reading a magazine. I went and stood under the awning behind Mattress World next door.

Quinton the tomcat was already sitting there, his paws folded under him, blinking as he watched the rain. Quinton has scars all over his big-jowled head, and one of his eyes only opens halfway. He's skinny and he limps, but he's my furry *bambino*. He gave me a hoarse chirp and rose to meet my hand when I bent to stroke the back of his head. There were always scabs under his fur.

I started to feel better. Animals are like that. They make you feel better without even trying. I wished I could adopt Quinton, but my mom's lease had a no-pets clause and Malu already snuck in an iguana. Anyway, it wouldn't be fair to take him away from his natural environment.

Purring, he turned his head so I could scratch him under his jowls. The rain came down harder. Tommy's driver shot out of the limo and ran around the back. He spread a huge umbrella, then opened a door. Tommy Zhang got out, talking on his iPhone, this time in fluent Thai. They walked towards me, the driver holding the umbrella over the star while he himself got wet.

'Mr. Zhang needs a place to smoke a cigarette,' the driver said, nodding at the awning. Apparently this meant I was supposed to leave. I was curious, though. I knew a little Thai because of Cake and Mr. B, and through watching endless fights on YouTube. I always hoped I could get over there to train someday. But Tommy was Chinese. Where had he learned Thai? I caught the phrases 'foreign journalist' and—he said this twice—'no violence.' Tommy sounded upset. Maybe somebody in Thailand had written a stitch-up of Tommy.

'Get rid of that dirty animal,' Tommy snapped in English. I stopped in the doorway and leaned back outside. The driver was making shooing motions at Quinton. Poor Quinton scurried a few feet on his belly, then stopped, ears flattening, and held his ground. He looked scared, but he wasn't running yet.

'Hey, take it easy,' I said, going out. 'That's only Quinton. He's the gym cat. See, he has a gold ring around his neck, like Quinton "Rampage" Jackson, get it?'

Tommy Zhang didn't laugh. He didn't look at me. He bent, picked up a beer bottle, and threw it at Quinton. The bottle shattered, Quinton ran, and I was pretty sure some of the pieces had hit him.

'Hey!' I shouted, positioning myself between Tommy Zhang and Quinton, who now shot off behind the cover of a dumpster. 'What's your problem? He wasn't doing anything to you.'

'You better go inside,' Tommy Zhang's driver said. He wasn't as big as the bodyguards—they were still in the gym, I guess—but he was a lot bigger than me. 'Mr. Zhang doesn't want to be disturbed.'

'Mr. Zhang already is disturbed if he abuses animals.' I feinted moving left and then shot to the right, around the driver. He tried to grab me but he was slow and let's face it, I'm really fast. I've had a lot of practice at avoiding being grabbed. I saw the door of the gym open, but it was only Eva sticking her head out to get a better phone signal.

I went up to Tommy Zhang and said, 'What kind of man are you? Don't you have enough money or you got to pick on some poor animal to make you feel all hard?'

'Get this trash away from me,' Tommy Zhang said to his driver, stepping back as if I had a disease. He held his lit cigarette poised like he was thinking about shoving it in my face.

'No,' I said. '*You* get away from *me*, bitch.'

Or something like that. The truth is, I never exactly remember what I say or do when a fight kicks off. I can only approximate. Like, for example, I can't remember exactly what he said to me next, or whether he made the first move, or whether the driver did. I don't know. I do know that one minute the hottest martial arts action star in Hollywood was acting like a cat-hating jerk-off and the next his nose was all splattered across his face and he was doubled over against the back door of Mattress World. Judging by the blood on my knee, I'm guessing I maybe left-hooked him first, because nobody ever sees my left hook coming. I must've grabbed his head and pulled it down and banged him in the face with my knee maybe two, three, eighteen times? The main thing is, his nose was good and broken and then he was one *stunned* cat-hating movie star.

I felt good.

All of a sudden there were bodyguards trying to grab me and people were yelling—Eva was videoing us with her phone—and I had to run before somebody creamed me.

I ran right into Khari's arms.

'Whoa, whoa, whoa,' he said. 'This is not good.'

There you go. Khari's always real astute at pointing out the obvious.

I Let My Ass Do the Talking

SO ME AND Eva got hustled into Mr. B's office behind the door with the white sparkly star and the name Bernard Jumsai stencilled under it. No biggie for me. I was used to being chewed out, detained, made to stand in line-ups. For Eva, though? Girl started to sweat and fan herself. She was worried.

'It's so stuffy in here,' she said, edging away from me. There wasn't much room in Mr. Big's office. Most of it was taken up by the desk, a cheap metal thing piled with papers and coffee cups and somewhere under it all, a keyboard and mouse. Mr. Big had a screen that showed him the CCTV views of the gym, and of course there was his special two-way mirror. He watched us train while he was wheeling and dealing on Skype, talking with promoters all over the world for hours at a time. The office had a back entrance, too, so you were never really sure whether he was in or out—or who was with him. Mr. Big liked to keep everybody guessing.

Behind the desk was Mr. B's shrine. In contrast to the rest of the office, the shrine was immaculate. Today there were fresh flowers and a pile of peanut M&Ms. A pair of Rangers tickets. I could never be sure whether Mr. B took his Buddhism as seriously as he seemed to, or whether he was just one of those people who want to cover all the bases. Either way, he never failed with the offerings.

There were dusty marks on the walls where pictures of Linda and the kids used to be. She'd left him two months ago for a carpet-cleaning franchise owner from Pearl River. Mr. B was upset. When I'm upset, I pound the bag until I can't move, then eat a whole carton of cookie dough ice cream, and then get over it. But Mr. B, he bought himself a consolation Humvee.

Seemed like we were waiting forever. I went behind the desk and pulled up one of the CCTV screens. The media people were standing out front, talking on their phones.

'Jade, what are you doing?' Eva hissed.

I turned up the sound on camera one.

'Yeah, his face was a mess. Looks like Khari Nkondo clocked him. Might have been a fight over this ring girl... what's her name? Eva Skye?'

Eva gasped when she heard this.

'Armando? Get me whatever you got on Khari Nkondo. Not just his fights, I want to know if he has a criminal record, any drug history, past issues of violence involving women... you name it.' The guy hung up and gestured to his cameraman to follow him inside.

Another reporter, standing close to the microphone pickup, whispered, *'Skye's real name is Kowalski. Leonard, check her out under that name.'*

I grinned at Eva, who turned pink.

'Kowalski?' My voice cracked with laughter. 'Why'd you change it? It's so much more romantic than Skye.'

She looked away. Her foot started tapping.

'I can go over to Mattress World and interview the staff. Somebody might have gone outside for a smoke and witnessed it. And I'll try to get the CCTV.'

Mr. B's voice cut through them all. He appeared in shot, making grand gestures with his arms.

'Thank you all for coming, we are so honored to have you all here today. As you may have heard, Mr. Zhang had to leave on an urgent matter. You can call his press officer. Meanwhile, I have to ask you all to go home. Mr. Zhang's people will be clearing the building.'

Chip the Viking started herding everybody, grabbing cameras and phones as he went. *'Right, everybody, let's all be cool. Nothing to see here, nothing to see. Sorry, was that your camera? Here you go.'*

'Where's my memory card?'

'I don't know where the memory card is, man, you must not have loaded one before you came.'

'Hey! Hey, that guy stole my pictures!'

'I'm not a thief,' said Chip in a rehearsed voice. 'I'm a security consultant. Do you wish to consult with me?'

'You'll hear from our legal department,' said the smaller man, backing away in a hurry. 'It's already all over Twitter, anyway. Ha!'

Me and Eva looked at each other. She was excited.

'You think they want to interview me?' she said. 'They think I'm playing Khari and Tommy Zhang at the same time. Wow. I could get in *People* for that.'

'Not so great for Khari,' I said. 'They all think he beat up Tommy Zhang, and he didn't.'

'I know.' She fixed me with pale green eyes. 'You did. What is wrong with you? Why you act like such a freak? Khari says you had some kind of bad childhood. Get over it.'

I felt my nostrils widen. I was about to unleash when Mr. B swaggered in.

'Girls, girls,' he said. 'This place is like Ringling Brothers circus.'

He reached out and patted Eva on the shoulder.

'You don't talk to nobody,' he said. 'Understand? Not one word.'

Her face fell.

'But Mr. B, they all want to interview me—'

Mr. B let out a grunt and held up one commanding finger. Eva seemed to shrink before his daddy act.

'Not. One. Word. One phone call from me and you never work again in this business.'

'But I didn't do nothing!' Eva protested.

'You keep your mouth shut. Simple. You come out ahead. They offer you work, fine. They interview you for *Cage*? Fine. OK. But you say nothing about today. Nothing. Get it?'

'I get it.' Eva looked at me pointedly.

'You can go, Eva. And tell Monika. No talking. To nobody.'

Looking grouchy, Eva started to go out. In the doorway she paused. Looking at me as she addressed Mr. B, she said, 'Why you give this girl so many chances? She is not so special. And by the way, Jade, I am not ashamed of my name or my homeland.'

She shut the door. Mr. B turned to me. I gave him my detention-center stare. He shook his head, sighing.

'Don't you get it, Jade? You know I want to change image of fighters as thugs. I'm trying to go upmarket so I invite a high class, A-list celebrity to our gym to raise our profile on *Battle of the Bitches*, and—hello, anybody home?—this what pays rent for nobodies like you. And what you do? You embarrass me.'

'But...'

'But what? But he's a jerk? But he's fake? You think this is some kind of excuse?'

No, actually my excuse is he's a... what's the scientific term for cat-hater? Like *homophobe*, but for cats. There has to be a word. I'll ask Malu later.

I said nothing. It had been a rhetorical question, anyway, because Mr. B plowed on.

'I know Tommy Zhang is all image. I know he can't fight. You know it. Deep down, he knows it. But we all got to keep up his front. He's a movie star. Tommy's career depends on image. Don't you get that?'

Still I said nothing. What could I say?

'You change your attitude or pick a different business. This ain't no sport, not no more. We are in show business. That means putting on a show. Tommy Zhang is huge. He's starting up a new fight circuit give those criminals in Las Vegas a run for their money. It's going to be big, and it's going be clean.'

He was referring to the underworld connections of Cage Federation, the biggest fight organization in the country. Some people said the whole business was corrupt and based on backdoor dealing. Of course some people would say that about boxing, too. I didn't care. I just wanted a little piece of it, a chance to do something with my life.

'Come on, Mr. B,' I said. 'You're not telling me Tommy Zhang is putting up his own money? Who's backing him, and how clean are they? He didn't sound happy on the phone to Thailand just now.'

Mr. B waved that away. 'Zhang got all kind of big money contacts. And he got better TV promotion. But thanks to you I got to go kiss his ass, make a fool of myself, and pray what really happened don't get out. Or we got headlines saying: "Tommy Zhang beat up by girl."'

Well, I thought. *If the pants fit...*

'Everybody on our side been sworn to secrecy, but you never know what little rat might decide to cash in. Now Tommy's gotta reschedule his photo shoot.'

I had to work so hard not to laugh. Mr. B saw my face and got really mad. 'He can't take pictures with a damn black eye, Jade. You're costing me all kinds of money with your fucking childish temper!'

I winced when he dropped the f-bomb. One thing about Mr. Big is that he almost never swears. I better watch out.

I looked down at the cigarette burn in Mr. B's carpet. If I thought about anything else, I might crack and start to cry, and no way was that going to happen. No way.

'I am so close to giving up on you. Anybody else, they'd be gone already, and I would tell Tommy he can press charges.'

I said nothing. Mr. B's tone changed. 'You know you are like my daughter.' I felt my cheeks getting hot. 'Your mom and Linda are best friends. Your mom came to me when you got in trouble with the police. I took you on. I talked to your school to take you back, I helped you get that job you need. Me and Linda got our differences, but we promised your mother we would look out for you when she went to the Dominican Republic. Your mom didn't want to leave you here. She let you stay because of *me*.'

'And because Malu moved in to my house,' I added. 'You kept me so I could train.'

'Exactly. You're talented, only a year away from turning pro. But you're not eighteen yet. You got to listen to us, Jade. Me, your mom, your cousin Malu, all of us are your family. If you don't listen we can't help you.'

He was expecting me to look at him or say something. I was still concentrating on the cigarette burn.

'Jade?'

'I'm sorry,' I whispered, finally, without looking at him. 'I'm really sorry. I didn't think.'

I felt my throat tighten as I let myself think about what this gym meant to me. My future here, all my hard work, my dreams of a pro title... I blinked back tears, refocusing on the carpet. Nothing can get through to you if you focus your attention on something very specific and refuse to let go. Nothing.

'You ruined the deal,' Mr. B. said. 'Tommy Zhang won't do business now. If I keep you, he'll find a way to hurt me. If I get rid of you and somebody offers you money to talk, and then the whole thing comes out.'

'I wouldn't! I wouldn't talk, I swear—'

'You're just a kid. You don't know this business. *Cage* will find out. Somebody will find out. I got Khari wiping out all the memory cards. But Tommy Zhang hates us now.'

'He might change his mind,' I said. 'He must be worried, what if somebody finds out he got beat up so easy? If he stops doing business with you, he has to tell people why. There's the show. His lawyers will want to know. What's he gonna say? There must be a way to make it right. What can I do? Can I apologize? Send flowers? Should I grovel? What can I do, Mr. B?'

Mr B snorted. 'What can you do? I don't know. Leave the country?'

He threw up his hands dramatically and spun around to turn his back on me. His elbow bumped into the gecko statue he kept on his shrine. I saw it start to fall. Before I even knew what I was doing, I'd lunged across the room and caught it.

He turned around and looked at me, astonished. Hell, I'm fast. I'm not bragging, but I got the reflexes of a fighter pilot.

I held the statue out to him.

'OK,' I said, giving him my biggest, cutest smile.

He didn't take the statue. He just looked at it, then at me. His face crunched up like he thought I was playing some trick on him.

'What you mean, OK?'

Good question. What did I mean? Think fast, Barrera.

'Um... don't you want your lucky gecko back?'

He took the gecko and nervously replaced it on the shelf. He made sure it lined up just right next to the incense holder. Then an idea flashed across my mind.

'OK, I'll leave the country,' I said. Actually, it wasn't even like I said it. I was totally talking out of my ass. Yeah, my ass must have said it. And the words came spilling out so easy they almost sounded plausible. 'How long should I go for? Two weeks? Three weeks? Until it blows over and the shows are under way and everybody's focusing on something else?'

Mr. Big rolled his eyes. He didn't believe I was serious.

'A month? My last exam is on Thursday. After that I could go stay with my Nana in the Dominican Republic, but you know she's sick. And I wouldn't be able to train there.'

When I said it I realized how much I was missing my mom. And how sad I was that Nana was dying and I'd never see her again unless I went out there...

Mr. B shook his head. He looked at the gecko. I knew I had him now. I saved his gecko. Or did he have another motive?

'Thailand,' he said suddenly, narrowing his eyes. 'You go anywhere, you go there. No age restrictions. You can fight pro there. Then we find out how tough you really are.'

This wasn't what I had in mind, but I nodded, still letting my ass do the talking. 'I'll ask my mom. Only thing is, I don't have airfare.'

'I buy the ticket. You go in my cousin's camp. You train. That's it. No beach, no party. You train. And you fight.'

'Got it, boss,' my ass said. 'When?'

He shook his head. Went to his laptop and started looking up flights. Was he serious?

'You got a passport?'

'I think I know where it is...'

'Your exam is Thursday? You leave Thursday night,' he said. 'Cheap ticket on standby. Until then I don't want to see you. Give me your phone.'

'My *phone?*'

'You don't talk to media, you don't talk to nobody.'

'Not even my mom?'

'Leave her to me.'

I thought for a second. If he didn't tell my mom what I'd done, he was saving my life. Because she would flip out in an epic way. But me going to Thailand, *alone?* There was no way she was saying yes to that. She still holds my hand crossing the street to ShopRite.

'You don't need this in Bangkok. What you gonna do, play games on there? Twitter? No. This is serious. No distractions.'

'Mr. B, please, not the phone...' But I said it weakly.

'You put up your hood and go out the back door. You don't say goodbye to nobody. You go to school, take your test, act normal until Thursday. I set it up with Coat.'

'Coat?'

'My cousin. He coaches, like me. Small gym, some good fighters. He's Cake's trainer, you know?'

'Isn't he the guy who doesn't want Americans in his gym?'

'That's him.' He handed me a printout. 'Your flight. Go home. Call me later.'

He reached in his desk and pulled out some Tiger Balm, spreading it on his forehead and closing his eyes.

'Thanks, Mr. B. I promise I won't let you down this time.'

He kept his eyes closed. 'I got a feeling you will, and I'm making a big mistake, but I got a soft spot for you, Jade. Now leave me. I got lot of brown-nosing to do and I hate that.'

I was leaking tears when I closed the door behind me. It always makes me feel worse when people are forgiving, and I guess Mr. B knew that. If somebody had belted me in the head, I would have been able to deal with it. The 'straighten up your act and by the way here's a cookie' approach totally threw me.

I took a deep breath and filled my mind with images of the good Jade I would become. The dedicated, sportsmanlike Jade. The non-vengeful, smiling, tolerant Jade. Helping old ladies cross the street. Turning the other cheek. Getting splashed on by buses and not swearing and kicking the bus. The New Jade. She would be me. Starting right now.

Khari intercepted me just outside the locker room. He grabbed my arm and pulled me against him, held me steady. Ooh, is he nice? In the next couple of seconds I flashed a mini-movie starring me and him on the mat. We're working on grappling, but then it all turns horny. Images of Eva walking in on us, turning even paler than she already is, and Khari saying, 'Sorry, Eva, but Jade's all the woman I need.' Images of Eva then shooting herself in the head with a pair of sixguns and in a final, glorious picture, me and Khari are lying on the mat, arms and legs all mixed up, drinking Gatorade while Eva's blood pools under the weight rack.

So much for the good Jade.

Unfortunately, Khari wasn't cooperating with my fantasy because when he leaned down to murmur in my ear, instead of offering to work naked submissions with me, he just said,

'Whatever else happens, I just wanted to tell you that was a sweet left hook, you know what I'm saying? Sweet. I'm gonna remember that one, girl.' Then he let me go, put his finger to his lips, and walked away slow—OMG what an ass!

'Thanks,' I whispered, forgetting all about the New Jade.

Damn.

The Forest

'FASTER, MYA,' MR Richard gasped. 'I can't stay here long.'

Mya's muscles burned with the effort of dragging the injured man. Beside her, Mr. Richard did nothing to help. The altitude had set him gasping for breath from the moment Mya's meditation had brought them to the forest. In the outer world it was rainy season, but everything was different here. Sometimes when Mya came to the immortal forest she found lush mangroves, sometimes bamboo jungle. Today it was cold and the air was thin. Trees spiked the blue sky, ending in the snowfields of the Himalayas. There were fir needles under her slippered feet.

The young man's skin was fever-hot in the cold air. His face was bloody, clothes slathered in mud. Johnny and the boys had already beaten him into a stupor, and then Mr. Richard had injected the night orchid extract into his neck. The night orchid grew in the immortal forest, and Mr. Richard used small amounts of it himself to cross the border between worlds. A big enough dose would send a person into the forest even without a guide— but it was a poison. Without the antidote they could not return to the living world.

When the needle went in, Mya had expected the young man to disappear. But he didn't.

Something in the young reporter had resisted.

That was why Mya had to bring him here herself. Now she tugged on his filthy arms. He was skinny but tall, a dead weight. His head lolled back, long hair falling away from his handsome face. There was foam in the corners of his mouth and his eyes were half-open, unfocused.

He needs a doctor, she thought.

But he was dangerous. Johnny had said so when he brought the unconscious man to Mr. Richard's house. Mya had been cleaning the tiny room that passed for a lab when Johnny carried the man and dumped him on the covered porch.

'We caught him spying, sir,' Johnny had told Mr. Richard in English. 'Sending pictures of the house back to a paper in London. He was Marco's translator but he didn't give up when we took care of Marco.'

Then he had handed Mr. Richard a silver phone, saying, 'It's password-protected.'

'You disappoint me,' Mr Richard had said. 'If you knew there was a translator why didn't you remove him?'

Mr Richard's voice was soft and sweet. He trembled when he moved, and his body was weak. He had a long, sticklike nose and crooked yellow teeth. He had brown spots all over his pink skin and a few strands of white hair on his head. The old Englishman didn't look as though he could harm an insect, let alone an overfed American ex-soldier like Johnny. But Johnny was as afraid of Mr. Richard as the servants were.

'We have been looking for him, sir,' Johnny had assured Mr. Richard, pacing up and down the covered porch of the stilt house and glancing out into the trees in the twitchy, slightly-paranoid way he had. 'You want him to disappear? There's always the river.'

'No. Bodies have a way of washing up. He must go where Marco and the others went. There must be no evidence left behind.'

Mya scrubbed a beaker with assiduous attention. After only two years in Thailand, she understood both Thai and English but spoke both languages only haltingly. She didn't let Mr. Richard know how much she understood because English was the language he used for speaking his secrets.

She had learned her first words of Thai from Som, the monk who had come to the prison camp and offered to sneak Mya and some other children across the river to Thailand—for a better life, Som said. Som had told Mya's parents she would be safe in Thailand, for there was a kind Englishman who ran an orphanage there, a good Buddhist. Mr. Richard wouldn't mind if Mya 'travelled' in meditation. He would see that she was cared for until the violence in Myanmar was over.

Mya could still see the look on her mother's face. 'Work hard and pray we will see each other again, but don't disappear,' her mother had said. 'You know what I mean. Don't go to your forest. It's dangerous.'

Forbidding Mya to go to the forest was like forbidding a fish to swim. The forest called her. Her mind would merge with the trees and plants that were nearby, and then she would simply slip over the edge of *this* world and into *that* one—she'd wander for hours among immortal animals and unreal flowers beneath great, brooding trees. 'I don't know what's worse,' her mother would say, exasperated. 'The way you disappear when you are supposed to be watching Thiri, or the fact that you see ghosts and they don't frighten you.'

No wonder Mya had been the daughter that was sent away. But Som had not taken her to the orphanage with the others; instead, Mr. Richard had welcomed her into his own home. He had encouraged her to disappear. He needed her to harvest the medicines of the otherworld that she could enter so easily. He needed her to guide him when he took the night flower extract himself, so that he could visit the forest and return home safely with the help of the antidote. And sometimes she came on her own, to deliver packages to other children who had been sent into the forest from their masters in other parts of the world. She was a part of something; she'd known that for a long time. Until now she had believed she was part of something good.

But now she was helping Mr. Richard abandon this young man who was not yet dead, who had no means to escape the immortal forest on his own.

Mya's throat was tight. She couldn't believe any of this was happening. The young man was only a translator for Marco; half-Thai, half-British, according to Johnny, and probably innocent of whatever wrong his boss had done. If they left him here alone, he would die.

The forest was moving around her. There were immortal beings here instead of earthly animals. Things with big eyes, iridescent scales, flashing claws. Creatures that dissolved as smoke, then reappeared somewhere else, as bright and unreal as reflections on still water.

Mya could go no farther. She stopped dragging the man, as if to catch her breath. Mr. Richard caught her up.

'We have had a narrow escape,' he said. 'Why do you look at me like that?'

Mya said nothing.

'This fool would have destroyed me and turned you over to the Burmese army. The orphanage would have been closed down, and then what would happen to all the refugee children I care for? Mya, the small-minded are always a danger to people like us. After this man's soul has grown and learned, he will return to the world to try again in another life. Do you understand?'

Mya nodded, even though she didn't understand why someone who wasn't dead in the first place had to reincarnate. She offered a silent prayer for the man's protection. When Mr. Richard led her away, she tried hard not to look back, but she couldn't help taking one little glance over her shoulder.

In the darkness between trees, she saw golden eyes and a black mane. The lion's gaze followed Mya.

Mr. Richard was not well. He appeared insubstantial, even as the apparitions in the trees were becoming more solid all the time. A group of deer were soundlessly keeping pace with the humans. Their coin-colored eyes flashed, and one of them assumed the form of a young woman just for a moment. She smiled at Mya.

Embarrassed, Mya looked away. Mr. Richard staggered a little.

'I must return,' he said. 'The night orchid hurts me.'

He sank to his knees. His eyes closed. He wrapped his arms around his gut, clutching the pain from the plant extract he had injected in himself to come here. Tears streamed down his face.

Mya felt suddenly alone. She had lived her first ten years in a forest village and she was at ease with the smells and subtle sounds of the earthly jungle, but this forest was not the same. It was a place of many moods, and she would never understand it no matter how many times she came here. Now the trees seemed to crowd around her. They were huge and green with moss. Their leaves hissed and muttered. The deer girls had gone, but Mya knew there were other creatures living here, beings from stories and songs. You never knew what was waiting for you in the shifting green shadows.

Like that face. She could just make it out. A child's face, hovering in the air above the suggestion of hands and a body. A boy, not much older than Mya.

A ghost.

The ghost looked at Mya and before she could look away, he had appeared right beside her. Quick as a thought. He was vividly present, complete with the smell of rotting flowers.

'Do you know what he is praying for?' said the boy. Mya shrank away, shaking her head *no*. 'Protection from ghosts. He has murdered so many, you see. Even a monk.'

Mya reeled. 'That can't be. No one would hurt a monk.'

'I was like you once,' the ghost said. 'You think if you do everything right it will get better. It won't. You will never be free.'

Mya shrank away, quivering. The ghost's ill-will flooded over her like cold water.

Mr. Richard got to his feet. The boy had gone without a sound. Mr Richard reached over and gripped Mya's hand.

'Let's go,' he said in Thai, reaching into his pocket for the envelope containing the antidote he needed to return home. His movements became quicker and more frantic as he didn't find it.

Without the antidote, the night orchid that had brought him here would damage him—even kill him, as he was trying to kill the young stranger.

'Mya, where's the envelope?'

Mya stared blankly. He always carried some of the antidote with him. It was a blue powder made from the venom of a naga. Mr. Richard had all sorts of pills and ampules and atomisers in his many pockets. He was a chemist, after all.

His face was strained.

'Help me look,' he said. 'Must have dropped it. Retrace our steps...'

They began to search the forest floor, but Mya wasn't even sure which way they had come. She couldn't see any marks made by the young man's body where it had been dragged. Mr. Richard moaned and clutched himself and began to froth.

'I can't see,' he said. 'I'm going blind. I mustn't die here. I am so close to immortality...'

He fell down. She stopped and went to him. She'd never seen him like this. He must have taken too much of the night orchid.

'What do I do, Mr. Richard?' she said, kneeling on fir needles. The boy's ghost formed over Mr. Richard's head and she shuddered.

'Leave him here,' snapped the ghost. 'It's what he'll do to you one day, if he doesn't sell you.'

Mr. Richard didn't seem to hear. He let out another groan.

'Do what we always do,' he managed to say. 'Make the passage back to my house. Help me through... I need the antidote.' He coughed.

'Leave him here,' said the ghost urgently. 'Don't you know he's nothing without you? He can't come here, and he can't leave. Not without you.'

Never listen to ghosts, Mya reminded herself. Anyway, she wanted to be back in the solid world, with its heat and smells and safe walls. With her heart and mind as well as her hands, she felt for the way back through the foliage. The forest began to tremble as its reality gave way.

'Don't leave me,' Mr. Richard begged.

The ghost mocked, 'Ah, now you know how it feels, yes?'

But Mr. Richard still didn't hear the ghost. He clutched at Mya, who closed her eyes and focused her mind on the place where she had come from: the covered porch of Mr. Richard's stilt house. The forest began to open. She stepped out of the forest and on to the wooden floor, leaving the angry ghost behind.

She was back in the heat of Mr. Richard's wooden house in the forest. Under the stilt house chickens were squawking, and clouds of insects moved through the dappled sunlight where the forest met the covered meditation porch. Everything in the forest might have been a vision in meditation—except for the clumps of mud that lay on the wooden floor, fallen from the journalist's boots as he had been dragged out of the world.

She saw the envelope with a little of the blue powder spilling out; it must have slipped from Mr. Richard's pocket. Mya snatched it up and turned back to the immortal world, still hovering in the air. The pathway lay up high, among the branches of the earthly forest, so that she seemed to be floating off the porch into thin air. Again she entered the chill of the immortal world.

Mr Richard lay on the fir needles, writhing and moaning. She tipped a little of the powder onto his tongue. He stiffened, and although his eyes did not focus, he grabbed her hand and pulled it to his mouth. The powder spilled on him, on the dirt. Some made its way into him. He put his palms on the dirt and licked the spilt powder up like an animal.

Mya tugged at him and he managed to crawl after her. He crawled out of the forest and between the wooden rails of the raised porch. There he lay on his back, breathing harshly at first, then deeply. In time the twitching subsided.

Mya did not know what to do. If he woke up and found her in the wrong place, doing the wrong thing, he might forget that she had saved his life. He might forget that any of this had happened. He was like that. The medicines he took made him kind and gentle, the sort of person one would do anything for. But without the drugs he could be ugly. Everyone feared him. She had no name for what he might do, no picture in her mind. Only a falling sensation in her stomach where imagination failed her.

She sat very still until the incense burned down to ash. Then she started to creep across the floor. Every time she moved, she sneaked a glance at Mr Richard to see if he was stirring. He wasn't. The flesh of her legs stung as the blood began to return.

There was a stuffed monkey sitting on top of the apothecary chest, its glass eyes covered in dust. The monkey looked sick. Lots of its fur was missing. *Mange,* she thought. She wouldn't touch it.

Mr Richard had dropped the phone on the floor. He lay so still she wasn't even sure he was breathing. She had the urge to go over to him and poke him, but she would never dare.

Mr Richard did not move.

Then, without Mya thinking about it, her arm shot out and took the phone. She found herself slipping into the work room that smelled of herbs and incense. On the shelves above the apothecary chest were skulls of animals and jars of dark liquid. There were crocks of dried herbs, and dolls with sad faces. Blue computer light spilled over the high-tech equipment and shone on the dolls' black-feathered hair.

When she opened the phone, lights came on and a chiming noise sounded. It had a touch screen in English.

One of the house servants was coming up the stairs. Mya held the phone behind her back, heart pounding.

Daeng came in, saw Mr Richard, and gasped.

'Ploy!' she shouted down the stairs. 'Hurry, Mr. Richard needs us. Mya, why didn't you call us? What happened to him? Quickly, quickly!'

Ploy helped Daeng carry Mr. Richard to his bed, where he

remained unconscious for three days while they fussed over him and called a succession of doctors, and sent and received a flurry of jerky video calls from Mr. Richard's computer.

Mya was largely ignored. She climbed the bodhi tree outside the house and standing on a branch too narrow to support anyone but her she peered through the window. While Daeng video chatted to Mr Richard's wife in L.A., Mya sat on the branch pretending to talk to her mother on the password-protected phone.

As if Mya's mother had a phone in the military camp. As if everything were different.

Charisma in a Bottle

MR RICHARD STAYED in bed for a week. For Mya it was a holiday. No prayers. No helping in the lab with acids that burned fingers, no bitter smoke. No hours spent listening to Mr Richard's teachings while the stuffed monkey watched over them with its dusty eyes.

Mya had placed the phone by Mr. Richard's bedside and she had tried to forget what she had seen. She helped Ploy and Daeng with the housework, and for a change they treated her kindly. She was allowed to eat her meals with the women and watch TV at the same time. They gave her a beautiful red dress to wear.

This didn't make her happy. She kept remembering the ghost boy.

You will never be free.

'When will Mr Richard send me home?' Mya asked Ploy one night, when they were down in the cool room watching a particularly emotional episode of the soap opera *Nang Rai*. And Daeng, who had been blotting her eyes with a napkin already, now covered her mouth and ran outside.

'Your family have bad karma,' Ploy told Mya over the sound of the electric bug-zapper. 'You must do your work here if you want to gain merit for your family.'

'I don't understand why I can go to the forest if I have bad karma,' Mya said.

'Don't be cheeky,' Ploy said sharply. 'You are very rude. Of course some children can go in and out of this world. Some of you are only halfway on this earth. That is the danger.'

Over the popping of dying mosquitoes, Daeng could be heard making a strangled noise just outside.

'Aunt Ploy, please tell me, why is Aunt Daeng crying?'

'Aunt Daeng is not crying, mouse.'

On screen, two men were engaged in a long and tense staring contest. As this dragged on a bit, Mya whispered:

'When I am thirteen am I old enough?'

'Go to bed,' said Aunt Ploy.

On the screen a hi-so woman with bright makeup and tall, coiffed hair was now attacking the pure and kind farm-born heroine by throwing a succession of vases at her.

They feel sorry for me, she thought. *It seems they think I'm going to die.*

Mya tore herself away from the screen and went outside. Aunt Daeng was nowhere to be seen. The chickens were asleep in the open space beneath the stilt house.

High overhead, the silver slip of a jet eased across the dark sky. Mya watched it, wondering if her mother could see it.

From the big open window above she heard Mr Richard's scratchy voice on the phone. Probably to America, at this hour.

'It's too far for me to travel in my condition. Why can't you come here?'

A pause. Then:

'You ask too much. You swear to me you had nothing to do with the reporter? Because I will find out if you are lying.'

His tone was shrill. Mya wondered who he could be speaking to. He sounded childish.

'Don't pretend you ever loved me. You used me to get out of your sad life. I was younger then, and you were beautiful—but don't forget where you come from. My wife knows everyone in L.A.. She can make you or break you at a word from me, and I expect cooperation. I expect loyalty. If you disappoint me you know the consequences.'

There was a long pause. Mya could hear Mr. Richard pacing slowly up and down.

'All right, then,' he said at last. 'Where are you? Yes, in about an hour's time. Wait for me there.'

Mya heard him put the headset down. She slipped behind the bodhi tree. But he knew she was there, listening. He knew everything. He called out the window.

'Mya. I know you are awake. Come up.'

The long rest seemed to have done Mr Richard good. He was not so pale as before, and his lips were no longer purplish gray.

'You have done well,' he said. She dared to glance up at him, just a peep, and for a moment her heart seemed to spread tiny frail wings of hope. 'I am glad I chose you among all the orphans.'

But I am not an orphan, she wanted to say. *My family are prisoners of the army in my country.*

'You brought me back with no help. Your mind is strong.'

Mya kept her gaze down, nodding meekly again. She waited for him to say the words she hoped for, but he didn't. As he continued talking her heart seemed to shrink, and her hope folded its wings, confused.

'Mya. You must never travel to the forest without me. Its nature is mysterious, and there are many doors that can take you from the forest, but those doors don't all come here. They can lead to places all over the world. You would soon be lost without me. Sometimes children think they are old enough to do things on their own. Those are the children who get lost in the forest. There are many spirits. Many ghosts, and they are hungry. Do you understand?'

Mya nodded, trembling. Mr Richard was at his gentlest. He spoke slowly and clearly, as if he didn't realize how much English she understood now. He knew many hidden things, but maybe he didn't know about the many hours of YouTube she had watched while he slept.

'Do you see that tree out there?'

He pointed to the bodhi tree beside the porch. It shaded a wide area near the house, and some of its branches came right down to the ground, where they had rooted to make new trees.

'This bodhi tree was once another kind of tree. The bodhi seed germinated high up the branches of the other tree. Over time, the bodhi tree grew until it swallowed the other tree and became great—immortal, even. See how it puts down new roots?'

She nodded, wearily because he had spoken of this before.

'I am the bodhi tree, Mya, and you are going to be the little tree inside.'

This made no sense. What did he even mean?

'I have been working for a long time to make the final medicine for us. When it is ready, this medicine will let me give you a great honor. When my body wears out, my power will move to you. You will come under my branches just like the mortal tree came under the bodhi tree. Look at it! Isn't it beautiful?'

Baffled, she said nothing.

'But for the moment we must think of practical matters.'

He reached into his pocket and produced a fresh vial of the night orchid extract. Then he took out a paper envelope sealed with wax.

'I took too much last time,' he said. 'If that ever happens again, you must give me this antidote. I keep it in the third drawer down.'

He held up the envelope. 'You know that this powder comes from the venom of the naga. It is very precious. I always carry it with me when we go to the forest, but I was distracted by Johnny's incompetence, and I forgot.'

'I understand,' Mya said. He was trying to show his gratitude. No wonder she had been allowed to watch *Nang Rai*. She tried not to squirm.

'Mya. Something is troubling you. What is it?'

Oh, his voice was the softest. Such a dangerous question. She summoned all her courage.

'Will I... will they...?'

'What is it, child?'

'Please, I only wondered... may I go back to my family now?'

He inhaled sharply. He had been leaning toward her with kind concern, but now he pulled back. Insulted.

'Ah. I see. But you have not understood. You think nothing of your family with your selfishness. Your duty is here. You belong with me now.'

Her mother always complained that Mya disappeared when she should be working. She saw things no one else could see and believed they were true. Mya's disobedience would ruin her, people said. Her lies would ruin her. But they had said these things gently, and with humor; Mya had been funny and strange, but her family loved her. Would they not want her back?

I would never go to the forest again if I could be back with my family, she thought.

Mya kept her eyes focused on a knot in the wood of the floor. She would not break. She would not cry. She would not beg. Those things would only arouse his anger. She thought of the beaten man abandoned in the forest.

'My body cannot suffer these medicines forever, child. There will come a time, soon, when instead of dying my spirit will take a new body. And you, my child, you will be the house for my spirit so that my work can continue. My identity will pass into you. And my power.'

Mya fought to control her trembling body. She kept her eyes downcast. Just like the virtuous girl in *Nang Rai*.

He put his hand on her head, and the touch soothed. The medicines he took ensured that he had such power over people. She found that she forgot to be afraid.

'Mya.'

Mr Richard's voice was always soft, but now it had an extra quality. Like sugar. Like magic. Like stars.

The hairs on her arm stood up with attention.

'Mya, you have nothing to fear when you are with me. You have a great destiny, and I will let no harm come to you. When the time comes, my power will be yours and you will be my eyes and hands in the world. We will become more than human. We will be immortal, just like the bodhi tree.'

She stared. The medicines he used made Mr. Richard so big. Not big like Johnny the hard man, but big like the sky, big like sunlight and wind. He seemed to fill in all the places where she was lacking, so that she could lean into him and trust him to make her safe.

Until the medicine wore off, and then she would just want to run away.

'Now,' he said brusquely, and waved a slip of paper at her with an address on it. 'Let's go. We have to see an old friend and hand out some charisma in a bottle.'

Mr. Richard was always concocting medicines in the little room beside the prayer room. Money flowed in through invisible banking transactions and in the form of information or favors by video link or encrypted message, and medicines flowed out. In the time that Mya had been working for Mr. Richard, most of the medicines had been passed along through the forest. Mya handed packages to people who waited in the doorways among the trees. Doorways to other places, the places where Mr. Richard had warned her not to go alone. Sometimes she took other children chosen from the orphanage across the forest to new homes. Sometimes she met other children and gave them the medicines wordlessly, with an exchange of shy smiles. The forest played host to a network of transactions that were invisible in the outer world.

Mya waited on her prayer cushion facing out the window. Mr Richard's body shuddered when the night orchid extract went into his blood.

She poured her mind into the forest all around, out into the leaves that gave shape to sunlight. She could find the forest anywhere that green things were growing. She reached toward Mr. Richard and he took her hand.

They were standing at the base of a fir tree caught in the act of falling by the branches of its neighbours. The tree hung suspended with its roots exposed. It was still alive, and there were mushrooms all over the shadow-side of its trunk. Mya paused to pick some of these; Mr. Richard could use them for their unearthly properties.

'We need to go somewhere new,' Mr. Richard murmured, spreading a pungent salve over his nostrils. 'The place is called Combat Sports Emporium in New Jersey, USA. Focus, Mya. Help me find it. I am not as strong as I was.'

Mya peered into the forest, expecting to see the boy ghost, or the dying journalist. She willed herself to keep thinking of Combat Sports Emporium, until at last the salt smell of sweat came to her. She reached out and parted the spatulate leaves of an otherworldly fern, and a gust of air brought with it not the smell of dirt, but a smoky, chemical musk.

She could see an opening in the shadows of the half-fallen tree. The room beyond was small, dark and cluttered; its air had been breathed in and out too many times. There was a ficus plant in a pot in the corner; it needed more light and it wasn't watered enough, but it was alive. Harsh music thumped through the walls. In a sliver of light Mya could see an altar with photographs, a chipped Buddha statue, and a porcelain gecko. She could see piles of cardboard boxes, stacks of file folders and a wall of trophies with a white towel draped over the largest. She had never been to this place before.

A slim person was standing just outside the frame of the light, shifting from side to side nervously. Through the opening in the worlds the person spoke to Mr. Richard in English. The voice was soft and low, and it could have been male or female.

'Richard, I swear I have never spoken to anyone about you,' the shadow murmured. 'I would never betray you.'

In a shaking voice Mr. Richard said, 'Don't forget it was me that got you out of Bangkok. And I can bring you down any time I want.'

Then he was pressing a little black plastic bag into Mya's hands.

'Give it over and come straight back,' Mr Richard said. 'Hurry up.'

Mya slid through the gap between worlds into a gust of cool, smelly air from Combat Sports Emporium. She set the bag down on the floor, ducking her head respectfully. She glimpsed a glass-covered window. Instead of letting in light from outside, it let in fluorescence from another room. Bare-chested Westerners in shorts were skipping rope on the other side of an empty boxing ring. Some were hitting hanging bags with muffled smacking sounds and shouts.

'Thank you, little one,' the person said softly in Thai. They didn't give her anything in exchange. Mya retreated to the warmth and floral smells of the forest.

'I am tired,' said Mr. Richard. He reached for her hand. 'Take me back, Mya, before I get sick again. I look forward to the day when I can leave my body behind and come with you. My spirit will be so happy in the house of your body.'

His chilly fingers were the color of old paper.

Escalating Fuckup Series

AT MANDINO'S THAT night I told Chrissie I had to quit without notice. I offered to work one last shift. She chewed me out some and then she ended up getting all teary. She said that if it didn't work out for me in Thailand she'd always have a job for me. I guess she's OK. I mean, I work hard and I don't steal, and I never hit anybody at that job, so I guess I'm a good dishwasher. I think she thinks I'm cute. If only she knew.

I was just closing up the kitchen for the night when Cake showed up, all fresh-faced and smiling.

'Now don't take this the wrong way, Jade.'

That's his opening. I hate it when people do that. I'm already taking it the wrong way.

'Let me guess, you've come to laugh at my pronunciation,' I quipped, hefting the bag of pig swill out of its container. 'All the times you've tried teaching me to speak Thai and I suck, right?'

I dropped the bag on the floor and started dragging it towards the back door. Cake sidestepped neatly. He looked all spiffed-up, freshly showered after training, clothes ironed, not a hair out of place. I looked like a rat under a hair net. I was finishing up my shift, which means leaving the kitchen clean. Everybody else had already gone home, except Manuel who was running the vacuum in the foyer.

'I want to talk to you about your temper,' he said, following me out back. He has a soft, singsong voice—kind of high-pitched, too—and he's only about five foot seven in shoes. If you know how to look, you can tell he's strong, but a lot of people don't know how to look. People think 'Cake' stands for 'Cupcake' or something.

It don't.

'What temper?' I heaved the bag into position for pickup and started stacking cardboard boxes to make room for the rest of the garbage. It was a warm night and I could hear Eminem's 'Go to Sleep' coming from the open windows of a car stopped at lights.

'It's OK,' Cake said. 'I am not passing judgement, I only want to share something with you.'

Sometimes it takes my brain a little while to catch up with my mouth. The truth is, in the time I've known Cake, he's never given me any kind of advice, he's never criticised me, and he's about as low-key as anybody I've ever met. He studies engineering at Stevens Institute and lives in Mr B's basement. He sends money home to Thailand. He's never been anything but humble, even though we all know that in a standup fight he could take anybody in the gym except maybe Khari, who outweighs him by about 80 pounds.

I sighed, wiped my forehead with the back of my filthy hand, and let myself flop against the stucco wall. It smelled bad out here but at least it was dark.

'OK, *pana*, what about my temper?'

Now all of a sudden his face screws up and he can't look at me straight. He's embarrassed.

'You see, in Thailand it's not like New York. People aren't...'

'What?' I said, laughing. 'Loud? Rude?'

'Sort of. Yeah. They won't respect you if you always show impatience, act pushy. You won't make no friends. You need friends, Jade. When I came here, I didn't know anybody except my uncle. Everybody was so angry here, so rushing all the time, nobody talks to you. If you ask them questions they are rude. Where I come from, people are good people. If you try not be so... aggressive, then you will be OK there.'

'I'm not aggressive,' I said.

'If somebody upsets you,' Cake said, 'You got to just relax. Don't worry about it. Flow with the go.'

'Cake, I'm a fighter.'

'Me, too. Remember?'

We both laughed and I said, 'OK, OK, true.'

'In the ring is fighting but after we smile and hug. We are kind to each other. You understand?'

I sighed again.

'Jade. It's too much. You would fight your own shadow. You only end up hurting yourself.'

'I don't know, Cake. I was brought up on attitude. That's how I got where I am.'

'OK, OK, no problem,' said Cake, and he literally backed away. 'Just some good advice for you. I hope you will be happy in my uncle's camp.'

Now he was walking away from me, through the kitchen, stepping carefully so he wouldn't get his shoes dirty on the trail of slime that the pig swill bag had left on the tiles.

'Wait,' I said, following. 'Is there anything else I should know? Can you teach me some curse words?'

'Keep practicing,' he said, flashing a smile over his shoulder. Then Chrissie was there, an envelope with my cash in her hand, and he was slipping around her while she started asking if my cousin Luis could do anything about the ignition in her Mercedes. Then he was gone.

I went home and told Malu what Cake said. She listened while she fed the fish and skimmed their tank.

'You, learning to take it easy? That could be asking too much. On the other hand, this could be an opportunity for you.'

'Have you been talking to my mom again?' I closed my eyes. Mom had called me on the restaurant's phone—she's resourceful, right? I wouldn't be surprised if she took out skywriting to get her message across: STAY OUT OF TROUBLE, JADE. She yapped away in my ear. Was I sure? Did I promise to be careful? Would I call her every day? I decided to let Mr. B explain to her that I had no phone.

Now Malu flashed her eyes. 'As a matter of fact, I did talk to your mom. And I had to swear upside down and sideways that you'll be safe on this trip. So you better. Don't get into it with anybody.'

'Fine.'

I thought I kept my voice neutral, but she gave me her Look.

'*What*, Jade? Spill.'

She knew me too well. Me and my cousin had been close since my mom moved from Queens to Union City to get away from my dad. Even in those days Malu was big and womanly-looking and smart, but she got pushed around by pretty much everybody because she never stood up for herself. I was scrawny and truant and back in Queens I'd had a lot of fights. I picked fights because I liked everybody to know that I might be small, but I was no pushover. I was Malu's bodyguard for years, and she made me do my homework.

Then Malu got a scholarship to private school and we were separated. We lived in different worlds. Malu lived away from home, where she got educated and cultured. 'You're like a butterfly coming out of your cocoon,' I used to rag her, and Malu would say, 'You're like bullshit coming out of a bull.'

Then my aunt and uncle moved to Virginia, but Malu stayed to go to college in the city. I was starting eleventh grade when our grandmother was diagnosed with Stage 4 lung cancer and my mom went back to the Dominican Republic to take care of her. Malu moved in to keep an eye on me, and she was doing that literally right now. She was *drilling* me with her eyes. I didn't flinch.

Eventually she said, 'You know you're going to tell me.'

'Nothing.'

Malu snorted.

'Nothing!'

'Uh-huh.'

'OK. OK, but it's stupid.'

She raised her eyebrows, waiting.

'I'm scared of Thailand,' I said.

Malu rolled her eyes. 'Come on. You've been wanting to go to Thailand to train ever since you started in with this Mr. Big dude. Now you do something really stupid, hit a movie star who could have you arrested, and with your luck you manage to turn it around so you get what you wanted to do anyway, which was to go to Thailand. Where does the scared part come in?'

'I know it doesn't make sense,' I said. 'You're right. I have always wanted to train there. It's just that everything's happening so fast. And I'm... scared. Of myself.'

'Yourself.' Malu can lay on the mock about three feet deep just by the tone she uses. I ignored her tone. I said:

'I think I can feel a fuckup coming on.'

Malu sighed. She went in the kitchen and came out with a plant mister. Malu is an earth-mother type. She keeps plants, and fish, and of course there's Coltrane the iguana, who she sneaked into the apartment without Irene the super finding out. As she started spritzing the Norfolk pine, she had a disapproving pout on her lips.

'Seriously,' I said. 'I can feel it building, you know like an electric charge before a thunderstorm. Probably my biggest yet.'

'What have I been telling you about thinking positive, Jade?'

'I'm not trying to make it happen. It just is. I mean, bad things happen in threes, right? Well, I've messed up twice so far, you know? First when I stomped that girl's head. Second, I lose my temper and knock out the world's second biggest kung fu movie star. This is definitely an escalating fuckup series.'

'Number three doesn't have to come,' Malu said quietly, pulling some dead leaves off a spider plant. 'This is your chance to stop it. Go to Thailand. Change.'

I shook my head. 'You don't get it. I don't have a choice. My fuckups never quit until I'm all out of options.'

'How do you think I felt when I went to boarding school with five pairs of Walmart underwear and there were girls there with their own polo ponies? You get used to feeling freaked out all the time. Being freaked is just a sign you're challenging yourself.'

'For real now?'

'For real. Go with it. So tell me, are you going to that big place where all the Westerners go?'

'Fairtex gym? No. It's a tiny place. Mr B said they don't have a website.'

'So it's authentic. Are you going to be in a little hut somewhere in the forest, picking fruit off the trees?'

'It's in Bangkok so I don't think it's a hut. It better not be a hut. I need a real bathroom. Especially with all that unfamiliar food and my... um... delicate stomach.'

'I'm way ahead of you,' Malu said. 'I bought you Imodium AD on my way home. Four boxes. You won't shit the whole time you're out there.'

Got Smelly Bottom

Rain dripped through the leaky roof of the PortaPotty and plopped on my head. I was holding the last three sheets of toilet paper in my hand, trying to save them until I was sure the eruption in my guts had ended. So far that wasn't happening.

This kid called Pepsi was banging on the door and calling to me in a piping voice.

'Come out now, Jade!'

Sweat dripped off my eyebrows as another spasm gripped my intestines. It felt like a bunch of snakes were biting me all up and down my guts, poisonous snakes with fangs who also did that boa-constrictor-type thing that snakes do. At the same time. I just wanted to run away from my insides and leave them to shoot rocket fuel out my butt without me.

But running away from my own insides was not an option. I opened my eyes. It was about 379 degrees outside and pouring rain in the building site adjacent to the gym. There was no seat, so I was squatting. My legs trembled with exertion and my teeth were chattering with that shivery feeling caused by shitting and hurling almost at the same time.

'Please go away!' I yelled. Malu had given me a Thai language book to study on the plane, but I'm not good at learning from books. So far I'd been getting by with gestures and English and the bits of Thai I'd learned over the years from Cake.

'Time to eat, Jade,' the boy sang, knocking again. I knew he was laughing at me; they'd all been laughing at me since the minute I got here. It was like I was some kind of traveling freak show. First I got on the wrong bus from the airport, then I got on another wrong bus to try to fix it. I'd walked about six miles, jetlagged, in the rain, until I found some college students who spoke English. They were so nice I almost cried, especially when one of them helped me buy this incredibly yummy fruit drink with salt in it.

When I got off the bus I changed my mind about the college students. They must have tricked me. This couldn't be the right place. Who builds a boxing gym in the most polluted area of the city, in open air under the arches of a superhighway? The air reeked of exhaust. Rain was pouring down in sheets from the roadway that passed overhead. Instead of houses there were makeshift shacks, and outside one of them two men squatted on the ground passing a bottle back and forth.

I'd stood there in the warm dawn listening to the roar of traffic and shifting the weight of my bags on my shoulders. I could see the boxing ring and the bag alley, right out in the open by a railway siding. This couldn't be it. A gym like this couldn't have any association with Mr. B and his Humvee and his gold chains. No way.

A tired-looking woman in flip-flops and a skirt had opened the doors of what looked like a shed and started sweeping the concrete. I remembered to make a *wai,* a polite little bow, before I showed her the address.

She examined the paper. She didn't smile, but her voice was soft.

'Jade Barrera. I'll get Coat.' She turned and walked away.

When I heard *Coat* my stomach had taken a dive, and my guts started to boil. This was the gym where I was going to spend my summer vacation?

I'd waited on the wet pavement trying not to choke on the diesel fumes. I hadn't expected Fairtex with clean mats and air conditioning and famous boxers, but I had expected to be able to breathe. Then I heard voices.

Kids started pouring out of the dorm. They were all boys, from teenagers on down to eight and nine year olds, more than a dozen of them. They were wearing shorts and filthy sneakers, no shirts, and they were all laughing like everything was one gigantic joke.

'What is this, day care?' I said. 'Where are the adults?'

A tall, stocky man showed up wearing a Fila t-shirt and shiny basketball shorts. He looked me up and down and sniffed, then gestured for me to join in the run. The woman took my bags and I was off, running along the railway siding through clouds of bluish exhaust in a neighborhood that made the Port Authority bus terminal look like the Ritz. I hadn't slept longer than 20 minutes in the last two days, and I'd only eaten snacks from food carts off the street—and that fruit juice cocktail that had tasted gorgeous at the time.

I knew a 10k run was a standard part of the day in many camps, but I didn't expect it to kick in on the first morning. Maybe it was a test. Well, guess what? I failed. Because after only a couple miles I'd fallen behind the rest—even the eight-year-olds. The air was like hot sludge, and I was regretting drinking that juice. All the way back to camp, I was wishing I'd taken that Imodium before I started running. The only thing that kept me going was fear of messing myself in public.

Finally it was over. We turned down an alley and returned to the highway, passing beneath its shelter and back to the open-air gym.

'Please!' I panted in my pathetic Thai, staggering after the others. 'Where's the toilet?'

The boys all started giggling. Like they were embarrassed. I was the one about to mess myself—did I not have the right word for toilet? What was so embarrassing?

'You want the day care toilet?' A kid was speaking English with a huge smile. 'Sure, no problem. I am Pepsi. I will be your guide. Come this way!'

Great, I thought. I was rude, so now they're going to take advantage of my delicate stomach and play games on me. I couldn't blame them—I'd have done the same. But no way was I following him.

Luckily I spotted a PortaPotty, which they obviously didn't want me to see. It stood crookedly among tall weeds in what looked like a building site next to the gym. The bottom of the door had been kicked in. Snarling at the boys, I went in and held what was left of the door shut.

'No!' the English-speaking boy was shouting at me. 'Not there!' He grabbed at the door but I closed it and held it shut.

Just in time.

It smelled like something died. And there was no seat. Just a hole.

There's no feeling quite like squatting in an unfamiliar toilet knowing that a stranger outside is holding your passport and wallet and phrasebook.

I was helpless.

'You OK in there?' said Pepsi in English. 'You need some help?'

'No,' I gasped. I held that door shut for all I was worth. I could just see the Instagram post: *Jade Barrera on PortaPotty, Bangkok.* Nobody was getting a picture of this.

The boy went away and came back. This time his hand reached under the broken edge of the 'door' and shoved half a roll of pink toilet paper at me.

I burst into tears.

'Oh, thank god,' I sobbed.

'We going now,' Pepsi said in English. 'Better hurry. You miss training.'

When I finally showed up, the training was in full swing. The gym was open-air and everything looked like it was about to fall apart. Two older kids were doing pad work in the ring and others were drilling pads on the concrete around the ring. Some were working bags. Some were doing sit-ups and lifting concrete weights held by ropes in their teeth. Some were jumping rope. Coat lounged against the ropes and watched the older fighters.

I felt weak. I took a few swigs from the bottle of water in my bag, but it barely kept me on my feet. I'd thought the rainy season would be cool, but the place was like a steam bath. Everyone ignored me, so I decided to do bag work. The bag was hard, and where the filling had settled at the bottom it felt like concrete.

All around me a random chorus of shouted 'Ay's' and 'Oh's' sang out as the boys trained. 'Ai-ai-ai-aaaaaay!' they'd yell as they let off a series of shots. The older boys were real hardbodies. They prowled around, stalking each other, one guy holding the pads and the other hitting, sometimes clinching, sometimes even throwing. They weren't training in anything like all-out fight mode, but there was no way I could keep up with them the way I was feeling right now.

The gym might be shabby, but I had to admit the standards were pretty high.

'Jade.'

I hadn't noticed Coat coming up behind me. Winded, I stepped away from the bag I'd been working on and *wai*'d to him; he'd squared up to me with a set of pads on his forearms. Towering over me, he nodded for me to hit.

I was blowing hard by then, and nothing I did had much effect. Coat signalled the shots he wanted from me but kept his evasive footwork going so that I didn't have enough time to get in. He was definitely checking me out, and I was coming up lacking. But I tried. I landed a couple of good round kicks, and I was aware that some boys had stopped training to watch the foreign girl. Coat turned to them and said, 'keep working,' with a smile, and they did.

At last he let me rest. 'Pepsi!' he called. Pepsi ran over, looking eager to please. Coat handed me his belly protector and pads and I slipped them on. Coat indicated that Pepsi should train with me.

Pepsi backed off, shaking his head and looking at the floor. He said something in Thai, and Coat laughed.

'What's going on?' I said. Coat didn't answer.

'Bad luck train with girl,' Pepsi answered in English. 'Jade, you train with Pook. Not me.'

I could feel my blood pressure rising. I was ready to snap; but nobody else got upset. No shouting. No swearing. Pepsi smiled and looked at the ground, ducking his head. Not looking at me.

'I train her,' Coat said. 'Am I bad luck?'

Pepsi scuffed the floor with his toe.

'OK, Pepsi. OK, come on.'

Pepsi flushed. The other boys were giggling. He gave in.

Coat showed us what he wanted us to do. Pepsi started putting his shots into me. He wasn't messing around, that's for sure. He might be young, but he was ferocious, and he didn't get tired. Coat corrected me a couple of times on the way I was using the pad to signal, but overall he seemed pleased.

He nodded to me, said, 'OK,' and then told us we could take a break.

'I gotta go toilet,' Pepsi said loudly in English, jumping up and down like some kind of pee bunny. Then he shot me a sly look and went across the gym to a door in the wall behind the boxing ring. He opened it like a game show hostess revealing a prize. There was a clean toilet and sink inside.

I felt like crying. And maybe if I'd cried, things would have gone better for me.

But I didn't cry. I stalked across the gym, grabbed Pepsi by the throat and shoved him against the wall.

'You wanna fight me, Pepsi?' I snarled. 'You think you're funny? Let's get in the ring and find out how funny I am.'

He tried to shake me off, but I'm not that easy to shake, not when I'm mad.

'I not fighting you,' Pepsi said. 'You unlucky foreigner, got smelly bottom, I not fighting you.'

If I hadn't been so mad, 'got smelly bottom' would have broken me up laughing. But I don't back down.

Coat had to pull me off him.

'You fight in ring, not each other,' he said. Then he added

something more complicated in Thai, to Pepsi, and I wondered what it was, because Pepsi shut up after that.

'Take a break,' Coat said to me. The way he said it I knew I'd done wrong, but I'm damned if I know what I was supposed to have done instead.

I peeled off my gloves and followed Pook.

'You want to stay here?' she said, softly. 'Or go back to America?'

I felt about two inches tall. I gulped. 'I'm sorry. I didn't think.'

Why do I always fuck up? Why? Why? *Why?*

'Cake sent me a text about you,' Pook said. 'I see he was not kidding.'

'I'm sorry,' I said again. 'Please let me stay. I'll be very quiet. I won't argue.'

'You must do better. We see how it goes.' She showed me the corner (literally) I was sleeping in, and the table where everyone ate meals. And where the extra toilet paper was kept.

She showed me the toilet paper twice.

Smart Phone

LONELY AND ANXIOUS weeks followed the incident with the journalist. Mr. Richard was growing increasingly electric and unpredictable. He was working on the thing he called 'the final medicine' in his lab as though his life depended on it, and maybe it did. He had been sickly since the incident with the night orchid extract, and now he looked at Mya assessingly, as though judging her strength. He talked to people all over the world in many languages. He worked in the lab. He slept only fitfully, when he could no longer resist the hushing music of the rains on the roof of the forest house.

He never mentioned the young journalist again, and he didn't even try to get into the phone. It just sat there, unnoticed amid the mess of vials and papers, even though Johnny stopped by and offered to take it to a hacker he knew in Bangkok. 'What the journalist found out is immaterial,' Mr. Richard told Johnny. 'He's not coming back.'

Mya couldn't be sure whether Mr. Richard really didn't care about the information stored on the phone, or whether he just didn't trust Johnny. He didn't seem to trust anyone lately. Something was happening to him. This was not quite visible, but almost. Once when Mr Richard was sleeping she saw a ghostly image of him rise from his body and drift towards her, wavering, until it disintegrated like smoke.

She did not want to share her body with him.

One night she woke to the sound of distant music. It seemed to be coming from the meditation porch. Mya rose and slipped her red dress over her head. As she made her way barefoot through the blotchy, leaf-tossed darkness she realized the sound came from beyond, from the little work room adjacent to the open porch. Mya hesitated. The masks on the walls were shrouded by shadow, but the blue computer light emanating from the laboratory made the stuffed monkey's glass eyes gleam. A bitter smell came with the light. Mr. Richard must be working again.

The music was a tinny little melody, repeating endlessly.

The mysterious password-protected phone was ringing.

Mya's breath caught as she saw Mr. Richard's body slumped across the desk. As she approached, she saw with relief that he was breathing. A smear of saliva lay on the formica counter by his open lips. Jars and bottles were open. The sleeping computer screensaver cycled images of gods and animals from old temple artwork.

The phone rang and rang. Mr. Richard had obtained a charger for it and plugged it into the wall socket. Did password-protected mean you needed a password to answer it, or just to make calls?

Mya picked it up and pressed the green button. The ringing stopped. She said nothing, but listened.

The voice was familiar, like the back of her hand, like the edge of sleep, like—

'Mya? Mya, I know you are there.'

Mya *knew* this voice. And the woman was speaking *Burmese*.

Mya's heart fluttered. 'Mother?'

There was a silence, in which Mya decided that maybe she was wrong. Maybe the voice was not quite right. But it had been a year since she'd heard her mother's voice. Maybe...

'Mother?'

'Mya, listen. There isn't much time.'

'Where are you? Mother, where are you?'

There was a pause. Mya burst into tears.

'Stop crying. Listen to me. Write this down. Quickly. Write down this password.'

'Password?'

'For the phone. Write it down.'

Mya grabbed an envelope and wrote down the Western letters and numbers with a ballpoint pen.

'Now listen to me. You have to get out of there. Take this phone and go. Now.'

'But, Mother, where are you?'

'It's not where, it's when... Mya, I can't explain. Just go!'

The line cut off. Tears streaming down her face, Mya pressed buttons randomly in a desperate attempt to get the voice back. But it was no use.

Mr. Richard stirred.

Mya was sweating but her fingertips felt icy cold. As if he suddenly sensed her there, Mr. Richard jerked awake. He recognized her and relaxed.

'What time is it?'

Mya had slid the phone behind her back, but it was still plugged in and if he woke up properly, he'd see the wire trailing to Mya's side. And she still had a pen in her left hand. The slip of paper sat on the table beside the keyboard, the nonsensical selection of letters and numbers that would unlock the reporter's phone.

Where was she supposed to go? Her mother hadn't told her anything. Mya couldn't just run into the woods...

A memory came to Mya. Her mother's voice, the words she had spoken while they were in the prison camp.

'When the soldiers first came I should have sent you to run away into the forest. You might have had a chance, then—the forest is your place, Mya. Here there is no chance. If I could do it again I would send you to the trees.'

Mya took a long breath. Her mother hadn't warned her to run back then, but the voice on the phone was telling her to go to the forest now. It was a sign. She could run blindly, just take off and leave it all behind.

With a quick, sneaky tug she pulled the connector out of the phone behind her back. The cord drooped noiselessly. Mr. Richard was rubbing his eyes and turning in his chair. Taking the paper with its inscrutable letters, she took a half-step back. A smell of decaying meat roiled around his body.

'I need to take something,' he murmured, patting the surfaces around him for medicine. 'I'm so tired.'

Then his eyes lit on the scrap of paper in her hand. She had taught herself English letters, albeit not very well.

'What are you writing?' he said, and in the same moment he spotted the dangling power cord. 'Did you touch that phone? Where is it?'

Mya backed away, into the prayer room. This was her last chance to make an excuse, hand over the phone, cooperate with Mr. Richard in his magic.

'Mya, what are you doing? Give me the phone,' he rasped. The drug he took to make himself so wonderful and big and magnetic—it had worn off. Suddenly he looked and sounded as withered as he truly was.

He came toward her with grasping hands, and for all his age he out-maneuvered her. The door to the room was behind him. The window was open but high above the ground.

She had to get out of here. She suddenly felt sure he intended to devour her in some way. She couldn't stop herself.

'Put the phone down, Mya,' Mr Richard said in a flat, deadly voice. He wasn't sleepy now. 'You don't know what you're dealing with. Put it down.'

There was only one place she could go. Mya projected her consciousness into the dark-leaved trees outside the window, focusing on their deep roots.

She was not permitted to travel to the forest alone. But she knew how.

'No, Mya!' His face tightened until it looked stringy. 'Do not leave me!'

Mr. Richard made a lunging grasp for the phone. He seized her arm, but she kicked and bit. Her heart was already outside, among the trees, and he had no drug to help him.

Mya slipped between molecules of air and into the wood of the trees. She passed through them and out the other side. The prayer room was gone. Mr Richard was gone. Moonlight tickled the edges of the big star-shaped leaves in the forest, and the stolen phone was still in her hand. Mya's heart turned over like thunder.

Where's Waldo?

to: shadowboxer@coolpost.com
from: malu.baines@thenewschool.edu
subject: re: staph infection photo

Stop oozing and taking pictures of yourself. You know I'm delicate. Can you write your mom more often? She calls me, like I'm supposed to know what's up with you. She says Nana won't be with us much longer. Your mom's having a bad time, she needs to know you're doing OK.

Khari called to ask about you. I said I wasn't in the loop and btw why don't you dump Eva and ask Jade out? Just kidding. He's too old for you.

xx Malu

to: malu.baines@thenewschool.edu
from: shadowboxer@coolpost.com
subject: re: staph infection photo

I skyped my mom and Nana. I can only get online at an internet cafe, I don't come here much. My skin is almost better so I'll be cleared to fight soon. Tell Khari ~~I want him so bad~~ I said hi.

My only friend here is a cat. He seems to be a stray. He's gorgeous. Not a Burmese, not a curly-tailed cat like you see here. He's big and long-haired and all black. He shows up at camp and watches us train. He's so cool. Sometimes he appears like out of nowhere. I call him Waldo because you never know where he'll show up.

*   *   *

I WAS MADE of bruises. I was always hungry, always on the toilet, and always homesick. After talking to my mom every day, or at least chatting to her online, it felt terrible to be cut off. I pictured her freaking out missing me, but the truth is I missed her like crazy. I had no friends here yet. Pepsi tried to be nice after our bad start, and he introduced me to his older sister, who often came by with her ladyboy friend Jane to watch pad work. It was kind of weird how Jane was more feminine than I am even though she's technically a boy. I knew that ladyboys were a normal thing in Bangkok because years ago Cake had showed me a DVD about Nong Toom, a famous boxer who was born male but felt like a girl on the inside. She had fought in makeup and a bra, then saved up her fight money for surgery to become a woman in body. Jane wasn't talking about surgery, though; I had the impression she wanted to keep her options open. I liked her and she was nice to me, too, which was more than you could say for Pook—the only other woman at camp. Pook wasn't mean or anything, but she kept away from me. I was sure she didn't like me.

Luckily Cake's advice finally was starting to sink in. Don't confront people, and don't get angry. Coat told me a phrase for it: *jai yen*. Cool heart.

Why was a cool heart so hard for me? I guess I was afraid that if I stopped being angry and confrontational, there wouldn't be anything left of me. I wouldn't be Jade anymore.

I already felt like my identity was getting erased. The language was hard to pronounce and I was struggling to say even simple things, to act the way people were supposed to act here. It was the opposite of everything I knew. I think somehow, when I came here I thought it was going to be like going back to San Cristobal, where everybody knows me. Where things are familiar. In Bangkok, nothing was familiar.

So I threw myself into training. Every morning we ran, then trained for two or three hours, ate, slept through the heat of the day, and trained again in the evening. Then ate again and slept. There was no chit-chat, not with my limited command of the Thai language. No TV, no video games, no Twitter. The insides of my nostrils were black from diesel fumes. And the inside of my head started to go quiet.

Back home, I was used to thinking of myself as hard up. We never had much money, even before my mom ran away from my dad. He put her through a lot of shit, and I didn't make it any easier by acting so much like him. Malu's folks stayed married, got good jobs and ended up doing real well for themselves, and I knew that Malu was on a fast track to a better life. But that left me looking around at all the money and trying to figure out how to get me some. Isn't it funny how the people who talk about material things not being important are always the people with plenty of options?

In Thailand, I wasn't broke. My little bit of money that I paid Coat, it wasn't a little bit of money to the camp. The kids I was training with had nothing. Half of them were orphans. Everybody's sneakers had holes in them. There were soap operas on Pook's little TV that showed rich people in designer clothes weeping on each other and living in fancy houses, but the people in our neighborhood made their living selling stuff on the street, including their bodies. The kids hoped to make their living beating each other up in public.

And people smiled a lot here.

It made me wonder. Maybe 'tough' wasn't what I thought.

One afternoon in between training sessions I'd gone looking for a clean t-shirt. Pook had just come back from her job in a restaurant to cook and do laundry for the camp. She had laid out washing lines for everyone's clothes to dry, but in this humidity they were always damp. As I reached up to take down my shirt, Waldo started winding around my legs like cats do. Getting all flirty with me.

'Hey, *chico guapo*,' I said. 'Are you my only friend here?'

Waldo sat on his haunches and looked up at me, blinking. Like I told Malu, he wasn't a typical curly-tailed slum cat like I'd seen around here. He was long-bodied, long-haired, all black with golden eyes. He had a kingly way about him.

I reached down to pet him. Waldo rose to head-butt my hand, making a purring cry of greeting.

I startled when I heard Pook's voice from the other side of a set of bed sheets.

'That's not an ordinary cat. He must be pedigree. Maybe he got lost from a high rise.'

I was stunned. Pook *never* spoke to me unless she had to.

'He reminds me of Kala Sriha,' she added, a laugh in her voice.

'Kala Sriha?' I echoed. My Thai was improving, but I didn't know these words.

'Kala Sriha. From legend,' she said. 'He's a lion but they say he doesn't eat meat. This cat likes fruit, did you notice?'

She was probably pulling my leg. But I said, 'Like mango?'

Pook bundled up the washing and started to go in. I guess that was the end of the conversation. She didn't like me. I felt my loneliness like I felt the rain falling.

'Figs,' she said over her shoulder. 'They are his favorite. I have been feeding him for a few days now.'

She opened the door to the dorm. I heard myself say, a little desperately, 'Please, I help you? I not busy.'

She turned and looked at me but I couldn't read her expression.

'There's always work to do,' she said with a wry face. Almost a smile.

Pink

to: malu.baines@thenewschool.edu
from: shadowboxer@coolpost.com
subject: fight!

I'm on the fight card at a stadium near Chiang Mai! The staph infection is better but I inhaled bug poison the other day. They send around these guys with masks on spraying clouds of poison gas down into the storm drains. To get rid of roaches I guess? There are a lot of roaches here so I can't see how it helps much. Maybe they will mutate and we'll have GIANT MUTANT ROACHES of DOOM... don't rule it out as a crunchy breakfast treat.
If I win a few big fights maybe I can come home.
luv, me

to: shadowboxer@coolpost.com
from: malu.baines@thenewschool.edu
subject: re:fight!

GOOD LUCK! Kick ass/don't get killed. OK? And you can come home whenever you want. Mr B is not God.
love & hugs,
Malu
PS How's Waldo? Send cat pictures!

WE RODE TO Chiang Mai on the same bus as another Bangkok-based club, a bigger outfit with heavy hitters. The kind of club

Mr. Big could have sent me to if he wasn't into nepotism and trying to bust my chops. They had two fighters on the card, Flexmaster Flex (aka Sangsidt Phongpaichit whose real name I can almost pronounce now) and a middleweight called Gold Kwanchai. Coat said Gold could give Boo in his heyday a black eye. He said it to tease Pepsi, who is a big fan of Boo. It upset me a little, too. I mean, there were good fighters and then there was Boo. Gold, winking, offered to go a few rounds with Pepsi and Pepsi told Gold he should be afraid, very afraid, but his voice cracked and everyone laughed. Then Pepsi fell asleep with his head on my shoulder. I guess that made me one of the team?

The sound of the rain was soothing, and I must have drifted off, too. When I woke up we weren't on the expressway anymore. The bus had stopped in the middle of nowhere. We were pulled off the side of a winding road going through forest. The driver was outside looking under the hood.

Oh, great.

He'd picked a terrible place to stop. The road was winding, and we were on a sharp bend. There was an enormous tree by the side of the road. It had vines climbing up the side of the trunk that made it look sinewy, almost as if it had muscles and tendons. Tied around the trunk were dozens of bright ribbons. Tucked into the ribbons were little toys and dolls. It reminded me of the way people put flowers by the road where someone has died.

I poked Pepsi and his eyes opened. I pointed to the tree. He shuddered.

'It's a bodhi tree. Ghosts live there,' he said.

'Have many people died here?'

'Don't talk about it. You'll attract the ghosts. Why are we stopped?'

He got up and pulled his hoodie up before stepping out into the rain.

I sat looking at the tree and the green forest beyond. The leaves were lacy with moth holes. Water beaded on the colored ribbons. It didn't feel spooky to me, only sad and strangely calm.

'Fan belt,' said Pepsi, returning. He offered me a little can of M-150 energy drink. It's powerful stuff. I shook my head.

'I get it,' he said in English. 'You don't want to peak too soon.'

I laughed and forgot about the ghosts.

'Where are we?' I said. 'Shouldn't we be in Chiang Mai by now?'

'Pook wanted Coat to stop by her husband's farm and check something.'

'Pook has a husband? And a farm? Since when?'

'Her husband is sick. She doesn't like to talk about it,' Pepsi said. 'Coat says we must get back on the main road or be late for the fights.'

But he looked out the window wistfully as we drove off.

'I would love to live on a farm,' he said. 'My uncle used to be a bee keeper. What a life. Clean air, and all the honey you could eat.'

'Why would Pook work in a restaurant if she owns a farm?' I asked.

But Pepsi pretended to be asleep again.

It was dark when we finally rolled in to town, and the 'stadium' turned out to be more like an outdoor nightclub. It was at the end of a little alley with bars all around. There were go-go dancers circulating in a crowd of mostly Australians and Russians. Betting was going on in a low-key kind of way.

I was whacked. Fights didn't start until after nine, and mine was the last on the card. They'd matched me up with a local girl who stared at the ground while our trainers discussed us. She was heavier than me but about the same height. All the extra weight was muscle, especially in her legs. She might even have been younger.

'Pink got a 4-0-0 record,' Pepsi confided later in English, while we were killing time waiting for the fights to start. 'Three of her wins by knockout and one TKO when she broke somebody's rib. Watch out!'

'Pink?' I said. It wasn't my idea of a name.

He shrugged. 'Jade?' he said, grinning.

'That's my real name. It's on my birth certificate.'

Coat came over and gave me one of his 'wakeup' massages that feel like you're a piece of meat being tenderized. When it was over I felt better. Because it was over.

'Keep her on the end of your left hand,' he instructed in Thai. 'Don't let her clinch. Use your teep. Whatever happens, no clinch.'

My teep—a pushaway front kick—was OK, but I hated to rely on it. It doesn't do damage.

'What if she clinch me?' I said. 'What I do?'

'Don't get caught. Pink was trained by Pot, so she is dangerous in the clinch. You can't handle her there. You don't have the strength. Understand?'

'Ha, ha!' I bleated, not like 'ha, ha!' how funny but 'ha, ha!' like, I am so screwed.

The quality of the fights got progressively higher as the night went on, which is normal. But the girls' fight was the last one on the card because the promoters didn't want our femaleness to spoil the luck of the ring (I know, right?). So my fight wouldn't even start until around 1 am. I usually go to bed at 8:30.

I wandered away from the crowd thinking maybe I could take a nap leaning up against a wall, but there were mangy dogs begging for rice and they made me think about Waldo. I was missing him. And Quinton.

This was what I'd gotten for protecting Quinton. I could be back washing dishes for $8.50 an hour and training in Secaucus and living with Malu, going to student films with her for free and meeting her brainy friends who argue about micro-banking and intersectionality and which of Mary J. Blige's songs belong in the canon, whatever that is.

If only I hadn't beat up Mr. Hollywood because he was rude to a stray cat.

The only way I could get my own back now was if I made

a name for myself over here. If I made Mr. Big want me back, because I was a good fighter. A proven fighter. And if that meant being a small fish, then I'd be a small fish in a big pond. I'd be the guppy with the biggest teeth you ever saw. I'd be Hell Guppy.

Pepsi won his fight by knockout. I felt sorry for the other kid. When I was ten I thought ten-year-olds had every right to beat the shit out of each other, but now I cringed when I saw those little kids whacking each other. Flexmaster Flex won by judges' decision; there was heated last-minute betting on that one, and Coat looked amused because FF's win was a real upset. More fights, then Gold lost on points against a title-belt holder called Superman, but gave Superman a lump on his head that looked like a duck's egg. Conclusion: Gold is good, but he's no Boo.

Just before my fight I took two shits and then puked. Coat said, '*Mai pen rai*,' which kind of means *de nada*, I guess.

The ringside orchestra was already playing. Traditionally, it would be the soundtrack to all the fights. Thai boxing music always sounds off-balance and sort of aimless to me, but it has a way of getting under your skin. Even in the noisy drunken crowd something happened when the tempo started to increase, driving the fighters on. It was like the music opened a window to another age and brought the air alive. You couldn't help feeling it.

Pink and I started our *wai kru*. I had only been practicing the ceremonial prayer dance for three weeks. I must have looked like a dying chicken.

Pink's *wai kru* was good. Ouch.

Whatever. We're not dancers; we're fighters. I tried to look her in the eye but she wasn't going for it. I just stared at her and thought, 'I'm gonna nail yo ass to the canvas, Pink.'

The bell rang.

Pink came out slugging. She was slow on her feet with her heavy thighs and low center of gravity. She would've made a great wrestler. But she had long arms and she could outreach me. Nothing got through to my head but that didn't matter because her body shots were savage. She bruised a rib on the very first punch. Breathing was tough after that.

I teeped her away from me and went on the attack, working simple combinations and trying to weaken her by repeatedly attacking her lead leg with my low round kick. It was like kicking a log. Her leg was solid. I felt like a bird throwing myself against a window.

I could hear Coat shouting at me from my corner, but I was inside my own head now. I'd never been beaten. Been hurt, but never defeated. Been dragged off people, but never knocked out. Never conceded. Never. And this wasn't gonna be no different.

But my shots couldn't seem to shake her. She was too solid, and she didn't seem to feel pain. The ring was sweaty and I was afraid to fire off a high kick or move too fast laterally because a couple times I slipped and almost went down. In my peripheral vision I could see money changing hands. I looked Pink in the eye and I couldn't see no emotion. It was like looking at a reptile. Studying me. Sizing me up, getting ready to eat me.

I don't think so.

Halfway through the round, I made my move. I went for her head. And I got her. Pushed her against the ropes. She took a series of punches to the head. Any one of them would have knocked out anybody else I ever fought. Pink didn't even seem to blink.

You think you're tough? I thought, throwing my shots even bigger. *Watch this. Here comes the guppy from hell.*

Then she clinched me. As she grabbed the back of my neck I tried to duck under, but her right knee must have come up to meet my face just as she turned my head with a savage jerk. All at once her knee and my face said hello, goodbye to each other.

Especially goodbye.

VOICES WERE TOO loud, an intrusion from some nasty place I didn't want to be.

Oh, yeah. Reality.

It took me a while to figure out I was on the floor of the bar. Coat was squatting beside me and my head seemed to be in Pepsi's lap. The doctor was there, too, with his latex gloves and little flashlight. I couldn't see out of my left eye even after the doctor took the ice pack off it. It was totally swollen shut.

I closed the other one.

'I'm OK. I want to get up.'

They wouldn't let me up.

I couldn't believe it. Coat kept reassuring me, telling me *You're OK* and *mai pen rai*—I mean, *mai pen rai*, come on! What isn't *mai pen rai* with you guys? I wanted to say.

But you know, honestly? I wasn't that upset. It happened. I got knocked out. I wasn't dead. She caught me. That's all. She was the tougher fighter.

It was almost a relief. Got that over with. I was just going to have to get better.

After the bar closed, we all hung out while our coaches gossiped. Our camp would go to the bus station and sleep on benches because Coat was too hard-up to get us rooms somewhere. Flexmaster's camp would go to some hostel, where they'd get to sleep a few hours before the bus came.

Pink came out of the bathroom wearing a maid's uniform for a hotel. She sat down next to me, got me a Coke from the bar even though it was closed, because she knew the owner. Her voice was soft and she smelled of limes and something floral.

I asked her why her ring name was Pink. She smiled and showed me her nails. They were bubblegum pink.

'Favorite color,' she said.

A Ghost Called Luck

MYA FOUND HERSELF on a steep hillside in the silver twilight. The land sheared away to her right, and from below she could hear the echo of water falling between rocks.

The air was warm, but she couldn't stop shaking. Her teeth were chattering. She had disobeyed. She had stolen. What would he do to her when he found her?

Because he would find her. He knew everything. He controlled people.

Mya stumbled to a halt, doubling over with a stitch in her side.

'You can slow down,' the ghost said in her ear. 'He isn't coming after you. He can't.'

Mya flinched. 'Are you sure?'

'He can't come by himself. He'll need a new helper.' The ghost was markedly friendlier now. 'He'll have to find a child who can bring him here. That will take him some time.'

Mya had never thought about it that way. Mr. Richard *couldn't* follow her!

'He will be lost without you,' the ghost said. 'He seeks immortality for himself. He was going to use your body to house his spirit.'

While she was thinking about that the ghost pointed to the phone Mya was holding.

'Didn't that belong to the reporter?'

Out of the corner of her eye Mya could see a huge serpent sliding through the trees from the direction of the river. The being had the face of a serene infant.

'Open the phone,' the ghost urged. 'Does it work? Are there numbers in it?'

'I didn't have time to try the password.'

'Show me. I want to see.' He was too eager, which alarmed Mya. Ghosts had their own appetites. But in the end she turned on the phone and entered the password. Lights came up and thin music played. The writing on the screen was Western.

'It has video,' the ghost said. 'Cool! Let's see!'

There was only one clip in storage. When she opened it, the camera was moving jerkily; then the person filming set it between some crates so that you could only see through a slit. The view was dim, but it looked like an industrial setting: steel roof girders, stacks of boxes, machine background noise. These were known to Mya only from TV and photographs. She had never been to a big town.

An old monk wearing glasses came into the shot.

'It's Som,' Mya breathed. 'He brought us across the river in a big inflatable tube. To the orphanage.'

A tall, handsome young man approached Som, apologising for the delay.

'Your translator,' said the ghost.

'I didn't recognize him.' Mya struggled to match her memory of the filthy, battered body to this living image. Then a linen-suited white man stepped into the line of the camera and began asking questions. The young man translated into English for the older one, who nodded a lot, his wispy hair stirring in the breeze. Som spoke softly about the records of the children at the orphanage, and how Mr. Richard had been abusing his privilege as a patron and removing children without 'proper authorisation.' He handed the older journalist something small... a flash drive?

The young man kept glancing at the camera, as if he knew it was there and he was worried about it. After a moment he excused himself and disappeared from the shot. The monk and the middle-aged man were left standing awkwardly, unable to communicate.

A whisper up close to the camera.

'It's not a good shot. The light's weak…'

A finger passed across the aperture, then the camera shifted position a little. It steadied, and there was the linen-suited man nodding and trying to thank the monk in clumsy Thai.

Offscreen, someone shouted. Som shrank back in fear, and the linen-suited man stepped in front of the monk protectively. Then Johnny was in the frame. He drew his arm back and hit the older journalist across the side of the head in a whipping motion. She glimpsed some kind of weapon—whatever it was, the man crashed to the ground, out cold.

'Oh shit,' whispered the young man into the microphone.

In the shot, Som tried to scuttle away, but Johnny caught the monk by one skinny arm and stopped him.

'I regret ever helping Mr Richard,' the monk said. 'The children are not his to take—'

Johnny cuffed Som across the head with the same violence he'd used on the journalist. Now there were two men on the ground.

Mya cringed, biting her lip.

Then Johnny reached into his jacket and took out a hypodermic needle. He injected the white-suited reporter in the neck. The man's image blurred a little in the camera's view; then he simply vanished.

Close to the camera, there was a sharp intake of breath from the young man.

Johnny turned his attention to Som and performed the same act; the monk, too, was gone. Johnny straightened up, looked around, ran his fingers through his brown hair, and walked away.

'Jesus Christ,' whispered the young man into the phone. The recording shook, then cut off.

Mya closed the phone and stared at it. This phone had taken those images. This phone had witnessed two people die.

'It's true,' she said. 'Mr. Richard has killed a monk.'

'I told you,' said the ghost. 'Som passed through the forest, but he has moved on now. So has Marco.'

'And the younger one tried to spy on Mr. Richard, but Johnny caught him.'

Mya's heart clenched. She had brought the young man here; his family would have no body to bury, no explanation.

'Oh, him. He is still here. Barely. Kala Sriha has been sniffing around him. I'd wish *I'd* been taken by one of the immortals. Then I wouldn't be stuck here. But no. I have to stay and watch everyone else move on.'

Mya was only dimly aware of the ghost's self-pity as she held the phone. It was warm, like a living creature. She felt as if some echo of Som's spirit was moving into her fingerprints and capillaries.

'What am I going to do?'

'Well,' said the ghost. 'If you want to survive, you need food. And not the food of this forest. That will turn you into an animal like the others. You must find a door back to the human world. Follow me.'

The ghost led her to where blue-tinged light flickered through a gap in the forest. Mya must have left this way open after she delivered medicine to the shadowy person in Combat Sports Emporium. Not far from the gap, Mya could make out the humpy outline of a shelter where someone had propped branches against the slanting trunk of the fallen tree. It was not much; Mya could have done better herself. The ground had been trampled by man-sized shoes, and there was a shallow fire pit with flat stones around the edges.

'Your translator made this,' said the ghost. 'He seems to sense he is close to an opening to the mortal world, but of course he can't get through it. Now, listen, Mya. You have a good door here. If you are careful, you can pass through, find food, and come back to the forest. Just find a tree or any living plant on the other side, and pray to return. The forest is connected to all plants, everywhere in the world. You can be free to travel.'

'I want to go back to my family.'

'You don't know where your family are now? None of them?'

'A military camp somewhere across the river. It didn't have a name.'

'That's too bad. They could be dead by now.' He said the words without pity. 'Still, you have plenty of options. Mr. Richard's children have already made many passages, and some are easy to open. Most of them go to places in Europe or the US. People want the powers his medicines can give them. He keeps it all secret. No border control, no paperwork, no government. He's killing people because those reporters were close to finding out what he's doing.'

'I just want to go home.'

'Forget it,' said the ghost. 'We all wanted to go home. It can't happen.'

Mya was close to tears.

'Why?' she said. 'What happened to you, anyway? Why are you hanging around haunting this place?'

'I'm not finished with my anger for what he did to me. They call me Luck—that's pretty funny, right?'

Mya didn't laugh. She turned the phone over in her hands again.

'But I can help you...' Luck smiled again. 'Really, I know a lot of stuff.'

'No, thank you.'

Even as she said it, she was distracted. Someone else was here. Someone was watching her. She scanned the undergrowth until she saw two golden points of light; wide-set eyes were tracking her from the shadows beside the shelter. Although they were some distance away she felt as if whatever intelligence was behind them had slipped inside her mind already. The golden irises had vertical pupils like a cat's, and thick black smoke surrounded the eyes. As if the smoke were congealing to become solid, the body of the animal developed an outline: it was a black lion of enormous proportions. It had some sort of prey drooping from its jaws, dragging between its legs as it walked.

Luck released a series of curse words and shot up among the branches.

'Heads up, Mya!' he called to her. 'It's Kala Sriha, and he's got your translator!'

Gecko Me Up

to: shadowboxer@coolpost.com
from: Malu.Baines@thenewschool.edu
subject: Quinton
att: Quinton.jpg

It is my duty to tell you that Senor Quinton has been to the vet and his tomcat days are over. Aunt Christina took him to Yonkers. Also, we de-flead him. He seems OK with it. See photo.

to: malu.baines@thenewschool.edu
from: shadowboxer@coolpost.com
subject: re: Quinton

I won four fights in a row BABY!!!!! That makes my record 4:1. Coat says I'm coming along. So I forgive you for going behind my back with Quinton. Is that shrimp he's eating in the picture?

I WAS DOING sit-ups with a weight plate when Coat interrupted me, clutching his phone and practically jumping up and down inside his own skin. It was like he barely had himself under control.

'I got you in Lumpinee,' he whispered, beaming.

I wasn't sure I'd heard him right. I stared.

'No way.'

He nodded like a jackhammer. There were practically sparks flying from his white teeth. He motioned for me to follow him into the kitchen, where Pook was doing dishes.

'Me? Lumpinee? *The* Lumpinee Stadium? I mean, there isn't another one, is there? Like at a strip joint or a sugar plantation?'

Pook snorted. 'Only one Lumpinee Stadium.'

Then Coat started talking so fast I couldn't keep up. I looked at Pook helplessly.

'You only have three rounds to do the job,' she told me, scrubbing the rice pot. 'You want a knockout. She is bigger than you, but slow. Use your high kick. Keep the fight fast, keep pushing her.'

'Her? Her, who?'

'Beatta Jorgensen,' they said in unison.

I put my hand to my mouth.

Jorgensen is a Dutch former champion. Turns out her American opponent had broken her hand in training. Jorgensen still wanted to fight, and apparently I was the best girl available in Bangkok on three weeks' notice. We weren't even in the same weight division, but the promoters wanted two Western women and Coat said I'd been very, very lucky.

I wasn't asking questions. I was too ecstatic. Lumpinee Stadium? Forget *Battle of the Bitches*. Lumpinee Stadium is the Carnegie Hall of Muay Thai fighting. It's got the prestige factor.

Coat looked worried. I guess it was understandable. Jorgensen is a seasoned fighter and I'm... well... not.

'Jade,' he said slowly. 'Don't be afraid to hit her.'

'Afraid? Me?'

Coat and Pook talked softly among themselves. Then Pook said, 'In your last three fights, you won on points. We feel you are holding something back. This time your opponent is bigger and more aggressive. She will dominate you. You need an early knockout.'

'OK,' I said.

They were still looking at me. Pook had that uncomfortable face, like Cake when he'd tried to tell me how to act.

'When our cousin sent you, he said you are like his daughter. That's why we let you come. He told us you have anger problems.

You are angry, but this is not coming out when you fight. Maybe you are afraid to hit a girl?'

I snorted. 'Of course not!'

I'd hit plenty of girls in my life, in the ring and on the pavement. They were crazy if they thought I was afraid. I took a deep breath, searching for words in a language I was only beginning to learn.

'I not stop. I hit, I no stop.' In my first fight I'd actually tried to attack the ref, but luckily Mr. B had intervened before I could get going. 'Mr. B say, Jade, be good. Or he throw out me. I try, I want stop, listen rules. Become real pro like that.'

I waved at the wall of photographs of former champions who had trained here. They had started with nothing. Their smiling faces and gold championship belts filled the wall.

'You must *fight* Jorgensen,' Coat said. 'Fight, not spar. Fight to hurt. You have to want to hurt her bad. Or you lose. Can you do this?'

I thought about it. It was tempting to laugh and say, 'Of course,' but it wasn't that simple. I'd been trying so hard to do the opposite, to become a technician, to be cool-headed. I wasn't sure I could turn the Old Jade back on.

'Cake say I fight my shadow. He say be nice when I go Thailand. I try nice, good, go easy? *Jai yen?* And I try fight smart.' I tapped my forehead. 'That why I here.'

Coat grunted at Pook. She dumped a stack of plates in the sink and wiped her hands.

'Come on, Jade,' she said. 'You and me. Put the gloves on.'

Five minutes later I was bouncing off the ropes while Pook, suited up with belly protector and pads, stalked me around the ring, picking me off from the outside, her cool eyes fixed on me like a tiger looking at lunch.

It was unreal. Pook, who had to be 45 at least, who did the cooking and cleaning, Pook was one shit-hot pad man. She was all business, and she pushed me until I had no choice but to come back at her full fury. Either she was out of condition and getting tired, or she was surprised by my sudden ferocity, because I finally got her in a clinch and started laying knees into her. Coat called it off.

When we broke up I was burned out. Pook was also breathing hard, but I'd landed some real bad knees into the belly protector and if she was hurting, she wasn't showing it.

'Pook, I not know you fight!' I gasped.

She shook her head. 'Fighting is not recommended for girls. I learned from my father, like my brother learned. Then I got married. My husband is a businessman, always traveling. He keeps a second wife in Chiang Mai. It wasn't working out with us. So I came back here to help my brother. My son is a champion, you know Cake?'

'You're Cake's *mother?*'

It was the first time I'd seen her really smile.

'I did a good job, right? I train you now. Keep the gloves on, we have more to do.'

It's funny. All that time I'd been looking at Pook like she was some kind of servant, and it turned out she was a better trainer than Coat. Thai pad men are revered in the West. Nobody ever told me about pad women.

'Forget your shadow. You are not fighting that. You are fighting Jorgensen. I will be Jorgensen. You be you. What do you think she will do first?'

'Uh... try break my head?'

And off we went. She only had three weeks to get me ready for the Lumpinee fight, and she crammed more into that time than Mr. B. had done with me in the years I'd been training in New Jersey. She was full-on.

I helped Pook clean and cook so we'd have more time together. Pepsi teased me that I was 'not American anymore' and said 'at last she do woman work'. I threw my sponge at him.

We dragged out Coat's Stone Age laptop and looked at all Jorgensen's fights. We talked, brokenly, about how she would be training to beat me. And then we played out the scenarios, over and over. Pook couldn't fake being six inches taller than me, but she brought in fifteen-year-old Benz to work with me as a simulated-Jorgensen. He was about the right size.

Benz might be only fifteen, but tell that to my bruises.

'Learn to take punishment,' Pook told me. 'Remember Pink? When you hit her, she didn't care. You need strong defense, too.'

I've been in street fights as a kid. I've been on the ground and kicked by a crowd. I know how to tune out pain, how to detach. But working with Benz taught me to take punishment and still fight back. And he taught me to protect my head.

Pook also made me work on my *wai kru*. Somehow I thought that training in Thailand would include my effortlessly mastering the ceremonial prayer-dance that the fighters do before every match. The reality was that I looked and felt stupid. I don't know what my Dominican aunts and cousins would say if they could see me doing these fussy poses that have to be exactly perfect, right down to the position of your fingers and eyes. I tried. My aunts probably would have peed themselves laughing at the sight of me trying. Pook made lemon-faces.

'A Lumpinee stadium fight is a big honor,' Pook said. 'You must make respects. Jorgensen has a weak *wai kru*. You can get the audience on your side before the fight begins.'

'Audience? Why?'

'Lumpinee is special, Jade. You need the support of the audience. You will feel it when you get in the ring. It's a kind of power. Now practice your *wai kru* again. Make it more sincere.'

Four days before the fight I was trying to sleep, but Pepsi and the kids were playing *takraw* in the empty lot outside. It's kind of like hacky-sack but with a plastic ball. I was wrecked from training so hard, but I tolerated the game until the ball came through the window and landed on my head.

'My ball,' I yelled in Thai, and the cat pounced on it. 'Be quiet, I sleep!'

They all came in shyly and sat on my 'bed.' The kids made me feel old because even after a hard day's training they still had the energy to play, and I just wanted to be a puddle. I gathered Waldo in my arms and let his purring soothe me.

'Hey Jade, tell Coat we want to go watch you fight at Lumpinee.'

'He know you want,' I said.

'Yeah, but he won't bring us. No money.'

'I will win,' I said. 'Then maybe Coat get more money student.'

'Jade, why did you come here?' Pepsi said. 'Everybody's rich in America, right? Why do you come?'

I laughed. 'I no rich!'

Pepsi grabbed my cheapo mp3 player and threw it to Moo, who stuck it in his ears.

'Why did you really come here?'

'Train. Get better. Be fighter.'

'No,' Moo laughed. 'You could have gone to Fairtex, Saisinprapa with the other foreigners.'

'OK, OK,' I said. 'I here because I got demon. In heart. People say I fight my shadow.'

Moo nodded like it made total sense.

'I must beat demon,' I said in my lousy Thai. 'I keep get disqualify. I fight dirty. I try be good.'

Pepsi shook his head in disagreement.

'If you are nice in the ring, your opponent will wipe you out,' he said. 'What is your demon?'

We were talking in a mixture of English and Thai depending on what words I knew. I struggled for words, and Waldo's eyes tracked the movements of my hands as I waved them around, gesturing.

I said, 'Hard to explain. My dad was boxer, American boxer, you know?'

'Like Muhammad Ali?'

'Yeah. My dad teach me boxing.' I mimed. 'I think he so great, but he got demon, too. He hit mother. We...' I was struggling for words to explain what had happened. My father's drinking. The night he almost killed her, broke her neck when he threw her across the room. The hospital, the social workers, the court dates. My mom's depression. Having to leave the city and move out to Jersey, hide from my father because they hadn't been able to catch him. In case he came back and she was weak because she still thought she loved him. They convinced her we needed to start our life over. Like witness protection. How do you explain that to a kid? At seventeen I still didn't understand it.

'Police come,' I said. 'My mother hurt bad. My heart... angry. So angry.'

They watched me with shining eyes. Waldo stretched out and I scratched his belly.

Funny, all the therapy I had, all the talking about it they made me do, I never said it simple like this. I never said it with the words sticking in the back of my throat, the tears so close to the surface.

'Then I doing bad stuff,' I said. 'Get... wrong friends?' Wrong boyfriend, to be exact.

'That's bad,' Pepsi said. 'Friends must help you, not make trouble.'

If only Malu hadn't gone away to school, maybe it would have been different. But she'd gone, and there'd been no one to hold me down.

'My boyfriend steal cars. I got in trouble police. Then Mr. B start training me. But... I still got demon. Angry.'

They looked at me sweetly. I felt ugly.

'No big deal,' said Moo with the air of an 80-year-old. 'Everybody has problems. You can find a way to live a good life.'

He was only twelve, but I wanted to believe him.

THREE DAYS BEFORE the fight Pook shook me out of that beautiful black pit I call sleep.

'Day off,' she sang in my ear. 'Get up! Hurry!'

I moaned. Sleep dragged me back down like quicksand.

'Jade! You deaf?'

'Mmm... day off, why I get up?'

She shoved me with her toe. 'Get up, girlfriend. Special day. Today you get a tattoo like other fighters.'

I was up!

'Really?' She must mean like when the monks tattoo a tiger on a fighter's back. 'Cool! Can I get bulletproof tattoo?'

Her mouth twitched. 'They say you have to be good Buddhist for it to be bulletproof. Are you a good Buddhist, Jade?'

'Um... OK, what about waterproof?'

The tattoo artist wasn't a Buddhist monk. In yet another instance of unfair treatment of the ladies, it turned out that the monks weren't allowed to tattoo women. Apparently we're lower on the reincarnation ladder than men. But higher than animals. When I found out, did I get mad and attack anybody? Nope. I am the New Jade. I flow with the *mai pen rai*.

I got my tattoo from a layman, a friend of Pook's called Mint. He spread out his designs on the pavement in the sun.

'Don't worry about it,' Mint said softly in English, bending over my right thigh. 'I can give you an invisible one, with henna. Office workers get them. Nobody will see.'

I laughed, but then said OK to the invisible tattoo. My mom would freak out if she knew—not about the ink, but about the unsanitary conditions. Besides, who can resist a secret power?

I'd decided to put it on my right glute. I'm not really into ink, but a Thai tattoo is special. You get an animal, and if you have that animal tattooed you can call on its power. The animal can even possess you, supposedly. Malu would say *Grow a brain cell*—but me, I like to keep an open mind. And in the Jorgensen fight? I'd take any advantage I could get.

'I was thinking a tiger,' I said to Mint in English. 'Or maybe a monkey. A monkey could be more realistic, like, closer to my animal spirit? You know what I'm saying?'

Mint pursed his lips. Then he shook his head.

'You need gecko,' he said.

'Excuse me?'

Pook intervened. They talked to each other a couple minutes. Then Pook said, 'This is how Mint works. He can only give you the animal he sees for you. They talk to him. The animal spirit must choose you, not the other way. You need the gecko.'

'Gecko? They're just little funny lizards. Who's going to be afraid of a gecko?'

'The gecko is a very lucky animal,' Mint said. 'Always warn you when there is trouble. Helpful and auspicious. You need the gecko.'

The idea of a gecko did nothing for me. 'A cat? Waldo?'

They weren't happy. I could almost see the *mai pen rai* forming on Pook's lips, and I knew that in a minute we'd be getting up and leaving and I wouldn't get any tattoo.

'OK, OK. Gecko me up. Does it hurt?'

The answer to that was yes.

Kala Sriha

MYA SCROLLED THROUGH phone menus with fierce concentration. She was familiar with Mr. Richard's smart phone even if he didn't know how much she'd handled it, but this one was more sophisticated. By the time she found the call register the sound of the lion's breathing was louder than the insects and birds, and a wind stirred her hair. The lion had dropped the translator on the ground. The man stirred a little, so she knew he wasn't dead.

She found the last number in the call register and redialled. *Please, mother, please, someone, tell me what to do...*

Now the man was completely still, but the lion walked around him in a circle. Kala Sriha was the size of a water buffalo, but black and long-haired, with the coiled musculature of a big cat.

'*Mya, you must never call this number again,*' snapped her mother's voice in Burmese. '*Don't even try. Next time no one will be here.*'

'Mother, please don't hang up,' she breathed into the phone. 'I promise not to call again. Please only tell me what to do.'

The voice on the other end sounded anguished. '*I wish I could. But it's too dangerous. Trust me as I trust you. Do what you must.*'

Could this really be Mya's mother, who was notorious for telling everyone what to do and expecting to be obeyed? What if the voice was just some cruel trick?

'*I can't interfere again. This is a turning point. You must act for yourself.*'

Kala Sriha's shadow lay heavy on the prone body. The immortal bent its rough-maned head and nuzzled the man's neck. Then it lowered its body until the man was covered in blackness.

Luck was excited. 'Kala Sriha is going to devour the translator!'

Mya turned her face away. She felt sick.

'I thought Kala Sriha ate no flesh,' she murmured.

'He does not eat flesh. He's going to take the reporter into his shadow. He must have done something worthy of Kala Sriha's respect to meet this fate.'

To the phone, Mya said, 'Make it stop. Please.'

'*I don't have that power, Mya,*' said the voice of the woman who was like-and-yet-unlike Mya's mother. '*I'm not even there. You are. If you want it to stop, you must make it stop.*'

Mya scowled at the phone. She looked at Kala Sriha where the god lay on the man's body. The zone where black fur met the man's filthy clothes was semi-transparent, so that Mya could see the lion through the man and the man through the lion. The lion was so huge it made the man look like a doll.

Mya stepped away from the tree and Kala Sriha's golden gaze took her in. There was a sensation as though a gong had been struck. Her bones began to vibrate. Her hairs lifted away from one another. The man tried to lift his head, and Kala Sriha opened its jaws to grip the man's skull.

'No!' Mya shouted, and threw the phone. It hit Kala Sriha in the face and bounced off, tumbling across the ground until it came to rest at Mya's feet again. Kala Sriha turned its attention on Mya. Which of them was the more surprised by what she had done could not be said.

'What are you doing?' Luck shrilled. 'Are you crazy?'

Mya picked up the phone. Leaving his shadow lying upon the fallen man, Kala Sriha rose and surged toward Mya. The immortal brought heat and a musky odor that made fear spark across the surface of her skin. The lion's breath on her face smelled like Mr. Richard's workshop when he was brewing drugs. Mya was shaking, but she would not let herself flinch away from the smell. Kala Sriha's upper lip curled back and she saw the end of a tooth as long as her forearm.

Luck remarked, 'He probably won't find you appetizing. But the sound of his roar can kill animals.'

Up close, Kala Sriha was enormous. She fixed her gaze on what was right in front of her: the shiny dark hairs that grew sideways across the lion's muzzle. Would they feel like silk if she touched them?

'I pray that you won't take this man,' she said to a black nostril. 'I brought him here. I will bring him back. He must not die.'

'Why not?' Luck said. 'He wouldn't be the first.'

Mya ignored the ghost. Kala Sriha sat back on its haunches, shifting position in a way that allowed her to see beyond the lion to the fallen man. A rumbling sound moved out of the lion and into Mya until her lips throbbed and the bottoms of her feet hummed. The phone felt hot.

Kala Sriha came into her mind and body in a way that shook her bones like the wind shakes a tree. The immortal mind was vast yet also familiar. Despite the creature's masculine mane, Kala Sriha's presence felt female. The immortal probed Mya's being. Mya's insides stretched under scrutiny, so that holes appeared in the cloth of who she was.

It is rare to meet a mortal who can come here. You are very old for one who lives on the earth.

Those weren't the words—there were no actual words, only residues of the immortal's passage through her, a suggestion of communication. She had the sense of becoming a thin, stringy net of ideas with big empty spaces in between, into which Kala Sriha inserted itself, contemplating what there was of Mya. Like blood through veins, the lion shot through all of her thoughts, until it came upon the question she had been harboring: *whose was the voice on the phone?*

There was a sense of laughter; not mocking, but truly happy.

You will find out one day, little star. Why do you protect this mortal?

It's my fault he's here, Mya answered. *Mr. Richard tried to kill him with the night orchid, but he would not leave the world. It was me who brought him here. His life is lost because of me.*

There was a pause while the immortal's mind enveloped Mya's, holding her soul like it was a baby.

The being belongs to me now. His acts are also my acts. I move in the world in many forms, and he is a part of me, now.

And again Mya felt the vastness of possibility yawn around her until her consciousness became a frail tightrope. The darkness of the lion was an immanence and an emptiness both. When it retreated she found herself looking through Luck, who faded in and out of sight against the seething green background of foliage.

Kala Sriha stood over the man once more. The man stirred and pushed himself from the ground. Around and above him crowded an afterimage of the black lion's form, like an overcoat. He moved toward Mya. His body seemed to get stronger with every step, and she wondered what the lion had done to him. He trailed a cloak of smoky darkness as he walked away from the lion, and little by little his form filled out so that he was more flesh and less bone. He came to a halt in front of Mya, his chest heaving with the exertion of walking. 'Thank you,' he said, and made a deep *wai* to her. 'I'm Shea.'

She shook her head. 'Not me. Please thank Kala Sriha.'

Shea looked confused.

'Kala Sriha... that's just a legend.'

Behind him, Kala Sriha's tail began to lash at his disrespect. Kala Sriha was becoming larger and diffuse, a black lion cloud. As its annoyance built the immortal emitted a smell like burning hair. Mya's chest tightened. She pressed her hands together at her breastbone and *wai*'d to Kala Sriha.

Thank you, thank you, thank you. Please excuse this mortal's ignorance. Thank you for his life.

A destiny lies on you both, Kala Sriha said. *But he is weak, starving. His strength of will alone sustains him, but it also stops him from accepting me. He will tear himself into pieces this way.*

Shea was sizing Mya up with quick, desperate eyes. He shuddered, his skin crawling away from the darkness that surrounded him; but it clung to him like fingers.

'I can't die here,' he said. 'There's something I have to do. Help me.'

He is closed-minded. He denies me.

Mya took out the phone and pressed it into Shea's hands.

'But—where did you get this?'

'Mr. Richard took it from you.'

'He drugged me. I keep seeing things. A black lion and lots of other hocus pocus.'

Kala Sriha rumbled with displeasure.

'Please don't say that!' Mya whispered.

I have shown patience with you both. Enough. There is a form waiting for him in Bangkok. He will be one of my animal servants.

Stricken, Mya said nothing. Animal servant? Was Shea to reincarnate?

'I would give anything to be an animal servant,' Luck whined.

'I have to go to Bangkok,' Shea said out of the blue, so that she was unsure whether the desire was his own or Kala Sriha's. He added, 'I have contacts in the police there. Come with me, Mya!'

He cannot go as a human.

Bangkok. Bangkok. Had she ever delivered anything to Bangkok? There was the time she had delivered cash to Mr. Richard's wife, slipping through the forest into the roof garden of the luxury high rise over the river…

'Please, take my hand,' Mya said. Shea's fingers were cool and he was shaking, teeth chattering. He staggered, bumping into her. She felt her way through the branches, seeking Mrs. Fuller's roof garden with its potted trees and its little fish pond…

In the air around them there was a change of pressure and light, like the rollover of clouds that comes with a rising storm. Kala Sriha.

He must accept me. But he does not.

'Kala Sriha, take me!' cried Luck. 'I may be only a ghost but you could put me in any animal body you like. I'd even be a turtle.'

The hot smell of Bangkok blew into the forest. Mya could see through the base of the palm tree in Mrs. Fuller's garden. She gave Shea a little push to guide him through, but Shea's legs gave way. He crumpled to the tile floor.

'Come on, Shea,' Mya hissed, bending beside him. 'Quickly, before Kala Sriha claims you!'

I know his fate. I can see around the corners of time. Did you think you could escape me?

On the other side of the carp pond sat an unusual-looking black cat with golden eyes.

'Is that Mrs. Fuller's cat?' Mya heard herself gabble. Wishful thinking. Of course Mrs. Fuller did not have a cat; all that fur would not agree with her haute couture décor. The cat stretched and then gathered itself. It sprang across the fish pool in a graceful arc, landing on Shea's back. There it lay down with a possessive air.

He is mine.

Kala Sriha was inside Mya's mind like blood in her brain. Yet she pleaded.

'Beloved Kala Sriha, he is still a living human.'

The young man has the beginnings of a powerful voice. That is why I came to him. But there is a price to be paid.

Beneath the black cat, a stain of darkness began to spread across Shea's prone body. When it had crept over his entire body, the blackness drew inward toward the cat, until there was nothing left of Shea but an animal crouched upon the blue tile above the noise and fume of Bangkok.

Mya's heart pounded with a kind of dread. What about the phone? The phone that had called her, Mya, and spoken to her in her own language, with a voice so like her mother's—what would become of it now?

The cat turned its golden gaze on Mya. She ought to be afraid; but strangely she found that she was angry. She had come so close to saving Shea.

'He won't accept you,' she said to Kala Sriha

She was right. The cat began to twitch and shiver, as though something were biting it. Its fur stood on end as it startled and skittered sideways across the balcony. Snarling, it ran up the side of the banana tree and from there made a spectacular leap toward the roof. Mya gasped as the cat hung mid-air for a moment before it managed to catch hold of the gutter and scrabble its way up. Then it disappeared from view.

'What is going on out there?' The door to the penthouse apartment opened and Mrs. Fuller put her head out, wincing as heat slapped her in the face. She was speaking English. 'Michael, is that you?'

Mya was so startled that for a moment she couldn't think. She had escaped Mr. Richard only to be stupid enough to return to his wife's apartment! Her insides seized up as she waited for Mrs. Fuller to turn toward the banana tree and notice her, but at that moment a man's voice answered from inside and Mrs. Fuller glanced fractionally in the other direction. Mya focused on stillness, so that she could slide into the tree and return to her forest.

As she slipped away the last thing she heard was, 'I heard a rat or something on the roof. Michael, can you call maintenance?'

Bangkok was gone. Mya let out her breath in the safety of the forest.

But the forest was not safe anymore. The hot breath of Kala Sriha was on her neck.

You have meddled. You have disrespected. You forget what I am.

Mya turned, and the lion's golden gaze seared her face. The trees shivered in a powerful sound wave, low and droning. The beginning of the killing roar?

Mya clapped her hands over her ears and bolted blindly into the underbrush. She had to get away from the sound. She had crossed this forest to visit so many rooms in so many countries—any living plant anywhere was all she needed to make a connection—but to do this required composure. She had none. The sound was attacking her mind, and she reeled sideways.

With a painful jolt she collided with the half-fallen fir tree. Here was the shelter that Shea had made, close to the opening to *Combat Sports Emporium*. Here was the way out!

The lion's roar broke around her as she fell through the yellowing leaves of a neglected ficus plant and into a cluttered office in New Jersey.

Channelling Rocky Marciano

LUMPINEE STADIUM HAD a big reputation, but it didn't look like no Madison Square Garden. It was scruffy and low-key. The atmosphere was something else. Even when the crowd wasn't cheering or roaring, you could feel their background presence. I had the spooky sense that decades—maybe centuries—of fighting spirit had sunk into the walls, the floor, the canvas, the silk banners. I was part of history, now. The orchestra were playing their traditional melodies and sidewinding rhythms, just getting warmed up for the real action, and money was changing hands over me and Jorgensen. She was the odds-on favorite, obviously. But I wasn't thinking about that.

I was thinking about how I was going to beat her without getting disqualified. When I did my not-very-impressive *wai kru* I put my whole heart in it, praying I could do Pook and Coat proud.

Beatta Jorgensen's eyes were cold blue. She came out of her corner twitchy and predatory. I don't know what they were feeding her, but she looked even bigger up close.

When we first kicked off I fought her on the outside of her range. The strategy was to cut angles on her, to avoid her shots and land my own. What actually happened was that Jorgensen kept me away with her longer arms, and then when I was lining up for a round kick, she teeped me right in the chest, knocking me back across the ring. Her timing was better than mine. But she didn't move in to capitalize. She was just letting me know she could get me.

I struggled to adjust my strategy. As we moved around each other, each of us twitching and feinting, I could tell that she was just sizing me up. Letting me try out my moves so she could get my measure and figure out how to do me. Soon she'd be coming for real, and then I'd have trouble.

The key in a Muay Thai fight, Coat had told me over and over, is to strike more and strike harder. Unlike in MMA, there is no ground game. There's no punishment for being thrown or tripped, except the loss of a point—and in Muay Thai, you don't usually win by points. The idea is to knock your opponent out. That's what this audience was betting to see.

I had to get to her before she got to me. Jorgensen started to work her low round kick against my thigh. I ignored the battering and charged in straight, punching all the way. Caught her with some body shots and I knew I had to be hurting her, but she hooked me up and clinched me almost immediately. Slick with sweat, we wrestled for positional control; I tried to knee her in the ribs to make myself some space, and she wrenched my shoulder girdle over and threw me.

The ref separated us and re-started the fight—in MMA Jorgensen would have gone down with me and we would have gone into the ground fighting phase, but now we were back on our feet, moving around each other. And I was mad.

I went after her with my kicks. She couldn't shoot for a takedown, so I was free to assault her lead leg. I am blessed with a pain-seeking sense that lets me keep finding the same spot, so I knew it would be hurting her more and more each time. With every kick I imagined her femur cracking. Her leg didn't actually break, but I could see the shock of the blow register on her face, even though she tried to hide it.

Halfway through the first round, I was getting good and hot. But I still had the New Jade noise in my head. I wasn't going to break a rule. I didn't come to Lumpinee to get disqualified.

The music was speeding up, reflecting the increased pace in the ring. I was sucking air in through the holes in my gum shield, biting down with my jaw on every blow. Pook and Coat were shouting at me from my corner. 'No kick, go straight, go straight!'

In the rush of the mix, I didn't know what that meant. Did it mean 'go straight' like 'become a decent human being for once in your life? Do your homework, clean your room, stop running around making trouble?' Because I'd heard that before.

I was still bashing Jorgensen's legs enthusiastically with my shins when she kicked me in the face.

The teep, or front kick, is a move you do to keep the other fighter off you. It's a push-kick. But in Muay Thai, when you teep somebody in the face, that's an insult, because showing someone the bottom of your foot is symbolically saying 'I'm stepping on you, dude.'

I got the message. Jorgensen was telling me I was a joke. I'd heard that before, too.

The gum shield had saved my teeth, and I was so high on my own body chemistry that I wasn't feeling any pain. I charged in with my guard up, punching hard, and again she clinched me.

The first round bell rang.

Then came the moment of truth.

As the ref broke us apart, Jorgensen turned her back on me, but I still had her in my kill sights.

The urge came over me, so strong.

I wanted to push past the ref, jump on Jorgensen's back, and choke her out. Pay her back for the insult. I wanted to do it so bad.

How could she be so trusting? On the street you'd never turn your back on an enemy.

'Jade!' Pook was screaming at me like she could read my mind. 'Jade, get in corner! Now!'

I passed the test. Stomped over to my corner and flopped down on the stool.

'Listen, Jade.' Coat was talking to me now. 'Forget kicks. She can take every kick you throw, easy. You go straight. Straight in, keep hitting. Overpower her with punches. If she kicks, you catch it. We worked this—remember?'

Yeah, I remembered. You cover up the head against the high round kick, and this leaves an opening at your ribs. So when she kicks you in the ribs—and she will—you catch it and drive her back. It was simple in training.

But this was the fight, and Jorgensen was built like a rhinoceros. How do you drive *that* back?

'OK,' I gasped.

Pook said, 'The chance will come. You will see it. Remember how we trained.'

I wanted to laugh, but I was still getting my breath back. They squirted water on my face. They slapped my shoulders.

The bell rang and we were back in.

The clean hot rush of anger had done something good for my brain. Now I could think. Coat was right. I'd been stupid to try to beat Jorgensen at her own game. She was too tall, too skilled. But I always could hit hard. My dad had trained me to box since I was five. 'You don't got to be tall to knock somebody out,' he used to say to me, and we'd watch old Rocky Marciano fights and try out his style.

Like Marciano, I went in slugging. Coat was right; why worry about the clinch? Jorgensen couldn't take me down, all she could do was stop me momentarily. I'd just charge in again.

After this happened once, she tried to keep me away with her round kick. I covered up my head and she couldn't get through, so she went for my ribs and I caught the kick.

So many moves you work in training come to nothing in the ring. But this was sweet. With her leg under my left arm I ran her back, punching her face with my right. Spilled her on the mat and was about to instinctively jump on her when the ref pushed me back.

With a supreme effort, I restrained myself from attacking the ref. *Supreme effort.*

I champed on my gum shield and waited for her to get up. My flanks were heaving and the sweat was pouring off me. I was slippery, harder to clinch now.

Up she came again with those ice-blue eyes and I went for that sore lead leg of hers, catching her right on the bruise with a nasty round kick, and for a moment she dropped her guard just an inch or so as she flinched.

And there it was, gleaming like a diamond: the opening. I tasted it. It only lasted a fraction of a second, but for me the moment hung frozen, glinting with possibility. Jorgensen's head was exposed and lined up for my right hand. She had probably judged herself out of range. But she wasn't—not for the kind of wild overhand Marciano-style shot that my dad had taught me when I was little. I stepped in deep with my left leg and swung that right overhand from the outside, and maybe it was all those childhood lessons, but now it was like Marciano was in my body for just that split second.

My hand came over the top of Jorgensen's guard and I felt my fist accelerate through her jawbone and there was a jolt as I hit the resistance point and kept going. Then my hand was flying free through space and sweat was hanging in the air like a bead curtain, flung from Jorgensen's skin. Her head whipped to the right, and her body paradoxically started staggering left because her middle ear was confused. She was only half-conscious as she reeled and went down.

See that? There goes your champion. Down, baby.

The ref pushed me away and knelt at Jorgensen's head. It was over, and the entire stadium knew it. The crowd was on its feet. Ladies may be officially unwanted in this sport. We may have to fight last on the card so we don't make the ring unlucky, but people bet on us and cheer for us and the musicians play their hearts out for us, just the same.

I raised my arms in the air and howled along with the crowd.

We went to a nightclub afterward. Someone gave me a drink. It was the first time I'd had alcohol in months and after a few sips the room was bending and stretching.

Pook stayed close to me. I think she had the idea that I needed protecting, which is pretty funny.

'I'm not supposed to be happy, but I am happy,' she said.

I laughed. 'Why not happy?'

'My husband died recently.'

I stared at her, shocked. She didn't meet my eye.

'I much sorry,' I blurted. I mean, what? Dude must have keeled over in the run-up to the fight. Why hadn't she said something? I didn't know how to respond. My Thai was so terrible that half of what came out of my mouth was probably offensive and the other half just stupid. I knew Pook had left her husband but I didn't know how she would feel about him *dying*.

'Don't be sad for me,' she said. 'It could be an opportunity. Remember I asked Coat to visit the farm near Chiang Mai? It belongs to my husband's family. He hated it there, he took jobs overseas to get away. He left Cake this farm in his will.'

Why was she telling me this. 'You go back there? Or sell?'

'I don't know. If Cake were here he could start a boxing camp up there.'

'But Cake do engineering degree in America.'

She nodded. 'Probably we will sell. We don't have enough money for a camp. You should see it. So beautiful, on the edge of the bamboo forest. A peaceful place. Not like Bangkok.'

She waved her glass around the loud, smelly room.

'You miss Cake, yes?'

'Every mother misses her child, Jade.'

That made me feel guilty. What time was it in the Dominican Republic? Should I call?

Just then, Coat pushed his way through the crowd and handed me his phone.

'For you.'

He was frowning. Had Mom bawled him out? I knew she was worried about me, but—

'Hello?'

Mr. B said, 'I need you on a plane back.'

'Mr. B... hi. Um...What? Why? What happened?'

'Tommy Zhang is offering you place on fight card for *Klaxxon*.'

'*What?!*'

'You know. His new MMA show. In Vegas.'

'I know what *Klaxxon* is! Are you sure he wants *me*?'

'Oh yeah, he wants you. He's not mad anymore. He likes your skills. He wants to get a piece of your career.'

'I must be drunk. Are we talking about the same guy?'

'Jade, don't ask no questions. I tell him, Tommy, I say—'

'Tommy? You're on a first name basis? I thought everybody had to call him Mr. Zhang.'

'I said, Tommy, my friend, Jade is not interested in fame or money.'

'I'm not?'

'Jade is interested in the fight, I tell him. I say, Jade can be a great fighter if somebody gives her a chance. She's got a big heart, I say. She wants it. He tells me he knows you can't fight pro yet because of your age, but he's having a special exhibition match at end of men's event. He can get around the age rule that way. You'll be on pay-per-view, second to last event before the final round. He's getting Gretchen.'

I couldn't breathe. I was going to fight K-1 star Gretchen Van Der Hoef? On TV? MMA rules?

'Jade? You still there?'

I tried to talk but only a squeak came out.

'W-wait. What's the catch?'

'Catch? No catch.'

'But... Mr. B, why'd he change his mind? Did you pay him?'

'Jade! Bite your tongue. I never pay nobody. I simply go to him with news of your win and what Eva showed me.'

'Eva? What does she have to do with this?' Even as the words came out of my mouth, I remembered Eva and her phone behind Mattress World.

'Eva got video of you and Tommy. I tell Tommy it can be our secret. Eva is gonna be Ring Girl of the Month for *The Cage* this October. Two birds, one stone, right?'

'Mr. B, you dark horse.'

'I don't drive no Hummer for nothing.'

Hungry Ghosts

MYA SHOT ACROSS the messy office like a wild animal, half-expecting Kala Sriha to pursue her, hunting her down. She found herself in a hallway. To the right was an emergency exit, to the left a door leading back toward the gym, where music thumped. Opposite her were two doors with male and female symbols. As she stood hesitating, the door with the man's symbol started to open.

Mya hit the metal bar on the emergency exit and plunged outside, onto a colorless, glaring expanse of asphalt that smelled of diesel and garbage. A blue dumpster loomed to her left, and she ran around behind it. There were concrete buildings and engine noises all around, and the only growing things she could see were a line of weeds sprouting from cracks in the pavement. Planes moved in the bald gray sky. She cringed from the sense of exposure. She flattened herself to the ground like a frightened animal.

There was no green thing anywhere to be seen; no way back to the forest. Only the sickly ficus plant in the office back there; but what if Kala Sriha waited for her? Nothing could make her go back there, not now.

She cut across parking lots and side roads surrounded by gray sidewalk and rectangles of dead bright color. She had to find something that was growing. Cars passed like great, reeking animals. At last she came upon a row of scraggly bushes by the side of a building—not trees, but the closest thing to trees she had seen in this world of pavement and steel. She settled on the dirt and touched their branches. Her heart was racing.

She smelled frying meat. On the other side of the little hedge stood a row of trash bins. Just beyond them a building with a sign she recognized loomed in brilliant yellow. She'd seen the ads on TV: smiling uniformed girls *wai*'ing as they passed out food in paper bags through a window to the sound of pop music. In reality the place was dull, and there was a heavy man in the service window who did not smile, and the cars that drove up to the building were huge and gleaming and their drivers didn't smile, either.

She remembered what Luck had said about food, and quickly broke into the topmost black bag. Nothing smelled rancid, and there was plenty of brown paper for wrapping scraps of food. She darted into the bushes with her takings and reached with all her senses into leaf, branch, and root, praying that the forest would still be there for her.

DAYLIGHT HAD COME to the forest, lush and redolent of happier days in childhood. A warm breeze beat Mya's face, and swarms of insects speckled the air. Instead of fir trees, bamboo was everywhere. Filtered sunlight made everything glow green.

Kala Sriha was nowhere in evidence.

Mya opened the paper and began to eat the scraps of meat and other unidentified food with her fingers. She wished for rice, but there had been none. She ate carefully. In the prison camp Mya's mother had taught her children to eat and drink slowly when food was finally presented. She had taught them how to stay quiet and save their energy in the long gaps between meals. She had stroked their hair.

Mya wrapped some of the food for later and set off to find water. Bamboo gave way to mangroves, and there were flowers she'd never seen before. Then, as she parted the huge, spatulate leaves of a plant as tall as herself, Mya came face to face with a great red bird. She gasped and drew back; the creature also recoiled and spread its enormous wings, startling a couple of monkeys and sending them screaming away into the canopy. For a moment Mya was unsure whether the bird would attack or flee. It did neither.

Slowly it lowered its wings and turned side-on so that one emerald-green eye regarded Mya. It opened and closed its beak, and in a flash Mya understood quite clearly that it was hungry.

She opened the paper wrappings enough to remove a scrap of bread, soggy with sweet red sauce. She extended her trembling hand, and the bird bent down and snatched the bread. Then ran.

'It's OK,' Mya said. 'I won't hurt you. If you're hungry, we can share.'

She didn't know how she was going to get enough food for herself, let alone another creature. The thought of returning to the gray world of Combat Sports Emporium did not appeal to her; but if they had so much food there that they could just throw it away, it would be safer for her than stealing from Mr. Richard's kitchen.

The bird had not gone far. When Mya made her way to a small stream for a drink, it followed her. Its gait was strange and swaying, and every so often in a flash so brief it seemed imaginary, Mya glimpsed the lower half of a slim girl in a blue sari. Just a flash, and then the red bird was clearly visible.

When Mya bent to drink, the bird drank. Mya offered a little more and this time the creature was less skittish. Finally, when Mya lay down to rest, the bird lay down beside her. Its wing smelled like the most lovely perfume.

Just as Mya was falling asleep, out of the bird rose the ghost of a young woman. In clear Burmese the ghost said, 'Thank you. That is the first mortal food I've had in years. You make me almost feel myself again.'

Geek Alert

THE HARDEST THING about leaving Bangkok was saying goodbye to everyone, especially Pook. She had become like an aunt to me. She even found a nice cozy cloth travel carrier for Waldo and *helped me get him in there,* which was brave. I didn't like putting him through all that, but I just couldn't bear to leave him behind. Pook had offered to feed him, but I felt like there was this bond between us. I needed him with me and I was pretty sure he needed me, too.

I tried not to cry on Pook at the airport.

'Give my love to Cake,' she called as she waved me off.

I thought of Nana and my mom and stifled a sob. Airports. People leaving. Even when it's a good thing, it hurts.

MALU WAS MORE excited to meet Waldo than me. He didn't feel the same about her. When we got home, he shot out of the carrier and under the sofa, glaring and hissing when I tried to coax him out.

'I don't know, Jade,' Malu said. 'That cat is too beautiful to be a stray. I hope you didn't steal somebody's pet.'

'Pook and I took him to the vet and he wasn't microchipped,' I said. 'He slept in my room every night for the last five weeks. I don't know where he came from, but I couldn't just leave him.'

'What about Irene?'

'I'll figure something out. For now we'll just keep him inside so she doesn't see him.'

'If he lives on fruit like you say he does, I'm not cleaning the litter box,' Malu said.

I couldn't find any fruit so I left Waldo an offering of Fig Newtons and went to bed. My body clock was all messed up. When I woke in the middle of the night, Waldo was sleeping across the luggage I'd left on the floor. At one point I half-woke, thinking I heard a male voice from the next room. I rolled over and listened, but it must have come from outside the house because I fell asleep again. When I got up it was afternoon. Malu was gone. So was Waldo.

I texted her.

I didn't see him. Thought he was under sofa. He didn't get out when I left. I would have seen him.

Maybe you would've seen him, I thought. And maybe not. Oh, Waldo.

I started unpacking. I picked up the empty cat carrier to put it away. It felt a little on the heavy side. I upended it over the sink, expecting cat poo to topple out, but instead a phone clattered into the sink, which was thankfully empty.

What the hell? I sure didn't have a phone in Thailand, and I was pretty sure there hadn't been anything but Waldo in the carrier when airport security had checked—after all, isn't checking for stuff like that what airport security is for? I tried to find out who it belonged to, but the menus were all locked to a password, so I shrugged and dropped it in my gym bag. I'd ask Khari what to do with it. He's good with technology.

The plan was for me to take two days off training to recover from the fight and the jetlag. I needed the rest, but although I was around the apartment a lot, Waldo didn't show up and I had a lot of time to worry about that.

'He'll come back,' Malu said. 'Everyone knows our apartment is the best place to be an animal. Right, Coltrane?'

The iguana on her shoulder flicked his tongue in and out.

'I think Waldo might eat Coltrane if we're not careful,' I said. 'He was always chasing the lizards at boxing camp.'

'I thought you said he was a vegetarian.'

'Malu, don't be stupid. He's a *cat*.'

*　*　*

ON MY FIRST day back at the gym, Khari picked me up and hugged me, then cuffed me with a couple of light shots probably just to confuse my hormones.

'Mr B's in his office finalising your contract,' he said. 'Tell you what, girl. You got to work it, now. I'm not letting you mess this one up.'

Was I in culture shock, or was Khari unusually full of himself?

I came out the locker room with my head down, all business.

'What we doing?' I grunted.

'Standup, obviously.'

'But I really need to run through submissions. I ain't done no groundwork in months.'

'We can fix that,' Khari said. 'Mr. B got Mario Diaz coming in tomorrow. Dude be like Gumby, he'll put you through the subs.'

He put on the pads and I taped up my hands and got my gloves on. Khari got in the cage and motioned for me to join him. It was stupid. We didn't need to train in the cage. Why was he being so stagey?

I looked around suspiciously. Jamie Bell was talking to somebody new, a skinny guy with spiky hair. The guy was nodding like he was paying attention to what Jamie was saying, but he was actually watching us. I'd never seen him before. *Geek alert,* I thought. He was cute but extremely wimpy-looking. Very skinny—even by the Thai standards I was used to.

We started off easy because I hadn't even had time to warm up. I didn't know why Khari was pressing me to get in the ring so quickly, but it must have something to do with the two journalists.

The bullshit was starting up. I missed Bangkok already.

'Come on,' he said, moving in on me and making me hit going backwards. 'Two months in Thailand. What you got? You still the bad Jade?'

He signalled for the high round kick and I wanted to give up right there—Khari is six foot two and I'm five foot one-and-a-half. He was holding the pads way too high, and if I went for it I'd probably slip on the canvas and go down.

Was I still the bad Jade? Hell, yeah.

I ignored the pads and kicked him under their line, whipping my shin right into his exposed ribs. He wasn't braced for it and he staggered back, coughing.

'Ouch!' yelled Dedalus from the floor. 'Khari, man, don't mess with the Jay-D.'

I tongued my gum shield and kept going. Khari winked at me. He had done it on purpose! Was I that predictable? Now I knew for sure he was putting on a show for Jamie and his friend, and it was working. Jamie's friend was staring openly.

Yeah, I was back in the USA. Land of Bullshit and Opportunity. When we finished, people clapped. Jamie's friend headed straight for us.

Khari said, 'I gotta talk to Jamie for a second.'

I ducked out of the ring and went to the bag while they schmoozed. Khari is always friendly and entertaining even though he thinks Jamie's a dweeze. Khari's a star; all his successes just feel like the natural course of events. He's got what it takes. It's like an aura around him.

Kind of the opposite of what I have. Me and my shadow.

The bag alley was crowded and I could only get a piece of the end bag near the locker room, a battered old leather thing that had been re-stuffed god knows how many times, patched with tape, bloodstained. I started hitting it, making rhythms, working my knees mostly because of Pook's last advice at the airport. I wondered what Pook was doing right now. It would be night in Bangkok.

But I wasn't going to think about Thailand. Right? I had to stop thinking about it. I was home. This was my big chance. No messing around.

So I pounded the bag. I knew I was in bad form, but I couldn't stop until I was exhausted. Then I walked around in circles to catch my breath, hands on my hips and head thrown back. The thump of bass made the air shudder, and I was all heartbeat and sweat. This is where I like to be. Even the sight of Eva perched on a stool watching Khari train couldn't affect me. Eva had her new pole-dancing shoes on, the kind with four-inch heels made out of glass and wraparound straps that go halfway up your calves. She was clapping and going 'Whoo!' while Khari did sit-ups on the Roman chair. I don't know how he could stand it.

I turned away and someone was holding a towel out to me. The guy who had been with Jamie was standing there, smiling. Up close he looked young. Probably Jamie's latest intern.

'Hi, I'm Shea,' he said. 'Are you Jade?'

'Yup,' I said. I toweled my face so I could avoid making eye contact. He had a singsong accent. English? Not quite. Irish? Whatever. I wished he'd go away.

'Maybe Khari told you, I'm doing a feature for the *Independent*. It's a newspaper in London. It's going to be part of an ongoing series about women in the martial arts. *Battle of the Bitches* has been airing there on Sky TV and it's getting a lot of interest. Cage fighting is very popular right now.'

So he wasn't from *The Cage*. He was a mainstream dweeb. But way too young to be a writer. And there was something else about him. Something false.

'MMA,' I corrected, trying not to snarl. 'But lately I've been fighting Muay Thai.'

'Of course,' he said smoothly, his smile deepening as he acknowledged the mistake. 'Anyway, I was wondering if you would consent to an interview.'

'Um, I don't know,' I said. I began to wish hard Mr. B. would get the hell out of his office and get me out of this situation. 'I just found out about the match myself.'

'Well, I watched the qualifying rounds and a lot of people thought your disqualification against Kristi was a real shame. You fought brilliantly up until then. It was clever of Mr. Zhang to invite you into the new event to show what you can do. And think of his connections in the movie industry! Maybe with Mr. Zhang's help you'll be the next Gina Carano.'

That was pure bullshit. I shrugged at the flattery. 'I only met Tommy Zhang once, Mr. Shea. He seemed pretty down to earth.' After I flattened him.

'Just Shea, please. Everybody calls me Shea.'

He did have a great smile. The accent didn't match the face. His skin was brown and his features were a little bit Asian. He had glossy black hair, deep-set melty eyes, and some nice metal in his right eyebrow. And those cheekbones. He had the whole sculpted-hollow thing going—although, to be honest, he looked like he needed a few cheeseburgers in him.

I knew he was just playing me for a story. Everyone knows British journalists are manipulative. He didn't know anything about Muay Thai; he hadn't even mentioned Julie Kitchen, the most famous fighter in his country if not the world. He probably didn't even know the difference between MMA and JKD.

'So I hear you just returned from Thailand. Me too. How did you like it?'

'It was OK,' I grunted. 'I got to go. I'll see you later, all right?'

I could feel everybody looking at me as I went into the locker room—he couldn't follow me there. Female reporters get to go in male locker rooms, but it ain't the other way around. The old Jade would have turned around and said to the gym at large, 'What the fuck you looking at?' It took a lot of willpower not to be the old Jade. It took a lot of willpower not to tell Shea where to stick it, because I knew for a fact the only real reason he wanted to talk to me was to try to draw me out about the Tommy Zhang rumors.

Well, OK, I didn't know it for a fact, but I deeply suspected it.

Don't know where my *jai yen* went. It's like, I land in Newark airport and two minutes later I'm back to my old ways. There was just something about Shea. He made me feel unsure in my own skin. Like his eyes were looking into me too deep.

I went into the locker room, grabbed a clean towel and turned on the shower. Before I could even take off my t-shirt, Mr B came charging in with his hand over his eyes and goes, 'You get out there and talk to him or hit the road for good, get it?'

I turned the shower off.

'Sorry, boss,' I said meekly. I told myself not to be stupid. I got hormones same as the next girl, and Shea was cute, and he got to me. Big deal.

Shea was waiting for me in Mr. B's office. He started laying it on with a shovel.

'I don't want to embarrass you,' he said, and then went on to say a lot of embarrassing things. 'Mr. B told me you're only seventeen. He thinks you've got a major career ahead of you, and I'd have to agree. You have real raw energy.'

I didn't look at him. It was all BS, anyway. Especially with that goofy accent of his.

'The look in your eye when you fight,' he said. 'It's like a wild animal. It's predatory. You remind me of Tyson when he was young.'

I laughed. 'You mean like I might bite somebody's ear off?'

He didn't laugh. He said, 'No, that was the older Tyson, after he was getting desperate. And, yeah, it's a fine line between sport and the real thing. Some people see fighting as a sport and that's it. Me, the way I see it, if you can't cross that line from the game into the fight, then you aren't for real. I'm not saying people should cross it all the time, you know what I mean? Because we live in a civilized society, naturally. But the best fighters are the ones who really know how to go there, to that place. And you're one of them. I can see it.'

I looked up into his brown eyes and his angular face, perfectly shaven. These weren't his own words. These were lines he'd been fed by Jamie. This was a game. I thought, *OK, so he's messing with you. But no blood, remember?*

He held out a business card, just brushing my arm with it.

'Maybe this isn't the best time for you. Why don't you think about it and ask Mr. B to give me a call? I'd love to do an interview. Maybe a few photographs, if that's all right.'

He smiled and walked away. My arm was singing where he'd touched me. I stood there with nothing to say for once in my life. Like I'd somehow lost a battle.

Jai yen is a pain in my butt.

Kala Sriha has a Plan

OVER THE NEXT day or two the trash was a good source of food for Mya, and by coincidence or maybe by fate, she was just settling down in the shrubbery to find her way back to the forest when a car rolled up to the drive-through and she spotted Shea in the passenger seat.

She froze. No. This couldn't be. She had seen him vanish inside the black cat in Bangkok. *After* she had been foolish enough to give him the phone.

Another man was driving. They had the windows down and while the other man ordered, Shea glanced around. He looked directly at Mya. She stood up, unsure whether to run.

They just stared at each other. Then Shea held up his hand to her, gesturing for her to wait.

He turned to his friend and said something. After a minute the car pulled into a parking space. The two men got out. Mya hesitated as they walked towards the restaurant, but Shea turned and made the same *wait* gesture to her. They went in, and five seconds later Shea emerged. He jogged toward her.

'I know you,' he said. 'I saw you back in Thailand.'

'That wasn't... exactly... Thailand,' she said carefully.

'How did you get here?'

'I thought you were gone forever,' she breathed. 'I'm glad to see you are well.'

'But I'm not well. I'm hallucinating and I keep losing my memory. I didn't think you were real.'

She thought of his phone, the caller with a voice so much like her mother's.

The words burst out of her. 'Do you know my mother? We are from Myanmar. My family are in prison there, and I was brought to the orphanage. My mother's name is Kyi and my father is called Thura. I have a big sister Htay and a little sister Thiri. Have you spoken to them?'

He smacked his forehead and stared at her so intensely she recoiled.

'Richard Fuller—you're one of his victims... I mean... I'm sorry, I don't know what to say. We have to talk. Tell me how you got here. Last I saw you we were... in a forest? In northwest Thailand.'

'We were in between the worlds,' Mya said, disturbed that he couldn't remember. 'The forest of the immortals. Outside time. You were near death. You needed to return to the mortal world, but you are part of Kala Sriha.'

His face softened. 'I remember. We must have both been drugged. I woke up in a strange apartment near here. I had to call a friend in New York and make up a crazy story, and I keep thinking I'm a... you'll laugh, but... well, I keep hallucinating I'm some kind of animal.'

Mya didn't know what to do. It was hard to speak up, to contradict him. But his foolishness was too great.

'Mr. Shea. I lived with Mr. Richard. Please understand that he is a *mor phii*.'

'No disrespect to witch doctors, truly,' he said. 'But no. Fuller's not a *mor phii*. He's a criminal.'

'He has powers other people don't have. Don't forget about the things you saw. Kala Sriha has let you live. Please don't be arrogant.'

'Arrogant? Me?' Shea ran his hands through his hair, which was now clean and shining. 'Listen, I'm in the middle of a job. I work as a translator for a newspaper, but I have contacts in the police, too. I'm gathering evidence against Richard Fuller. He shouldn't be running an orphanage or going to Hollywood premieres with his posh wife. He should be in jail. How did he get into Myanmar?'

She didn't answer. *Police?* What had she done wrong?

He kept on talking, half to himself.

'You can't just wander around New Jersey by yourself. How did you get here? Who brought you? I knew this gym was involved. I knew it!'

Mya moved away a bit more in case he tried to grab her.

'I just needed some food. I won't bother anyone—'

He shook his head. 'I'm supposed to save you. That's the whole point of what I'm doing. If you come with me, we can talk. I can help you...'

Mya edged away further. He was in no condition to be 'saving' anybody.

'I should have brought the police in sooner,' he went on. 'I promised my boss a story if he could get money to the right people, but everything went wrong and my informant was murdered. It was terrible. I tried to get more evidence against Richard Fuller, but that American psycho caught me. I wish I knew what drugs they'd given me. I'm a mess. Look at this!'

And he pulled out his passport, opening it and showing it to her.

'There's no stamp in it. How did I get into the country?'

'You're part of Kala Sriha now. Maybe Kala Sriha has a plan for you. I don't know what the plan is, but you are here and you must be changing form.'

He shook his head.

'I woke up in this girl's apartment. She's one of the fighters at the gym over there.' He nodded in the direction of Combat Sports Emporium. 'She just came back from Thailand, and she took my phone. There's a connection between Richard Fuller and this gym, and I'm going to find out what it is.'

Mya thought about the delivery she had made to the man in the office. She thought about Kala Sriha, and how his roar could stun or even kill. If Shea could tell everyone about Richard Fuller, wouldn't that be just like Kala Sriha putting matters right with his roar? This investigation must be what the lion wanted.

'Maybe I can help you,' she said. 'Will you help me, too?'

'Of course,' he said. 'I wish I weren't so unstable. I'm exhausted all the time, and hungry.'

'That's because you have suffered,' she told him. 'You must please strengthen yourself, Shea. You need to have human experiences to stay here. Food. Life. Talking with other people. Things to connect you to life. Otherwise you will keep...' she bit back the word 'changing' and substituted, 'forgetting.'

'So... you know what I'm talking about? You've seen this effect of the drug before?'

'Something like that.' She hadn't wanted to go on arguing about whether or not Kala Sriha was real. There had been more important things to do. 'Shea, I need food for others who are... having problems like you. I need food for them. To make them better. Can you help me?'

He'd laughed. 'What, all you need is food? That's easy. I have to go talk to Jamie, the man I was with. He's helping me with the investigation. Come with me. We won't tell him who you are.'

She shook her head. No way.

'OK, then. Wait here.'

He went inside and came out with a hot, fragrant paper bag. Mya realized it would have been better to specify food that was not disgusting, but never mind. She took the bag and backed away, still leery of being grabbed. She would keep an eye on Shea and help him accept his relationship with Kala Sriha if she could... but for now, she stepped back into the tangled bushes and prayed herself back to the forest.

The last she saw of his face before she vanished, he looked surprised. Very surprised.

Duct Tape and iCarly

WAS I HALLUCINATING because I was hungry or because of jet lag? I don't know, but I kept thinking I saw Waldo out of the corner of my eye on my way home from work. It was probably wishful thinking. I was so hungry. And tired. One thing that sucked about being home was being broke. Malu's parents had been sending Malu and me money for rent, but we were covering the groceries ourselves. You gotta wash a lot of dishes to feed a fighter in training. They gave me free food at work, but most of it wasn't nutritious enough to support my training. I walked because I couldn't afford the bus.

At one point I stopped, turned, and squatted down. I rubbed my fingers together and made *psss psss* noises and called 'Waldo?' really quietly. Waldo didn't come. I felt stupid.

By the time I turned onto my street the gecko tattoo on my butt started itching like crazy. And it's not like you can walk down the street scratching yourself there. I trudged up the stairs to the apartment, dumped my gym bag outside the door, and leaned my head against the door as I unlocked it. As the door swung open my tattoo actually felt like it was burning. Freaking stupid gecko.

There was a light on in the living room, and the TV was flickering, mute.

'Honey, I'm home,' I called, kicking the bag ahead of me and shutting the door. 'What a day.'

I put the chain on the door and went to the bathroom, then came out to see what Malu was up to that was keeping her so quiet. I hobbled down the short hallway past the little kitchen, and then I stopped.

Malu was on the floor just inside her open bedroom door. She had been tied up and gagged with duct tape. Her hands were taped together behind her, and her ankles were taped to them. Her face shone with sweat, and her eyes were fixed on mine. My hackles rose.

'Hello, Jade,' said a deep voice.

Sometimes you get a voice that deep in a small body. But not this time. The guy who stepped out of my bedroom was a mountain of a human being, his hair scraped back in a ponytail to show off the piercing in his ears and eyebrows. He had a jaw like a professional wrestler. From the darkness in Malu's bedroom another guy emerged, as tall as the pierced mountain, but whipcord-thin. The way the second one moved set my teeth on edge. Both of them wore dark jackets with t-shirts, and Pierce had boots on.

My scumbag alarms were ringing the house down. I mean, Tommy Zhang's bodyguards were all show and blow with Hollywood written all over their sculpted muscles—in reality they were cowards just like him. But these guys *felt* menacing. They were probably psychos who used to be in the service. The kind who join because they like the idea of killing and then when their service is over, they hire out in civilian life with career titles like 'Threat Management' and 'Close Cover Operative.' Khari used to have a cold-blooded 'friend' like this and the stories he told made me sick.

They didn't even look comfortable around each other. Two of them, honestly, was overkill.

What had they done to Malu?

My bones started to glow hot from inside. I wanted to launch myself at them. It was all I could do not to look either of them in the eye. I was mad. I should have been scared, but I was too mad for that. I guess that's part of my whole problem right there. I never know how to be scared at the appropriate time.

Then I clocked the guy on the sofa as he stood up. He'd been only partly visible behind the Norfolk pine, or I'd have seen him sooner. He was Asian, older than the other two, and his eyes were moving all the time. He looked back and forth between me and the two other men.

I said something like, 'What the fuck is this?'

Pierce nodded to the skinny guy, who twitched aside his jacket so that I could see his holster. In a rumbly voice Pierce said, 'We're here for the phone. No games. Put it on the floor and back away.'

'Who the hell are you?' I was still staring at Malu. She didn't look right. I wondered how they'd managed to subdue her without the neighbours hearing. She didn't look bruised or bloody, and there was no sign that the room had been disturbed. Her pupils were dilated and her eyes looked bloodshot. Maybe they drugged her.

'You don't want to ask that question,' said Pierce. He oozed self-importance, so that without him actually saying so you felt that he was in command and everything was going to fall his way. The other guy said nothing, but I was watching him in my peripheral vision.

Pierce added, 'You have a phone that belongs to my client. I could accuse you of stealing it and punish you the way my client punishes all thieves, but my client is a reasonable man. Unless you give him a reason not to be.'

I was tempted to argue; I'm always tempted to argue. But the sight of Malu like that freaked me out.

'Wait,' I said, suddenly remembering. 'I *found* a phone. I never had a chance to turn it in…'

I pointed to my bag. I'd shoved it in there and forgotten about it, but how would anyone even know I had it?

The twitchy guy leaned across me and picked up the bag. I could smell him. My eyes narrowed.

'So,' I said. 'I'm a mule now? Who am I working for, because I didn't get paid for this.'

I felt like an idiot for letting myself be used this way. I was mad at myself for not remembering to show the phone to Khari. I'd been too distracted by Geek Boy.

The dangerous-vibe guy flipped the phone open and handed it to Pierce, keeping his eyes on me the whole time. I could feel him looking, not at me but through me. People used to say my dad had penitentiary eyes but this guy had something colder than that. I was looking up the barrel of his gun before I even saw him move.

I refused to go to pieces; I've been around guns before, and they scare me, but they don't scare me shitless.

Pierce said, 'Contact the authorities and we'll come for you. Not a word, to anybody. We will be watching you.'

I nodded, wishing he would just go so I could check Malu. He stared back at me until I stepped back; then he disengaged. I heard him thumping down the stairs.

I put on the deadbolt and the chain; then I went to untie Malu.

I had peeled the duct tape off Malu's mouth and was working on her arms behind her back when I heard a noise outside that freaked me. It was an animal noise, a roaring—not like a lion's roar, more like something out of Jurassic Park. It started me shaking all over.

For what seemed like several seconds, I couldn't move. Malu was hyperventilating and cursing, and now she began to thrash. I heard voices outside.

'Quiet,' I hissed at Malu. 'Don't make a sound. I'm going to look outside.'

I crawled across the floor to my bedroom window. The roaring sound had been close, and it hadn't come from the street below, but from somewhere high up. Like the roof.

I peered over the sill. On the sidewalk below the three of them stood facing me, looking up. I dropped my head again, thinking they were looking at me. Then there was a noise over my head, on the roof itself. Footsteps, the shifting of weight. Something was up there. Sounded like two men.

I didn't dare stick my head up again. I might end up in the crossfire.

Overhead a bass drone started up, a rhythmic rattling that vibrated in the roof of the building itself.

'Jade? Jade, come back here and untie me.' Malu was scrambling around on the floor.

'Shhh!' I backed away from the window and got a pair of scissors and a paper bag. I cut her loose.

'Breathe into the bag,' I said. 'When you stop tingling, get yourself a drink. I'll be back in a minute.'

She grabbed my arm, her big hand circling my whole forearm.

'Don't you dare go out there and get involved,' she said. 'Just stay here and stay out of it. I'm calling 911.'

I shook myself free and returned to the window on hands and knees. There was a part of me that wanted to do as she said, trust in the law and the overall righteousness of the universe to take care of shit. There was a part. A very small, tiny-tiny part. OK, I'm lying. There was no part of me that thought that. Get real! The universe doesn't take care of shit. And anyway, the person who takes care of my shit is me. End of story. Like an idiot I'd brought the phone into the house, endangered Malu and myself, and now I needed to find out what was up on the roof making the GI Joes look like they needed extra-large Huggies.

Gunshots popped off. One, two, three, four. Movement on the roof. There was a scrabbling sound on the tar paper, and from my position crouched on the floor under the open window I glimpsed something larger-than-man-sized go sailing overhead and collide with the tree in the yard next door in a flailing of branches. Leaves seemed to explode from the tree as a black shape went scrambling down—panther? Leopard? Very furry ninja?—whatever it was, it ran down the tree head-first in the darkness and the four men fled, led by Pierce with his ponytail flying.

The Thai dude was the last to flee. He turned and fired at the shadow as he ran, but his shots were wild.

The men cut across the street and ran between some houses, disappearing from sight. The shadow followed them without a sound.

Malu's voice. 'I need the police. Yeah, I'm in Cliffside Park—'

I dived across the room, grabbed the phone from her and killed the connection.

'What are you doing?' Her eyes and teeth flashed and she tried to get the phone back but I was too quick for her.

'They told us not to report it or they'd come back. Don't you get it? The police can't protect you from people like that. We have to just keep quiet, and lie low, and... I'll be right back.'

'You're crazy,' she shouted at me. 'Don't go out there! Hey!'

'Emergency services have to call you back. Don't answer it,' I commanded, standing in the half-open door. I grabbed the only weapon I could find, a collapsible umbrella. 'Don't talk to the police. You'll get us killed.'

Then I went. As I closed the door, she shouted, 'Yeah? You're not the one with duct tape burns on your ankles!'

I ran down the stairs. By now people were out on the landing, including the super, Irene, yakking into her cell and running her free hand through a giant mop of blonde hair like it was the end of the world. Who was I kidding? The whole neighborhood would be calling the police. You didn't get gunshots at nine o'clock on a Thursday night in Cliffside Park.

Irene put out a hand to me as I passed, but I dodged around it. Nobody touches me if I don't want them to.

'Hey!' she said. 'You know anything about this, Jade?'

'Sure,' I said. 'If it's gunshots, the black girls upstairs must know something about it, right?'

That shut her up. I went out.

I didn't follow them at first; I turned right coming out of the apartment and went up to Anderson Ave. like I was going to get a bus or whatever. I walked a couple blocks north and then cut back down the hill on a side street that I knew would connect.

You can't go very far east in Cliffside without hitting the cliff itself.

I heard dogs barking toward the bottom of the hill. I could track the men by the disruption they caused. I followed them north, towards Fort Lee. Maybe they'd left their car up there to be closer to the Turnpike.

I didn't have to go far. If I had, then I'd have had time to think about what I was doing and I'd have realized it was pointless, and dangerous, and the kind of thing that never ends well for me. But I'd jogged only a few blocks when I saw the automatic security lights come on behind a big house on the cliff, and I heard the muffled sound of a dog barking inside. I started up the driveway, waiting for somebody inside to turn on more lights or open a window or shout or something, but nothing happened. There was a Lexus in the driveway. From the back yard came a terrible snarling noise.

I stopped in my tracks.

It was an Animal Planet type noise, a roaring, slavering, complicated utterance that sounded like a very large predator having a messy meal. I shrank against the hedge separating the big house from its neighbours. Through the windows of the house next door I could hear the refrain of a Lady Gaga song. Nobody inside had any idea what was going on out here. The dog in the big house continued to bark.

The noises seemed to go on and on. Pretty soon I'd changed my mind about investigating shit further. I started edging away, trying to stay out of sight and hoping I was downwind of whatever the thing was. Then I heard footsteps and two of the men bolted past me. I could hear their ragged breathing. They were practically knocking each other over to get out of the backyard of the big house by the cliffs. It was Pierce and the Thai dude. They ran up the street and through another yard.

I got a pretty good look as they passed. Their faces were drawn with terror, and Pierce was holding something in one hand that it took me a few seconds to recognize. It was like a prop from a horror movie. He was holding somebody's hand, and part of the arm attached to it, dripping blood.

When I got home, the police lights had turned my block pretty colors. I was tempted to keep walking, but it would look bad. So I went right up to the building and stopped by the front door. I could see Lt. Perez leaning on his car and talking on his radio. I waited for him to notice me.

He took me in, squinted a little, said something into the radio and then put it down. He came over, pulling his whitest minty-fresh smile.

'So, Jade, how you doing?'

'I'm doin',' I answered, smiling fakely back in an 'aw shucks' kind of way. 'Is it safe to go in there now?'

'Where you been?' he said seriously. 'Your cousin's worried about you. You know something about this?'

'Me?' I said, pointing to my own chest. 'You know I'm straight now, Lieutenant. I don't know nothing. Anything. I don't know anything about it.'

'About what?' he said.

'The gun shots. We heard them, and I told Malu to call 911 and then I went to look around.'

'You went to look around. That was smart. That your official statement?'

'I just went to see what was going on. But I couldn't see nothing, so I came back.'

'You been gone a good... twenty minutes. You sure you didn't see nothing, Jade?'

'I didn't see nothing,' I said, looking him in the eye.

'OK,' he said, and the way he said it was so neutral I couldn't figure out what he was thinking about me but I figured it couldn't be good. I didn't think Malu would have caved so quickly, but Perez knew how to make me feel guilty just by looking at me. He always made me feel like I should be going to church with him and saying my Hail Marys. He's so... moral, which I find funny in a cop. He always used to be on my side, though, back in the day. I decided to try and play it through.

'Can I go upstairs now?' I said.

'Yeah, yeah, go.' I turned, not daring to believe it would be that easy—

'Yo, Jade, one more thing!'

I turned back. I knew it. Perez sauntered toward me, getting ready to spring whatever he was going to spring. But before he could say anything, his partner in the car put the sirens and lights on and gestured for Perez to get in.

Perez kept his eye on me as he jumped in the car and went. I watched the cop car do a U-turn in the road and squeal off down the hill, toward a big, fancy house on the cliff, where they'd find...

I tried not to think about what they'd find.

Malu was sitting on a kitchen stool doing shots of tequila. She'd had the presence of mind to put on a long-sleeved shirt and a pair of yoga pants that covered the marks of the duct tape, but when her sleeve fell away from her arm you could see a weal.

'I'm so sorry,' I said. 'I swear to god I don't know what any of that was about.'

She gave me a wounded look. Even though now she goes to the New School for Social Research and I go to the Old School for Kicking People's Heads In, still I tell her everything. She might be upset about being held at gunpoint and tied up and stuff, and she might be scared of what those guys could do to us, but the look she gave me now was the look of betrayal because she thought I'd been into something and hadn't told her.

'I swear,' I said again. 'I don't know who they are or why they wanted that phone—you know I didn't steal it or nothing, I found it and I forgot I even had it in my bag—'

Malu gasped. She had just taken a wedge of lemon out of her mouth and now she turned to look at me as she made the same connection I'd made earlier. She's usually a little quicker than that; being tied up and drugged must have put her off her game.

'Oh my god,' she said. 'You were a mule. That's why those guys wanted it back. You have to tell the police, explain what happened and that it was innocent. It happens to people all the time. Just tell the truth and—'

'Shhhh!' I hissed, so vehemently that spit flew everywhere. I slid past her into the kitchen and reached for a glass for myself. 'Why don't you talk a little louder so Grandma Bernstein can pick it up with her hearing aid?'

'Sorry,' Malu whispered. Then, hand trembling, she picked up her drink and took a long swig. She shuddered a little as it went down. She looked at me. 'You OK?'

'Me?' I laughed. 'I should be asking you that. Do you need to go to the hospital? They didn't... they didn't do anything to you, did they?'

She shook her head.

'Not that I know of. I was out of it part of the time.'

'They knocked you out?'

'They were here when I got home. I don't know how they got in, but they grabbed me as soon as I came in and put a needle in me. When I woke up I couldn't move, and that huge guy was asking me what I did with the phone. He called me Jade.'

I put my hand over my mouth. 'I'm so, so sorry. I swear to you, Malu, straight up, I'm not into anything here. The phone was in the cat carrier. I don't know how it got there.'

'I don't know about that Mr. B, Jade. You read the behind-the-scenes stuff on MMA, there's Mob money and stuff like that going on. I wonder if these guys are some kind of Thai Mafia.'

'What did you tell the police, anyway?'

'I said you heard a noise and went after them.'

'And Perez bought that?'

'I didn't know what else to say. You heard that scary guy. Even the other guy—Johnny?—even he's afraid of that guy. How can the police protect us from that?'

'They won't have to,' I muttered. The scary guy was now a dead arm. Ugh.

'You did the right thing, Malu. The last thing we want is for them to come back.'

'But... I still think I should have reported it. Won't the police take it more seriously if they know I was drugged?'

'They'll take it serious. The question is, do you want to go to the hospital and get checked out?'

Malu poured another shot. 'I'm all right. They'd better get the guys. Do you think they'll get them?'

I didn't look at her.

'I hope so,' I said unconvincingly. 'But we gave them the phone, so they have no reason to come back here.'

'Did you see where they went?' she asked.

I made a vague face. It's almost impossible to lie to Malu.

'You better call your grandma and tell her,' I said. 'You don't want her to see this on the news.'

'You saw something, didn't you?' Malu would make a great interrogator. I swallowed my drink. I don't really like tequila, but this wasn't the time to be choosy.

'I saw something but I don't want to talk about it.'

'Oh, no, don't give me that. You owe.'

I squeezed my eyes shut, wishing I could un-remember.

'You wouldn't believe me,' I said. 'And plus, it's gross.'

'Try me.'

I told her. She said, 'You smoking herbs now at that gym?'

'I'm so glad I tell you things, Malu.'

She said, 'What are we talking about here, werewolves? Vampires? Giant spiders?'

'Like I said, I don't want to talk about it.'

'So what about the guy's arm?' she said. 'What happened with that?'

'I think we can expect Lieutenant Perez to be coming back,' I told her. 'I just got to think what I can say to him.'

'Well, he can't accuse you of being involved in some supernatural shit. I think you should just tell the truth. There has to be a plausible explanation.'

I finished my drink. I could see the cop in the hallway, pacing up and down and talking on the phone. She was just babysitting us. But what if that man-eating shadow came back up here? Plausible explanation or not, I had the urge to call Aunt Yanira in the Dominican Republic, who practices *Las 21 Divisiones*. Maybe she could ask the ancestors to help me out with some kind of protection. But then my mother would find out. So... maybe not.

'You're going to lie, aren't you?' she said. 'You don't believe in telling the truth.'

'When the system's fair to me, I'll be fair to it,' I said, echoing what my dad used to say. 'Anyway, who would believe the truth? I told you, two of them got away, including that asshole with the piercings. Do you want them to come back here? What if they saw me see their guy getting eaten?'

'You actually saw people getting *eaten*?'

'Well, no, but I heard it. I definitely saw the dismembered member, you know what I'm saying?'

There was a silence. The tap dripped. Malu said,

'Let's leave. Let's go to my Grandma's house.'

Malu's grandmother on her dad's side was an OK lady, but she wasn't my Nana. I wasn't going there.

'Go to bed,' I said. 'I'll get rid of the cop. We'll be OK. We can deal with it.'

I don't know why after all these years of me fucking up my life and her succeeding in hers, Malu still listens to me. But for some reason, she does. She went to bed.

Birdhouse in Your Soul

THE RED BIRD-girl was called Hla. She was the first of many animal-children who came to Mya for human food. There was an elephant-headed bird whose body housed the spirit of a capricious nine-year-old boy, and a skittish deer girl who was afraid of the elephant head. And there were others, too shy to speak to Mya but no less hungry.

All of them had been dumped in the forest by Mr. Richard and his associates, but had been taken under protection of animal spirits.

'Are they alive or dead?' Mya asked Luck.

The ghost shrugged. 'Both. Neither. Like Shea. They could go either way.'

Luck told her that he'd been the first of Mr. Richard's children to travel to the forest. At first he had come alone, sent to find plants that Mr. Richard could use in his drugs. Later Mr. Richard had developed the extract of the night orchid that enabled him to come with Luck and explore the immortal land for himself.

Luck had helped Mr. Richard find ways to open the forest into specific places across the world. This allowed Mr. Richard to interact with other magicians. Luck had carried drugs and escorted children through these places. And he had trained other children to enter the forest—but eventually they outgrew the ability to travel here.

'We're expendable,' Luck told her. 'That's how we ended up here. Some were thrown away by their owners for whatever reason. Some were dumped by Mr. Richard when we outlived our usefulness. He had me train my own successor. Then when I couldn't come here anymore through meditation, they overdosed me with night orchid to send me here. I couldn't escape.'

'That's evil.'

'The night orchid poison is very painful. Your body disappears from the real world and you die here. Animals eat your body, but if the immortals don't want your spirit then your ghost gets stuck in the trees. Mr. Richard and his gang are clever. There's no evidence of a crime. No one can stop them because of this.'

'Not even the immortals?'

'I don't know,' Luck said. 'No immortal came for me. My body rotted. I'm stuck here.'

'I'm sorry,' Mya said wearily.

'It's my karma. I took many children through the forest for Mr. Richard, and they suffered because of me. So I'm stuck here now. I can't move on.'

Mya watched him keenly.

'That's why you're helping me? You want to gain merit.'

The ghost nodded. 'My betrayal of others holds me back.'

Mya swallowed against a painfully tight throat.

'I betrayed others, too,' she whispered. 'He told me they were going to be adopted by new families. I thought they were lucky.'

'He always says that.'

'What will happen to them?'

'It depends where they go. They might be adopted, but some clients are perverts. Mr. Richard is very well-connected. He's rich, but he doesn't care about money. He cares about power. He likes having power over the people who buy children.'

Mya felt sick.

'What am I going to do?'

'You could keep feeding them,' Luck said. 'They come closer to the human world when they eat human food, speak human languages. You can remind them of who they were.'

'What good is that?'

'I don't know. But they are hungry.'

Mya shivered.

'Mr. Richard is making a new drug,' she said. 'He says he will pour his spirit into me.'

'He has been working on that for years. He thinks he can escape the wheel of reincarnation by taking over the body of a child, so he can have power even over his own death. I've seen two boys and a girl die when he tried to possess their bodies.'

Mya looked around. The leaves and flowers were lush today, as though the immortal world were advertising its beauty that surpassed all beauty on earth. Mya decided that being a ghost here would be preferable to being possessed by Mr. Richard.

'Imagine it,' said Luck, a little gleefully. 'Imagine him in your bones and fingertips, imagine his breathing in your lungs, imagine your hands are his hands now... Mya, how close do you think he is to finding a medicine that will really let him do this?'

She swallowed.

'I think he probably has one by now,' she whispered.

Friendship Donuts

I KNEW I hadn't fooled Perez, but I had to stop worrying about police and giant animals that ate people's arms because Mario Diaz was on the mat. Like a lot of Brazilian coaches, Mario might be easygoing, slouching around murmuring suggestions in a really low-key way, but there was nothing low-key about the work. Nothing takes it out of you like ground fighting, and I hadn't done any for months. I had to work harder to make my moves stick. I trained with Dedalus and Cake, who are smaller guys but not small enough if you're me. I had to think my way around their moves in a way that's totally different from thinking on your feet, and Mario made it harder by restricting me to certain finishes during a given run. He'd call a given submission for each of us—say, 'ankle lock' for me and 'triangle choke' for Dedalus—and even if Dedalus offered me an arm bar on a plate, I couldn't take it. I had to go for the ankle, all the while stopping him from getting me in the choke. I learned about a dozen ways to get an ankle lock, though, so that was good.

After my water break Khari came over to talk to me, but I made myself just flash him a smile and walk on by. *Jai yen*, baby. I went straight to the sit-up bench and started in with my conditioning work. I was used to this by now. In Thailand we'd done all our push-ups, sit-ups and neck exercises at the end of a hard day. If this had been Bangkok, my training day would be only half over, but this was America, and Mr. B had scheduled a photo session for me this afternoon. I had to get my training done, take a shower, and change into clean fightwear by 2 pm. So I crammed in as much as I could. Two weeks is not a lot of time to get ready for somebody like Gretchen.

While I was doing incline sit-ups I could hear Mr. B talking to someone on his headset.

'I know Jade's no Gina Carano. How many girls who look like Gina want to fight? Gretchen's not bad-looking but she no Jennifer Lawrence either, so why you worry?'

Oh, no. He was probably talking to a sponsor about me. It was the looks thing again. Same old same old. How come nobody cares what Fedor or Tito or Wanderlei look like? How come women fighters have to also look good? Ever since Gina Carano had proved you didn't have to look like a dog to fight like one, promoters had been looking for the next Gina all over the place. When Cris Santos beat Gina I thought the pro game would open up for women, but sometimes it was just the same old bullshit. Promoters thought viewers just wanted a wet t-shirt contest, and most viewers weren't arguing. It pissed me off... wait, I'm supposed to keep that in the ring. *Jai yen*, Jade.

I was dreading the photo shoot. There was nobody to help me with my hair, and I was probably going to come out looking like George of the Jungle.

I finished my sit-ups and started doing kipping pull-ups. I was suffering through my second set when Monika appeared in my peripheral vision. She held a Tupperware box in both hands at chest height, like she was making a ceremonial offering, and she was smiling at me.

I dropped to the ground.

'Sorry,' Monika giggled. 'I am not meaning to interrupt. I want to give you this.'

I scowled. 'What is it?'

'We make donuts,' she said. 'They are called pączki. For you. My sister and I, we are such fans for you. We want to support girl power in cage.'

I felt my eyes widen and my lips twist. Fans? I flashed the thought that the donuts were poisoned. Eva might not know the exact content of my fantasies about Khari—like, she probably didn't know how many times she'd died a bloody death in my mind so that he could be with me—but she had to know we weren't friends.

'I don't know what to say.' I didn't take the box. Monika was so put together, standing there with her perfect boobs rising and falling with every breath, her perfect nails gripping the Tupperware, her spotless white capris and her windswept brown hair. She seemed to glimmer, and I felt more than ever like a human version of Quinton the tomcat.

'Please, take them,' she said, extending the box to me. 'We make special for you. We are excellent bakers! I promise! One day soon we open our own bakery, maybe in West New York. Serve all kinds of cake.'

'Really?' I took the box. Monika giggled and tossed her hair. She put her hand across her swelling chest like she was pledging allegiance to the flag. 'I am so admiring of you, Jade. I never have courage to get in cage like you. The woman power, we all stick together, we can do anything! I really believe is true.'

'You're opening a bakery?'

'Oh, yes, it is our dream since we were little. I bake, Eva does account books. She loves to bake but she never eats, you know.'

I grunted. No kidding.

'All our working is to raise money so we start the business. I go to school part time to become pastry chef, and Eva saves everything. We are going to buy the two family house and have many babies, help each other with business. Woman power!'

'Many babies... does Khari know about this?' I tried to picture Khari with his arm around a heavily pregnant Eva... ugh.

'Oh, Khari, he is so sweet! He is loving my cheesecake. We don't tell him our plans, he is not so bright, you know?'

I found myself smiling. I don't even know why.

She said, 'You look so skinny after Thailand, a little treat not hurt you. Anything else you need, I can help you in any way, you just let me know, OK? You are not alone, we all a team here.'

She actually reached out and patted my arm. I don't know what happened. In spite of myself, I was kind of starting to warm up to her. A little.

'Actually,' I heard myself say. 'There is one thing...'

'Just tell me! I can help you?'

'It's just, I got this photo shoot, and I look like I got hit by a truck...'

'No you don't! Come on. You get in shower, I go get my makeup bag. Everything will be OK. I am the hair genius.'

Perez came in while I was getting my picture taken. Monika had done my hair in cornrows, how it would be the night I fought Gretchen, and she'd also plucked my eyebrows, given me a facial, and put some subtle makeup on. My dark circles were hidden. She had trouble restraining herself from glamming me up, but I told her I had to look like a fighter. Still, I was wearing more makeup than I remembered having on since I dated Dmitri the car thief. And I have to admit, I looked pretty good. For me.

Malu texted me twice, once to ask me to pack her a bag and bring it to Mandino's, where her Grandpa Harris would pick me up and take me back to her grandparents' place in Teaneck. And again to say she'd forgotten Coltrane's iguana food when she'd taken him to Teaneck, so could I pack that too?

I didn't blame her for not wanting to stay in the apartment now. It had been agreed nobody would tell my mom, because she had enough on her plate with Nana. But it made everyone uptight and guilty. I felt terrible. Even though it wasn't my fault. I mean, it was more my fault than it was Malu's. Seemed like I was always bringing my problems on the family, and they never complained, and that made it worse.

I'd pack her bag, but I had no intention of going to Teaneck.

They made me stand in these dorky poses for the shoot, holding my hands up like I was fighting even though I don't stand that way in the ring. I tried not to look at Perez while this was happening. He watched the shoot for a few minutes, but he didn't stay. He spoke with Mr. B in the office for a while, and then he must have gone out back because I didn't see him after that. This made me nervous. It's like when you know there's a spider in the room but you don't know where. He was bound to give me a grilling. It was just a matter of when and where.

After the photographers left Mr. B cornered me. I expected him to start in with the whole 'why you not stay out of trouble with law' schtick, but he just said, 'Jade, you can finish interview before you go.'

'Interview?'

He meant that reporter, Shea, who showed up behind Mr. B. He must have been eating better because he actually had dimples when he smiled at me.

'I've got plenty of time. I'll go with you wherever you're going? Then I don't need to take up too much of your time.'

Mr. B put his arm around my shoulders. 'Oh, Jade got plenty of time! Go ahead, you crazy kids. Jade, see you tomorrow. I got Mario coming ten o'clock, so don't be late.'

I didn't want to bring the reporter back to my place, but I had to get a bag packed for Malu and get up to Mandino's before my shift started.

On the bus Shea said, 'You looked good in the shoot.'

I snorted. Then I remembered I was supposed to be professional, so I mumbled, 'Thanks.'

'Have you worked out your strategy against Van Der Hoef?'

Of course not. I hadn't had time.

'Yeah, we've got our game plan but I'm not going to talk to you about the specifics because Gretchen might be reading.'

'Oh, come on, you can tell me something. I understand she's highly effective on the ground. What's your feeling about that?'

I laughed, trying to sound light-hearted. 'You heard Mr. B. We've got Mario Diaz taking care of that aspect. Mario is Brazil's finest ground specialist.'

I sounded so fake. I just couldn't get into this interview. There was something too intense about this Shea guy. I mean, I never get interviewed. Why would some British newspaper want to talk to me, unless it was another 'ugly girl vs. pretty girl' article? But Gretchen isn't really pretty any more than I am. We're both just regular-looking.

'Is this a bad time?' Shea said. 'Your trainer was eager to have you do this interview, but I get the sense I'm imposing. Maybe I could take you to lunch tomorrow?'

'I'm training all day tomorrow,' I said. Then I realized I was stonewalling him again and Mr. B wasn't going to like it. So I said, 'It's OK, we can do it now. I'm just a little preoccupied. I'm rushing to get to work, so why don't you come up and we'll do the interview now?'

'Can't I take you for a meal? Make it more pleasant for you?'

I looked away. He had nice eyes.

'I can't, sorry.'

'You can't eat?'

'I'm in training? For the fight? My diet is strictly controlled.'

'Oh, yes, of course.' He glanced at the box of Monika's donuts on my lap. A wonderful smell wafted from it.

'Oh, these. Monika gave them to me. You want one?' He did look hungry. Maybe that was why he wanted to take me to lunch.

We got off the bus with Shea munching a donut, and a child in a red Chinese-style dress got off after us. She looked scruffy and almost as intense as Shea. I noticed her staring fixedly at us and I almost offered her a donut, too, but when she met my eye she turned and went quickly away in the other direction.

We walked up to my building. A police car was parked just down the hill. My heart began to thump. I opened the front door, listened, but heard nothing, so I hurried Shea through the lobby and up the stairs.

'Sorry about the rush,' I said.

I ran up the stairs, unlocked the door and held it open for Shea, and just as I was about to slip in I heard Irene's door open onto the lobby below. Irene stepped out into the hall, and Perez was with her.

I hustled Shea into my apartment, whispered, 'Go in the living room, I'll be right there,' and shut the door as quietly as I could. Shea looked freaked as I put my ear to the inside of my door and listened.

'Problem?' he said.

'Um, I have a thing that I need to handle,' I whispered. 'Let me just get rid of this cop, and then we'll talk. Can you wait in the living room?'

'Yeah, one of them is there,' Irene honked. 'I heard somebody go upstairs just now.'

So much for my plan of locking the door and pretending not to be home. I grabbed my keys, stepped out into the hallway and locked Shea in.

'Ah,' said Lt. Perez, coming up the stairs. 'Just the person I wanted to talk to. Jade, you wanna take a ride with me?'

I halted, trying to look surprised. 'Do I have to?'

'I'm not arresting you. I just want to talk.'

'Well, I got to be at work soon. I don't have much time.'

Perez glanced significantly at Irene-the-Super and Irene retreated into her apartment and shut the door.

'Let's go up to your place,' Perez said. 'If you don't mind.'

I shrugged. As I unlocked the door for a second time, my mind was racing with explanations for Shea being there. I was tempted to scream and point the moment I saw him. Then Perez would take him downtown and get him out of my hair. But Mr B would have me shish-kebabbed if I did that.

When I opened the door, there was a faint, almost subliminal smell: something damp and flowery. No sign of Shea. I put the box of donuts in the kitchen and looked around, but the apartment was empty. The doors to my room and Malu's were both open, and so was the bathroom door. The living room window was open a few inches.

'You shouldn't leave your windows open,' Perez said, leaning over and looking down into the backyard of the building. 'Especially after what happened last night.'

'Forgot,' I said woodenly. 'Malu's not here. She's totally freaked.'

'I know,' Perez said. 'She made a statement last night. But I never got your statement, because of the subsequent crime around the corner.'

'There's nothing to state,' I said. 'I didn't see nothing. I didn't hear nothing.'

Perez exhaled and the smell of coffee wafted across to me, mingled with his aftershave.

'It's always the same with you, isn't it? Hard to the end. You don't even know what you're dealing with, Jade. I'm investigating a homicide now. You sure you don't want to say something to me? Because what I saw down the block last night wasn't pretty.'

I winced. 'You want a cup of coffee?'

He shrugged. I went into the kitchen and got out the instant.

'So the cage fighting, it's going good?' Perez said, swaggering around the apartment looking at stuff.

'Yeah,' I said absently. 'And I'm still working at Mandino's. I'm all good now.'

'Right,' said Perez, picking up a copy of *Lonely Planet – Thailand* that was sitting on top of the TV. Shit, shit, shit.

'You just got back from Thailand, huh?'

I nodded.

'They do a lot of drugs out there,' Perez said. 'I got a homicide down the street, could be drug-related. An Asian man was seen earlier the same evening at your place. You say they weren't in the apartment. I got eye-witnesses seen three guys come in the building and go upstairs. So whose apartment were they in? Grandma Bernstein's next door? Or you?'

'Milk and sugar?'

'Two sugars. I can bring a dog out here and we can find out if they were here or not. Two of them are still out there. You think you can't talk to me because they'll come back here and kill you, something like that? That what you think? Come on, Jade. You know me better than that. I ain't gonna let you get hurt.'

I gave him the coffee cup and closed my eyes. Shit.

'They were here,' I said. 'They tied up Malu and said they wanted this phone I... found. They said they'd kill us if we involved the police. I gave them the phone. Then they went outside and we heard shots. They ran away. I tried to follow them but I got scared and came back. I told Malu not to talk. It's my fault. It's just that in my experience, Lieutenant, the police can't always help.'

'You should know me better than that by now, Jade.'

'Nothing personal, Lt. Perez. No offense, you know what I'm saying?'

'Sure, just looking out for *numero uno*, right, Jade? OK, I'm glad you come clean and talked to me because I already knew it. I took a statement from Malu and forensics have already been in. But I appreciate you telling me voluntarily. Now, what I want to know is where's the guy who was up here this morning?'

'Guy?' What was he talking about? I forgot my annoyance at Malu.

'You know who I mean. There was a guy in your window earlier today, maybe around noon. While you were out. I got my partner watching the building, so I know he didn't leave. Tall, skinny guy. Spiky black hair. Is he in the closet?'

Now I was confused. Perez must be double-bluffing me. Stoically I said, 'I don't know what you're talking about, Lieutenant.'

Perez went around the apartment opening doors and looking under beds.

'I know he didn't go out the window because my partner covered it,' he said. 'So where is he? You got an attic trapdoor or something?'

'I don't know what you're talking about,' I said again. Perez got down on his hands and knees and looked under the sofa, which sits only about six inches off the ground and isn't big enough for a child to hide under.

'Well, what have we here?' he said. My skin prickled.

He said, 'You got the super's permission to keep a cat?'

'Cat?'

He got up, dusting himself off—we don't vacuum much.

'Yeah, cat. There's a friggin cat under there—or are you going to deny that, too?'

I wanted to dance for joy. I looked under the sofa. It was Waldo!

'Malu's been feeding a stray,' I lied. I suddenly flashed the thought that if Perez knew I'd brought Waldo from Bangkok, they'd cut him open to look for drugs. 'I didn't know she was letting it in. Look, go in our kitchen. We don't have any cat food. We don't have a litter box. It's just some stray.'

'Uh-huh. Whatever. I'm not the cat police. Jade, I need you to be straight with me. This situation is nothing to mess with. I can get the information I need without your help, but I can do it a lot faster if you cooperate. Maybe somebody asked you to bring something back with you, and you needed money so you said yes. And now they want it and they don't want to pay.'

'It was just a phone. Nobody gave it to me. I found it in my stuff. I didn't even think about it.'

'They use a lot of expensive phones at this gym in Bangkok?'

'No,' I said sullenly.

He grunted. 'I been down to your gym to talk to Mr Bubba already.'

'Mr. Big,' I corrected.

'Interesting character. Anything funny going on with him, Jade? I understand he has relatives back in Thailand and you were staying with them. You see anything when you were over there?'

'Of course not. The gym is clean, Lieutenant. Mr. B doesn't tolerate performance enhancement drugs or none of that stuff.'

'Huh,' said Perez. There was a long pause while he rocked back on his heels and thought. 'OK, Jade. When you decide to talk to me, I'll be ready. You talk, I can help you. You give me trouble, then I won't stand in between you and the long arm of the whatever, you know what I'm saying?'

'Yeah. I know.'

'So where's the guy?' he said suddenly.

I groaned. 'There is no guy, Lieutenant.'

'I know what I saw.' He seemed very sure. He was making me a little nervous, because those assholes last night had said they would come back. What if one of them had been in the apartment while I was training? Did they think I had something to do with the... animal... that had killed their boss? It was all getting *muoy* creepy and I just wanted Perez out of here.

'Are you sure it wasn't somebody else's window?'

'And here I thought you changed,' Perez said. He handed me his coffee cup.

I shut the door behind him and leaned my head against it. I could hear Waldo purring. Waldo would be dangerous, if you were a little lizard or a bird. What if Waldo were really, really big? He'd be scary. I'd be scared of him.

He was winding himself around my legs like he used to do in Bangkok. Showing me he loved me.

'Oh, no way,' I said. 'No way is this happening.'

This whole deal was dragging me back into the old days of being in trouble, and I didn't want to go back there. Sometimes I feel like I'm in quicksand, and the harder I try to get out the more it's pulling me down.

It sucks. Pun intended.

What the Cognoscenti Say About Me

I ENDED UP being early for work. Perez had spooked me, and Shea vanishing had spooked me, and instead of making something to eat and taking a shower, I'd packed Malu's bag and gone out. I got the bus to work. I texted Malu telling her I was staying in Mr. B's spare room to be closer to the gym. Telling her not to worry. Then I texted Mr. B telling him I'd be staying in Teaneck for a few days.It's a junior high school trick, but it works.

I mean, come on, people. I've lived in Bangkok. I'm not going to fall apart just because of one little incident.

When I got off the bus, Shea turned up right behind me.

'What's with the disappearing act?' I snapped, unnerved. 'Did you *follow* me?'

Shea shrugged. 'I'm sorry—did that freak you out? I thought it would be better for you if I wasn't around to... er... complicate things with the police. Can we talk?'

I was hungry, so I let him pay for overpriced sandwiches and coffee. When he took out his wallet I said, 'Is that your ID?' and he showed me his UK driver's license. He had just turned twenty years old. He had long hair in that picture. It looked good.

'*Vijaralongkorn* Shea?' I said. 'You're Thai?'

'Nobody calls me that.' He snatched it back and handed the barista an Amex. 'My mother's Thai. My father's Irish. I grew up in Cardiff. That's in Wales. All clear?'

I relaxed a little. He was still very nervous, though. It's kind of fun standing next to a cute, nervous guy who is trying hard to get on your good side. Not an experience I'd had very often. OK, I never had that experience. It's not bad. Shea was wimpy, but cute, and he had an Amex and he knew how to disappear. Which could have been hot, in different circumstances.

'Aren't you a little young to be doing this kind of work?' I said. 'How many guys your age have their own expense accounts?'

He was not comfortable talking about his age. He stammered and stuttered and finally mumbled, 'I took a gap year in between school and university and ended up working for a... mumble mumble...'

'What?'

'Ahem. For a moderately famous investigative reporter. I was working as Marco Lewis' translator and research assistant in Asia, sort of an internship. I kept meaning to go back to London and finish my studies, but I've learned so much on the job that it never seems worth it.'

'That's funny,' I said. 'I just got back from Thailand. Well, you know that. But if you're Thai then shouldn't you know more about boxing?'

We sat down to eat, and he said, 'Are you a big baseball fan?'

'Me? Baseball? Couldn't care less.'

'But you're American, right?'

'Yeah, so?'

'Yeah, so, that's why I don't know about Muay Thai.'

'That's a stupid reason,' I said. 'You're bullshitting me.'

He was looking straight into my eyes. It made my stomach unsteady. I told myself I was probably just hungry; I picked up half a BLT and tore into it. He watched me for a little, and I gave him my *you got a problem with me?* look.

'Right,' he said, still in that funny, lilty accent that I now knew was Welsh. 'Here it is, then. You're right. I haven't been entirely truthful with you.'

'No kidding,' I said. 'Go ahead. Confess. You just want the female angle on Khari, right? Well, I ain't giving it.'

He frowned. 'I wish it were something so trivial. No. Here's where I bent the truth with your Mr B. I do work for the

Independent, but I'm not writing an article on lady fighters.'
He leaned forward, lowering his voice. 'I've been investigating
a criminal ring, and I got a lead that brought me to your gym.
I wanted to talk to you about your experiences in Thailand and
ask you if anyone asked you to bring anything back for them.'

Speaking of geckos. When he said that it felt like six or seven
of them were running up and down my back. I stopped chewing
and scratched my tattoo.

He added, 'But it looks like I was too late.'

'What do you mean, too late?' I said with my mouth full.

He shrugged. 'I read the papers. I saw the TV report. And I
know how to read between the lines. I'm concerned about you,
Jade. Shouldn't you be with your family or something? Should
you be going to work as if nothing happened to you last night?'

I swallowed. 'Nothing did happen to me,' I said. 'It was my
cousin. And I didn't bring nothing back.'

'I know what you gave them. The question is, where did you
get it?'

'Get what?' I batted my eyelashes cluelessly.

'The phone, of course. Who gave it to you?'

'How do you know so much?'

'It's my job to know things.'

'And how do you know what happened to my cousin last night?
Did you have something to do with that?'

He looked shocked. 'I'm not a criminal,' he said. 'I'm a
journalist. I'm a Buddhist. I'm a... a... I'm a vegetarian!'

I laughed. 'OK, you're a vegetarian. Does it offend you that I'm
eating this BLT?'

'Can we stay on topic, please?'

'OK,' I said, putting the sandwich down. 'If you're a non-
violent vegetarian journalist, how do you know so much about
the... item... I allegedly gave to a band of criminals? Were you
snooping around my place? Do you know who these guys are? I
don't want to mess around, Vija... Vija...'

'Everyone calls me Shea.'

'Shea.'

When I was done fumbling his name and spearing him with my wicked stare, I picked up my sandwich again and took a giant bite. There hadn't been any BLTs in Thailand.

'Those men are *not* my friends. On the contrary. I can't answer those questions at the moment, but I assure you my intentions are honorable.'

'That's reassuring,' I mumbled around a lettuce leaf. Insincerely.

'So will you keep my cover?' he said. 'I need to find out what's going on in your gym, what the connection is to the men who were at your place last night. And I assure you, there is one.'

I wiped my mouth, hiding a burp behind my hand.

'You gotta be kidding. Mr. B is like family to me. He took me out of the corrections system and got me into MMA. He gave me another chance. I know he's a little into the wheeling and dealing, and I know he's tacky, but he's got a heart of gold. There is just no way I'm not telling him about our conversation.'

I stood up.

'Sit down, Jade. You need to know more before you make that decision.'

'What more do I need to know? You're a fake, you're a liar, but it takes all kinds in this world, so thanks for the coffee.'

'Jade!' He stood up, too, in that reflexive, old-fashioned way some guys still have. It was kind of cute, bizarrely.

I sighed.

'Please sit down.' He said it through clenched teeth. He needed to work on his *jai yen*.

'You don't know squat about combat sports,' I said. 'You were just flattering me to get me to help you. You think I'm really that pathetic?'

'I'm sorry. You're right, I don't know much about martial arts. But I wasn't flattering you. I did my research and I found out what the cognoscenti say about your gym in general and about you in particular. I knew you'd just been to Thailand, where you won a very impressive victory over a Dutch champion in Lumpinee Stadium.'

I narrowed my eyes. 'The cognoscenti?'

'Yeah. Well, Jamie from *The Cage* told me most of what I needed to know.'

'Jamie thinks I'm that good?'

'Please, won't you sit down for just one more minute?'

I looked at my watch. 'Sorry, I can't. Late for work.'

I set off, and he followed me. I walked fast up the sidewalk toward Mandino's, but he had longer legs—much longer legs— and he kept pace with me easily.

'Jade, I don't want to compromise you but there's no way of preventing that now. I think you should know that the crime ring I'm investigating is into a lot of rackets, but the one I'm most particularly concerned with is human trafficking. Specifically children.'

I looked away.

'I can't believe you just said that. Are you talking about *selling* kids?'

'You know it goes on.'

'Yeah, I know it goes on, but Mr B wouldn't be into that stuff. And Coat is more likely to rescue kids who have been trafficked than anything. This whole conversation is so offensive, Shea.'

'I'm sorry. But you must understand that I have to look into it, and I can't do that unless everybody believes I'm really writing about cage fi—MMA.'

I shook my head. 'I don't know. You're not telling me everything.'

He spread his hands on the table. 'It's fairly complicated and I don't want to make accusations without evidence. Give me a chance. We can talk more. I'll fill you in as I learn. Please just don't blow my cover. And in return, I'll do everything I can to protect you and your cousin.'

I laughed.

'You? Protect me? You carry a gun?'

'No! I told you, I'm—'

'A vegetarian, I know. Look, Shea, I'll think about it. But if you don't watch yourself, I think you're going to be the one who needs protecting. Mr B's fighters are loyal. If anybody else finds out what you're really doing, you're gonna get messed up real bad.'

We had reached the entrance to Mandino's. He held the door open for me.

'You are not coming in here,' I said.

'Please, just give me a chance,' he murmured, bending down closer to me.

I shivered. There was a scent on his breath—not the coffee, something else. Kind of nice, sweet, and familiar... I pulled back.

'Don't push me,' I snapped, and stalked into the dark restaurant.

'I'm not pushing!' Shea called after me in that cute, lilty accent. 'I wouldn't dream of pushing you, Jade! Just think about it.'

'Ooh, Jade,' Miguel crowed from behind the bar. 'Just think about it, baby! Could this be the end of your long, long dry spell?'

'Shut up, Miguel, or I'll put glass in your cheeseburger.'

Raiding the Fridge

Mya followed Shea and Jade on the bus and then sneaked after them, waiting outside while Jade and the police and Shea came and went. Shea went into the apartment but did not come out, even after Jade was gone. So Mya went around to the back by the garbage cans and called up to him.

Shea did not answer, but a black cat that looked like a miniature Kala Sriha jumped on the windowsill from the inside. He peered down at her. Mya put her hand over her mouth.

'Shea?' she asked hesitantly. The cat turned and she heard a loud thump followed by Shea's voice, cursing, from inside the apartment. He must have changed then and there. Shea stood up and looked out at her.

'What are you doing here?' he demanded blearily. 'What just happened?'

A strange conversation followed. Again Shea made noises about 'authorities' and 'police' and then he reached into the pocket of his jeans and handed her the phone, the same one she had given to him in the forest.

'This is important,' he told her. 'Please keep it safe. Don't lose it. It's very important.'

'Why don't you keep it?' she said.

'Because I can't control... things.'

'You mean you can't control when you change.'

'You saved my life,' he said. 'I'm very grateful. But this is all too strange for me.'

'Strange or not, you must know it's true,' she told him gently. 'You know I can go to the forest. And you—'

'No, I don't know anything,' he said.

So she showed him. Putting the phone in her pocket, she slipped right through the potted pine tree in Jade's apartment.

The forest on the other side was still. Maybe too still: the air was hot and thick, as before a thunderstorm. But one thing had changed: the way she had used to get to Jade's apartment was now visible, like a passage through the air of the forest.

She clapped her hands together and let out a happy sound. Now she didn't have to go back to that gym or its awful parking lot. She could go from the forest to the apartment now, directly.

That was good, because whatever else you might say about Jade, she kept plenty of food in her house. Fighters were hungry, apparently.

So was Shea. When Mya returned to the apartment, he was gone; but he had taken half a loaf of bread. She cleaned up the crumbs from the hallway carpet. Then she gathered food to bring to the forest for the animals. The food smelled strange, but there was plenty of it. Mya felt badly about stealing. Very badly.

'I promise I will make up for it somehow,' she said to Jade's apartment. The place was so untidy and the food so plentiful that she hoped Jade wouldn't notice too much.

Mya felt responsible for Shea now as well as the animal-children. Kala Sriha had not come near Mya since uttering that one terrifying roar, but Mya nevertheless felt that she had unleashed Shea on the human world and needed to ensure his good conduct. He refused to believe in Kala Sriha even as the god infused his very cells. He thought he was being drugged, and he stayed doggedly faithful to his original purpose—the quest for justice against Richard Fuller.

Mya's quest was a different one. She was trying to bring the animal children back into the world. And to do this, she needed to remind them of their human lives. Food was the most obvious.

So here she was, in Jade's kitchen, tasting unusual things. Cold yellow noodles in the fridge with orange sauce all over them.

The remains of a chicken cooked in spicy marinade. She found a plastic bag and put fruit in it, then added tins of fish—she didn't dare steal a can-opener so she opened two cans and put them in the bag with their lids still attached. Brine began to drip out of the bag. Flustered, Mya cast about quickly for one more thing to bring back, and that was when she found the plastic box of sweet bread-things.

She opened the lid and sniffed at the sugary pastries inside. When she touched one, sugar came off on her finger. She licked it. Then she saw Baby Lek, the infant naga, come sliding through the leaves of the potted pine tree. He must have found the opening in the foliage that she'd made. Lek had no arms or legs, but he made an eager sound and lunged for the box of pastries with his mouth open. She shoved one at him before he could knock over the whole box.

'You've come back to the world,' she breathed, amazed. 'You can cross over!'

Mya had always felt sorry for Lek, because Mr. Richard used the naga's venom to make the antidote to the night flower extract. Every time Mr. Richard needed the venom, he commanded Lek to surrender it, and Lek always did. Now Lek could leave the forest... and anything might be possible.

Mya and Lek brought the box of pastries back to the forest, and Mya shared out the food. It had a miraculous effect. When they were eating, the other animals flickered back and forth between their mortal and immortal bodies. The transformations only lasted for a few seconds at first, but there was no doubt about it: right before Mya's eyes, the animal-children were remembering how to be human.

Itchy Gecko

'WHAT THE HELL happened to you?'

I slid into the seat opposite Shea at the back of the Palace Diner. He had a black eye and was awkwardly eating a salad with his left hand. There was a big bandage wrapped around the other hand. He smiled anyway when he saw me, and started to get up in that super-courteous way he had. But I was in my seat in a flash. He lowered himself slowly back into the padded seat of the booth.

It had been three days since he'd told me about his investigation. He had texted me to say he needed to show me something.

'So what's going on,' I said. 'You taking up fighting as part of your cover?'

He tried to laugh but I could tell even that was hurting him. Broken rib, maybe.

'I'm glad you came. I wanted to see you but I didn't want to be pushy. You must be hungry. What would you like?'

What I'd like wasn't the point. It was what I should eat to build muscle. I ordered a turkey sandwich without the bread and a skinny milkshake. Shea raised his eyebrows but didn't comment.

'You don't look too good, Shea.'

'Thanks.'

'I told you it would be you needing the protection,' I reminded him. 'What's the deal?'

He waved off the question. 'Misunderstanding. Some people tried to shake me down for something I don't have. Right. Well, you'll be pleased to know I've got nothing on Mr. B so far. It's very frustrating. There's no association between the gym and the... thugs who came after you. They've been sent to bring the phone back to Thailand.'

I reached out and touched his eyebrow. 'So did the Thai Mafia give you that?'

The bruise covered a good part of his face, and even the unhurt eye looked deeper and darker. It was kind of sexy.

What am I saying? Forget I said that.

'It's nothing.' Obligatory macho bullshit response. Very funny, coming from him.

'Was it the same guys who done Malu?'

He didn't answer, which I took as a yes. Our food came, and I took my eyes off Shea. I looked out the window where a pickup truck and a Volkswagen were going for the same parking space. There were only a few spaces in front of the diner thanks to some digging going on. Construction workers had left a fenced-in pit and a JCB behind, plus a couple jackhammers. I was surprised nobody stole the jackhammers.

'You should go to the police,' I said. 'I mean, you're on the up and up. They might even believe you.'

He shook his head. 'I can't. I have my reasons.'

The Volkswagen shot into the space and the driver of the pickup hit her horn so loud that everybody in the diner turned to look. She had to back out into the highway, nearly hitting a black SUV that was turning in. These drivers wouldn't stand a chance in Bangkok.

'That's stupid.' I crumpled my protein bar wrapper and chucked it on the place mat. 'You're doing a story, you get messed up by some guys who are already wanted by the police, so you go to the police with whatever information you got. See, Shea, people like me can survive without the cops, but people like you are soft. You need help.'

He looked miserable again. Man, I always know what not to say to a guy. He sighed.

'I know you're right, and normally I would, because I am

normally, er, a law-abiding taxpayer and all that. But there are some issues with my passport and I don't want to draw attention to myself. Homeland security and suchlike.'

'You came in illegally? Why?'

'It wasn't intentional. It just sort of happened that way.'

'How can you accidentally get into the country illegally?'

He took a deep breath. Put his hands flat on the table like he'd made a decision. Let the breath out. Then he said:

'I'm sorry, Jade. I can't tell you.'

'Omigod.' I swallowed the last sip of my shake and dropped my voice to a whisper. 'You're a spy. You work with MI-4 or is it MI-6. Stirred not shaken...'

'It's MI-5 and no, I'm not a spy. Although it's flattering that you would think so...' He grinned winningly.

'Do you always flirt with the people you're investigating?'

'Only if they're fit. And they seldom are. Which is what makes this such a treat.'

I felt myself grinning even though it was a stupid line. There was just something about him. Even through the aromas of coffee and frying burgers and diesel fumes, I could get a faint, intoxicating scent of him. Maybe he was getting to me subliminally. Maybe he had on spy cologne, with pheromones or something.

'Jade,' he said. 'I need to ask you a favor, and you're going to think it's silly, but I'm serious about this.'

'Oo-kay...'

He slid a business card across the table. On the back he'd written down an e-mail address and the name Parawat Ratanaruang.

'If you don't hear from me for more than a couple of days, can you get in touch with her and let her know the worst has happened.'

'Is this your wife?' Because, you know, I mean. Enough already.

'A contact who is working the case with me.'

'Oh, right. Sure. So let me get this straight. If you don't call me for... how long? Two days? I'm supposed to e-mail a total stranger and tell her I think you're dead? You're kidding, right? Because you know none of this is my business and there's no way I'm doing that.'

'Please, don't be like that, Jade. Because—and I don't mean to be macabre—but there might not be anything left of me to find. She needs to know.'

'Shea, listen. This is too much. I mean, I barely know you.'

He reached across the table and touched my hand.

'That's not true. You do know me. There's a reason we've met. I don't know what it is, but I can feel it's there.'

So... when he touched me? It's not like we're talking sparks, or electricity, or anything like that. It was more like... a melting sensation. I'm sitting there across from him and outside it's dark now. It's started to rain, and the highway is a blur of light. There's noise everywhere, but between the two of us there's a kind of stillness.

'Have a look at this,' he said. And he passed me his phone with a photograph displayed on the screen.

It was a skinny white guy, about fifty. Judging by the style of clothes, the picture must have been about fifteen years old. He was posed with a teenage girl who was tall enough to be a model. It looked like they were at a nightclub. She was heavily made up and wearing a short skirt and heels and a little fur jacket that she clutched around herself for protection. Fantastic beauty, but there was something else about her that made me stare at her and not at the man. She was familiar.

I knew that face. Where did I know her from?

Then my gecko tattoo started itching.

I stood up. 'Gotta pee,' I blurted. 'Back in a second.'

In the stall I gave the tattoo a really good scratch, but it only itched more. I came out of the stall and washed my hands, glaring at myself in the mirror. Malu would kill me for getting involved with this guy. *You have an instinct for trouble,* she'd say. *It's like a metal detector, only less profitable.*

I scratched a few more times. Then I opened the bathroom door and stepped into the little hallway between the main part of the diner and the back entrance. A gunshot snapped off in the diner and glass shattered.

'Everybody down!'

I startled but stayed put. There was a scrambling sound, then a hush. Through the round window in the swinging door that led to the diner, I glimpsed a dude in a jacket and balaclava moving past, hands extended in front of him gripping the gun. Under his jeans he had thighs like an oak tree.

I went out the back door into the darkness, then ran around to the front of the building, keeping my head down.

Everything inside the diner was lit up, so it was like watching a movie. None of the customers were visible; they all must be down under the tables or on the floor. The shooter had Shea by the hair and was pushing him toward the door. I scanned the parking lot. The black Nissan SUV was parked crooked, pointing toward the highway. Engine running, driver with his hood up.

I stumbled across the broken pavement, ducking behind parked cars, looking for a weapon. Any weapon. I fumbled at the pieces of broken asphalt but couldn't get a grip; then I saw a socket wrench, left behind by one of the workmen. It gleamed in the streetlights like friggin' Excalibur.

The gunman hustled Shea across the parking lot. I ran along parallel to them, staying down, until they'd reached the SUV. Then I darted up behind Shea's attacker. The gunman put his gun in his belt while he opened the back door of the car, keeping hold of Shea's hair with his other hand. He still didn't know I was there, and I'd been careful to keep out of line of sight of the driver.

You get one shot at this, Jade.

Gripping the wrench in both hands, I leaped up and clubbed him on the back of the head. Right behind the ear.

He went down like a sack of shit. I grabbed the gun, screamed, 'Run, Shea!' and shot out both tires on the passenger side.

Shea ran. But instead of running somewhere smart, like across the parking lot to the gas station next door where they'd have a panic button and lots of cameras, he ran along the shoulder of the highway in the other direction. Towards a little patch of scrubby woods where the highway bridged a big ditch with a stream in it. Meanwhile, the driver was getting out of the SUV and I was going to have to shoot him before he shot me.

All right. If that's the way it is.

I was about to squeeze when it hit me that he was ignoring me. He ran after Shea. Firing his Glock the whole time. I couldn't see his face, but from the shape of his body I was pretty sure this was Pierce—or Johnny, as Malu had heard him called. I didn't wait around for the first guy to come to. I chased after Pierce/Johnny, who chased after Shea, who by now had reached the highway bridge and disappeared down into the ditch. I couldn't tell whether he'd fallen or jumped.

I couldn't shoot and run at the same time. In fact, I couldn't shoot, period, not over any kind of distance. I'd handled guns and I'd fired a few, and I knew just enough to know that I didn't have a prayer of hitting Johnny at this distance. So I just ran after him anyway, because that's the kind of thing you do if you're me. He turned once and shot at me. The bullet hit the pavement near my feet and that was enough to send me reeling sideways to take cover behind a pickup. He was already back on his target. He fired another shot in my general direction, probably to cover himself as he climbed over the guard rail and disappeared down into the culvert.

I really didn't know what to do then. People were coming out of the diner now. I could hear shouts, and I saw that men were surrounding the fallen body of the would-be kidnapper. I'd lost the advantage, lost what little control I had. I had to go down into that ditch, but I didn't want to. Give me a dark alley any day. Woods always remind me of movies where psycho killers jump out and chop you up in little pieces. Where you gonna run for help in the woods? Who can save you? Nobody will even find your body. The woods are too freaky for me.

But I couldn't stay here. Police were coming. People would be asking questions. It didn't matter that I was a good guy this time; I was going to end up in big trouble. Everything about the situation was telling me to turn back and leave it alone.

Guess that's why I jumped over the guard rail and slithered down the bank into the trees.

There was water at the bottom. The stream flowed between steep banks lined with maples and sumac and thorns. The strip of land was only about forty feet wide, and it looked like the developers couldn't be bothered to do anything with it, so they just left it alone and built around it. The stream was channelled into a pipe about three feet in diameter where it passed under the road, but the water wasn't more than a few inches deep. It was too dark to see, but I could hear the sound of shots hitting the inside of the concrete pipe, and I knew that the two of them were in there.

Damn. If it passed right the way under the highway, that pipe would be more than fifty feet long and not big enough to stand up in. How could Shea not get shot full of holes?

I went right up to the opening and peered around the edge. Complete darkness. I whipped my head away, just in case Johnny was still bothering to shoot behind him.

I was going to have to get to Shea from the other end. Maybe, just maybe, there was a chance. After all, if Johnny wanted Shea dead he could have shot him on the spot in the diner. Johnny wanted Shea alive. If I was fast, I could catch them at the other end.

I scrambled back up and made a dash through the traffic. Got to the central meridian, climbed over the barrier, and stood there waiting for my opening. It took several seconds to come, and as I took off across both lanes of eastbound traffic I realized how tired I was, how much my legs were letting me down. All that lactic acid was weighing on me.

But I made it. A truck horn blared as I skittered down the bank on the opposite side. Here the slope was less steep, and instead of a wooded culvert there was only a gravelled ditch, man-made, that took the outflow from the pipe. I positioned myself so I was standing on top of the pipe where it opened out.

Someone was coming out as I got there. I couldn't tell in the dark whether it was Shea or Johnny. The edges of the man seemed blurry, almost like he was oozing black smoke. My eyes must be going. Then I saw he was dragging a limp man and I didn't wait another second. I jumped on his back, knocking him to the ground. I ended up straddling his back. I had the gun to his head and I was telling myself to pull the trigger before he could turn over, when the black smoke dissipated and my vision seemed to clear.

I shrieked. 'Shit, it's you!'

'Mmmfff,' Shea said. I rose and backed away shaking, still pointing the gun at him because I couldn't figure out what was going on. The other man's body lay half in and half out of the pipe, his arms thrown wide. No sign of the gun.

Shea picked himself up and I bent over the shooter. Pulled off the balaclava.

Under the mask Johnny's face was covered with blood. His throat was a mess. Ripped open. Blood everywhere. His eyes were wide, staring up at the orange clouds.

Girl in a Red Dress

I WAS STILL holding the second gun. Blue police lights reflected off the frontage of Auto Parts Galaxy. Sirens.

'You killed a man.'

I sounded so calm. Shea took in the sight of the dead guy. He started to back away, holding his hands in front of him as if to ward off the truth.

'I d-d-didn't...' His teeth were chattering. He was going to pieces.

'Shh! OK, calm down. What's done is done. The cops will be here any second. You need to calm down.'

I looked at the gun in my hand. My prints would be all over it, and my prints were on file with the police already. Of course, if they dusted down the diner they'd get prints, too. A vision of Perez floated into my mind. He was shaking his head like a disappointed altar boy.

I'd saved Shea's life. I didn't have anything to apologize about.

But who was Shea, really? And what had happened in that tunnel?

'Listen,' I said, 'I don't know what this is about, but I'm fighting the biggest match of my life next week, and I can't afford to get in trouble.'

'What?' His eyes moved all around, looking at everything and nothing. Like he'd just landed from the mothership. For a second I'd been afraid he would do something to me—who knew what he might be capable of, if he'd actually turned the gun around on his attacker? But the Shea I was looking at couldn't be capable of violence. He looked like he didn't even know his own name.

'I'm going to go talk to the police and hand in the gun,' I continued. 'You coming, or you going to wait for them to catch you? Personally, I suggest you cooperate. It was self-defense, and you got plenty of witnesses saw them take you at gunpoint.'

He looked horrified and shook his head. 'No. No police. Jade—don't leave me!'

I narrowed my eyes. It was like he was on drugs or something.

I put out my hand, saying 'stop.' He stopped, his face anguished.

'You can't run from this,' I said. 'Whatever happened here, the police are on the scene. Don't resist. This is America. They'll shoot you. Understand?'

He nodded woodenly, scared.

'Come on,' I said.

I talked to the police while wolfing down two more turkey sandwiches. The whole thing took hours because they didn't believe me but couldn't figure out what had really happened (neither could I). The CCTV footage would back up what I told the detective about my part in the whole thing, but when I told him about the socket wrench he looked at me like I had to be making it up. The police were talking to Shea separately. There were plenty of witnesses from the diner. The waitress who'd been through the whole thing was giving cops coffee now.

'You were fierce,' she whispered. And to the cop, 'You should give her a medal. She was fierce.'

I told the detective that I'd lost Johnny in the tunnel, and when I found Shea, Johnny was already dead. While I was going through every detail of this, and reminding myself to skip the part about black smoke and Shea not knowing where he was, Shea himself was getting bundled into a police car. I hoped he'd be all right. I told myself he was lucky to be alive, that nothing else much mattered.

The guy I'd clocked on the head was taken away in cuffs. I didn't recognize him. Which meant the third man from the apartment was still on the loose, and he wasn't going to be happy with me.

What the hell shit was I in the steaming middle of?

It was after midnight when Malu showed up to take me home. The look on her face made me cringe.

'You're coming to Teaneck until after the fight,' she said. 'Nothing to discuss. I know you want to stay with Mr. B but under the circumstances...? If any of this criminal activity might possibly have anything to do with your gym, then we have to keep you safe.'

'Malu, I can't stay in Teaneck. I'll be fine. You know I can take care of myself. Did the police tell you what happened? Criminals should be afraid of me, not the other way around.'

'Yeah, sure, whatever you want to tell yourself.'

'Malu, I need to ask you something. That reporter guy who came to the gym, the one I told you about.'

'The hot one?'

'Yeah, whatever. He thinks Mr. B might be involved in something pretty bad. I know he's wrong. I know Mr. B is straight up. And I know Coat and Pook are... well, they're the salt of the earth. But I have to talk to Mr. B myself, and I can't do that if I'm staying in Teaneck.'

Malu shook her head.

'This is such a bad idea,' she said. 'Have you talked to your mom?'

'You know I haven't.'

'Nana is on a respirator. They're going to give her last rites.'

She was crying. I put my arms around her.

'Nana is always in my heart,' I said at last, but the truth was I couldn't let myself think about her. I'd go to pieces. 'Let me do what I need to do.'

'Promise you'll keep your head down, Jade.'

I hugged her tight, but I didn't actually promise.

After Malu dropped me outside Mr. B's house I had to turn around and get all the way home again. I had to keep living the lie.

It was one o'clock in the morning when I got in. In Thailand everybody would be having a nap in the middle of the day. Even if my internal clock was confused, I ought to be able to sleep now. But I was too wired. I turned on Gretchen's fight mix DVD and watched it until my eyes bled.

THE NEXT THING I knew, my phone was ringing from my bag, sunlight was pouring in, and I had a splitting headache. I turned over and buried my face in the sofa. I thought I heard something in the kitchen. Rustling.

I groaned. I was so tired. I just wanted to sleep.

I opened one eye and checked the phone. It was morning, and Mr. B was on my case.

'Where are you? Mario is here. Let's go, Jade.'

'OK, OK, I'm coming. I overslept.'

'Champions don't oversleep. Haul ass *now*.'

There was a muffled crash from the kitchen. I closed the phone, peeled myself off the sofa and went into the kitchen with my eyes half-open. A box of cereal had fallen off the counter and was spilt on the floor. The fridge was half-open. But no one was there.

'Malu?'

I stuck my head out into the hallway. The chain was on the door. The window was open a few inches in the living room, but I'd been sleeping on the sofa right under that window, so it wasn't like somebody could climb in without waking me up.

I was getting wider awake now. Ideas were running through my head fast and thick. If someone had been in the kitchen and hid when I got up, the only place they'd have time to go was the bathroom, which was set in the short hallway immediately inside the front door. It shared a wall with the kitchen.

I stepped into the hall. The bathroom door was ajar. I listened.

A small, thin voice was singing softly. The sound was mesmerising. It was a girl's voice, very quiet. I could probably only hear it because of the echo off the bathroom tile.

I pushed the door open. Kneeling on the orange bath mat between the toilet and the shower-curtained tub was the girl in the red dress. From the bus. I'd know her anywhere. The dress was in a traditional Chinese style, heavily embroidered with gold thread—but now it was filthy. How many days had she been wearing it?

Her eyes were wide open and staring at the ivy plant that Malu had left hanging on the shower rod because supposedly the plant liked steam. Her palms were pressed together at her chest in prayer, and her lips were moving. She was maybe... eleven? She was a solid-looking kid—she'd grow up to be strong like Pink. Her face was gentle, softly swollen with health and perfectly symmetrical. I could have looked at her all day.

As I stared, I noticed that in her lap she had a heap of protein bars and a jar of peanut butter.

I didn't know what to do. The girl didn't seem to notice me. Her face was totally composed, and there was something so calm and serene about her that it seemed wrong to disturb her. Even though she was on *my* bath mat with *my* protein bars and *that deeply problematic* phone... but I'd given the phone to the bad guys. How did she get it? I had a million questions, but I couldn't bring myself to make a sound.

And then she just evaporated. Shimmered a little, like a mirage, and disappeared.

My bathroom smelled like a greenhouse full of flowers. The mirror was fogged up.

I could feel my heart racing. I rushed in. The mat where she'd been kneeling was still warm. I checked behind the curtain. Nothing. The bathroom window is only a thin strip of frosted glass, and it was shut.

I put my fingers to my lips. I thought of my Nana with her

plastic saints and her friendly banter with our dead ancestors, going away on her long journey.

My phone rang again. Shea's number came up. I turned it off. '*Madre de Dios,*' I said.

Baby Lek

With so many ghosts to feed, where to begin?

'You have to be strategic,' Luck told Mya. 'Mr. Richard will be back here soon enough. If you could get Baby Lek back to the human world, that would slow the old man down. He needs naga venom, after all.'

'Why does Lek help Mr. Richard? Can't he say no?' Mya asked.

'Mr. Richard sold Lek's mother to someone in Holland and she was sent back here pregnant. The Holland people didn't want her anymore. She gave birth to Lek in the forest, but she had lost her power to move between worlds. She went into the water to beg the nagas for help. She drowned, but Lek was taken under the protection of the nagas. Just like your friend Shea was taken by Kala Sriha.'

'Lek was *born* in the forest?'

The ghost nodded. 'His human part hasn't aged much. You can see from his face that he wouldn't be more than two or three years old. It will be hard to remove him. But he never actually died, and part of him is still human. Maybe the nagas will let him go. The only way you can find out is to introduce him to the human world.'

Born outside the world. Yet Lek had crossed over into Jade's kitchen once.

'I will do what I can. I will try.'

In the middle of the day, when Jade was at the gym, Mya cooked rice for Lek in Jade's kitchen. It took some time to figure out how to work the stove, and at first she startled at every little noise, expecting Jade to come back.

But it was the black cat who came back. The cat who looked like Kala Sriha. He sailed through the window and stood on the counter, blinking and licking his lips.

She offered him rice. Then she took the pot and backed out of the small kitchen.

When the cat began to eat, the air shifted and the smell of the forest came into the apartment.

Shea was crouched on the kitchen floor.

'Not again,' he groaned. Mya kept clear of him while he stood up, then offered him the rest of the pot. He took it and ate hungrily, sitting on the counter.

'The police talked to me.' Anguish tightened his face. 'A man is dead. They don't think I could have done it. But I'm starting to feel like maybe I did.'

'You are not evil,' Mya said. 'I think you are just confused.'

'How did I get here?' His gaze flicked to Mya and then away, as if he were afraid what her answer might be. She tried not to laugh.

'Do you remember being the cat? You came through the window? Big jump?'

He stopped chewing.

'No,' he said. She could tell he was lying.

'You need human experiences,' Mya told him. 'You have to feel what it is to be human, and then it will be easier for you to stay.'

'What it is to be human, huh?' Shea gave a muffled laugh as he chewed, shaking his head. 'I don't have time to feel things. I'm going back to Bangkok. But what if I have one of these breakdowns on the plane?'

'Plane? When?'

'Tomorrow, I hope, if I can get a new passport at the British consulate. I have a contact in the Bangkok police. I have to do something before Richard Fuller can make his next move. So far all I can get off the phone is the video, and it shows two people disappearing into thin air.'

'Do you believe this is what happened?'

'It's what I saw. It's what you say is true. But I can't justify it or prove it.'

'And if it is true, then it could be true you are also a part of Kala Sriha.'

He closed down when she said that. How could a person be inhabited by an immortal and yet deny it?

'It's not what I believe that matters. It's making a legal case. I'm relying on my police contact for that, but I need evidence.'

Mya said nothing, but she was thinking.

'Mya?' Shea said. He slid off the counter, brushing grains of rice off his clothes. 'You have an idea, don't you?'

'Addresses,' Mya said. 'The places where Mr. Richard sent each child. I saw the paper. You know, the children I brought through the forest? He wrote the addresses in English. Some of them had e-mails and phone numbers. Do you need these?'

'Do I need them? Mya—' He brandished his spoon excitedly. 'Is that all you remember? Do you know where he kept them? In his computer?'

She shook her head. 'Written down.'

'Mya.' Shea dropped to his knees so that they looked at each other eye to eye. Kala Sriha's intensity blazed in his expression like a clear fire. 'Can you remember them? Do you know where they were kept? If we can get that information, we have a chance of rescuing them. Without it... well, there's no proof they're even missing, let alone where to look for them.'

'I don't remember the details,' she said.

'Try to remember something.'

'I have to think about it.'

He saw her fear, but he didn't understand it, and his disappointment was visible.

'It's too much to ask of you,' he sighed. 'Forgive me.'

Mya frowned. He had no idea what he was asking because he didn't believe in the immortal world or her ability to move through it.

'Maybe I *can* rescue them...'

Now it was his turn to frown. He really didn't remember anything.

'Can you recall where the paper was? Do you know where he keeps his private documents? Does he have a safe?'

She nodded, and to get him to stop pestering her she drew on the back of an envelope a little picture of Mr. Richard's work room, showing where the safe was hidden under the lab sink. She wrote down the combination of the safe, too. She could feel the surge of electricity around Shea when he looked at it.

'Brilliant. This is brilliant. Thank you.'

'Shea, please remember. Mr. Richard is dangerous. He has ways of knowing things. He isn't going to be easy to catch.'

Shea smiled, and she could see him dismissing her completely. 'Leave that part to me. This is very helpful. Thank you. And what you said? About going to look for them yourself?'

'You don't believe I can.'

'I'm not sure what you can do. But Mya, please. Don't try to save anyone. What happened to them isn't your fault. None of this is your responsibility. The first thing I'm going to do when Richard Fuller is brought in is look for information on your family. You can't carry on in limbo like this forever.'

She bit her lip, stopping tears because she knew he wouldn't catch Mr. Richard. Shea was foolish to think he could.

'Where can I find you if I need you?' she asked.

He glanced away, at the floor, and she saw the pulse in his neck quicken.

'You said I need human experiences,' he whispered. 'So I guess I'll be here.'

It was embarrassing to think of Shea and Jade together. But he was trying to do the correct thing. Whenever Mya thought of the children she had led through the forest, she felt her heart crumble, like she was turning to dust inside. She didn't know what was happening to them, exactly. But it was bad, and she was responsible. There was no way Mr. Richard was going to give up the children's whereabouts to Shea, or the police. Mya considered the idea of rescuing the other children herself, one at a time. But Shea was right about documentation and the authorities. Even if she succeeded in bringing the others through the forest, what then? Mya herself was a fugitive, without family or papers. What would she do with several others like her, all displaced from nation and loved ones? What if they were thrown in jail? After all, her own family had been imprisoned for no reason at all.

So she should help Shea. This would mean going back to Mr. Richard's house. That was one of the very worst things Mya could imagine doing right now. It made her fingers turn cold and her teeth chatter.

No one who didn't know Mr. Richard could understand why going back there was like running into a burning building you'd just escaped. The house was soaked in his sorcery. That was why Daeng and Ploy feared and revered and hated but mostly feared him—and they loved him, too, in their way. So did Johnny. So did everyone who knew Mr. Richard. He could see the soft insides of your bones. He could move your thoughts as easily as stirring a drink.

That was why, even as Mya considered sneaking into the house, suspicions crawled among her plans. It was the nature of Mr. Richard to make you think you wanted to do things, when in truth it was Mr. Richard who wanted you to do them. You could never know what you really thought when he was around. And he wasn't around now... but Mya had lived with him for a long time, and he had trained her mind. He proposed to crawl into her very skin, and she wouldn't put it past him to lure her back. She knew he was afraid of the evidence on the phone. He would be bending all his energies toward getting it back. If one way failed, he would try another.

Was Mya's idea to steal the addresses all part of Mr. Richard's grand scheme? It might be. When Mr. Richard had taught Mya to play chess, he had told her stories of powerful people he had controlled and manuevered, just like the knights and rooks he tricked on the black-and-white plastic board.

Maybe it was Mya's own will that propelled her through the forest to the prayer room in the north of Thailand. Maybe it was Mr. Richard's manipulation. Maybe she was a hero; maybe she was a moth to a flame. She couldn't even tell the difference. All she knew was that, once the idea had taken hold of her, she couldn't make it go away. She had to see it through.

Mr. Richard had taught her about destiny. How events can pick you up like a tide and carry you. How it is all laid out before you, even though you don't see.

She thought: *if I don't do this, no one else can.*

Punishment and Crime

I WOULD MAKE an excellent stalker. I had Gretchen Van Der Hoef in my sights. My consciousness had become a laser beam focused on fucking up Gretchen.

I pictured her when I was doing my conditioning, like she was right there and I had to beat her at pull-ups and sit-ups. I had to do more than her.

I pictured her when I was hitting the bag. I felt her ribs breaking from my body shots. I pictured her when I was doing my omoplatas on poor Cake. *Destroy Gretchen.* That was my mission now.

Life can be so crazy, but in the gym what you got to do is clear. Punish yourself now so you can punish your opponent in the cage. It's solid and you can bank on it. Nothing else in life is clear like that.

I put Shea out of my mind. I put away all thoughts of missing pączki and little girls chanting in my bathroom. I went out of the gym feeling high and light.

Then:

'Hold up, Jade.' Khari was waiting for me in the parking lot. He took out his phone. I thought: if he calls Eva right now so help me god I'll take him out with a flying head-butt.

'You know that thing you were asking about the other day?'

My stomach dropped. I nodded. He handed me his phone.

'I thought you should see this. Mr. B deleted it—I guess he don't want the police to see it. I picked it up off his computer.'

'If you could take it off his computer, the police can, too,' I said.

'If they make the effort to look,' Khari said. 'But Jade.' He paused dramatically. Khari towered over me, his head ducking away as he rubbed the back of his neck like he always does when he's embarrassed.

'Somebody already doctored it,' he finished. 'You'll see what I mean. Take a look. But don't copy it. Mr. B don't even know I got it.'

He turned and went back into the gym.

The footage was grainy, and the screen on Khari's phone was small. But I could tell that I was looking down from the corner camera in Mr. B's office. You could see a little bit of blurred movement going on in the main gym through the two-way mirror, but nothing clear enough to identify. There was very little light.

A figure was pacing up and down just beneath the camera. The shot looked down on them at an angle that only captured their head and shoulders from behind, and in shadow. The rest of the body was out of shot. I strained my eyes, trying to confirm that it was Mr. B, but I really couldn't tell.

Then, right in the middle of the room, out of nowhere appeared the girl in the red dress. It was like she'd been edited to fade in. She was holding a small bundle in her hands. For a few seconds no one moved; then the girl stepped forward and put the bundle on the ground, and the shadowy person took it. The girl seemed to be saying something. She stepped back and faded away. The shadowy person slipped through the door without showing their face. I was pretty sure they were too slim to be Mr. B, but that's all I could really say.

It was dated weeks ago, while I was in Thailand.

I gave Khari his phone back. Then I hoisted my bag on my shoulder and went to the bus without saying one single word. I didn't hear nothing, didn't see nothing. I went to Mandino's and did my shift on autopilot, thinking. But I didn't get very far with that. If Einstein had been a dishwasher he never would have figured out relativity. It's just too easy to get distracted and cut yourself with a fish knife.

What was I supposed to think? People don't just pop in and out like that. Khari thought it had been doctored, but Khari wasn't in my bathroom when the girl pulled the same trick. The police weren't going to find any of this amusing.

How was I supposed to go into this fight with so many doubts about my manager? It was looking more and more like Mr. B was into something really despicable. Just my damn luck. Finally start to get a break with a big fight, and now my manager could be arrested any day for involvement in pedophilia and drugs. Great. The only hope I was clinging to was that maybe Mr. B didn't know.

He doesn't know, Jade. He doesn't know. Please, god, let him not know.

As SOON AS I let myself into the apartment I knew someone was there. I could smell that weird flower-shop smell again. A little zing of adrenaline rushed into my forearms and hands. After the incident the other night with Malu, I'd started keeping a baseball bat in the hallway just inside the front door, and I grabbed it now, flexing my fingers around its neck.

A voice called from the kitchen.

'Jade? Down, girl! It's only me.'

The voice was Shea's. He waved a hand out of the kitchen.

'Is it safe to come out?'

I lowered the bat as he emerged. He had a bottle of wine in one hand, which he waggled at me like I was a dog and it was a Milk Bone.

'How did you get in?'

He shrugged. He was unshaven and wearing the same jeans as the day before, although he'd changed the bloodstained shirt for a white t-shirt. His hair was a mess.

'Do you really want to know?'

'What about the police?'

'I don't want to talk about it. Look, Jade, I'm sorry about imposing like this. I wanted to see you, but I don't blame you if you don't want to see me.'

He was lying. That was obvious. The only thing is, I couldn't figure out which part was the lie. He was leaning against the refrigerator like he was trying to take up as little space as possible. How was I supposed to believe Shea was a killer? But what other explanation could there be?

'OK,' I said. 'We can talk about it over food. I'm starving.'

'I thought you worked in a restaurant.'

'It was too busy tonight to take a break. Move over and I'll make us something.'

'Have you got anything beyond those cardboard things you eat?'

'My protein bars not good enough for you? You want somebody's arm, or maybe a thigh...?'

He didn't rise to it. 'Actually, if it isn't too much of an imposition, could I use your shower? I'm feeling rather grimy.'

He looked way nastier than people look after a night in jail. He was lying so bad. Where had he been? I said, 'Didn't you go back to your hotel, then?'

'Er... no. The police gave me the shirt.'

'And here I thought you stole it.'

He even had the nerve to grin at me.

'What's so funny?' I said it with an edge.

The smile wavered. 'Nothing! I just... well, I thought if you were the type to prefer a bit of the rough, then maybe this would be my opportunity...'

'A bit of the *what*?'

Smile vanished completely. 'Never mind. I was making a feeble attempt to appear to be something other than the mild-mannered reporter I obviously am.'

'Towels are on the shelf,' I snapped, trying to untangle the string of words that had just come out of his mouth. Who talks like that? He was making my brain hurt.

While he was in the shower I started making a stir-fry. It gave me something to do with my hands. I was all jumpy and excited and... happy. Damn. And not 'damn' in a good way, damn for real. I was flying to Las Vegas tomorrow and Shea was *not* a mild-mannered reporter, and—*hey, what the hell happened to all the food in my fridge?*

I bent over and stuck my head deeper into the fridge to see if there was some chicken in the back, and *a feather* floated up against my nose. I'm not talking about one of those little tiny butt-feathers that sometimes get stuck to free-range eggs, which are gross but explainable. I'm talking about a big feather that could have belonged to a damn peacock, if peacocks were bright red.

Was my fridge being raided by a hungry showgirl? What the hell.

I closed the fridge and opened the freezer.

The phone rang.

'Hello?'

'Put your friend on the line,' Perez said.

New Kid in Town

A KNIFE-SHARP sliver of cool forest air came with Mya as she slipped into the prayer room by dark of night. Rain thrummed on the roof of Mr Richard's stilt house, and the air was saturated with moisture. The windows were shuttered against the rain, and the only light in the prayer room came from the computer monitor in the adjacent work room. Mya stiffened, afraid that Mr. Richard was working late. But the monitor was running a screensaver, a series of photographs. Mr. Richard shaking hands with a film star. Mr. Richard at the orphanage, surrounded by smiling children. Mr. Richard and his wife on the red carpet at a society event. Mr. Richard receiving blessings from a bishop.

The address list she'd seen had been in the work room. She remembered exactly what it looked like, and it wouldn't be hard to find because Mr. Richard wrote very little down on paper. The work room had more test tubes and jars than it had paperwork. Tonight, in the intense humidity, the acrid smell of the medicines he had been concocting hung in an invisible pall. The smell struck fear in Mya.

She had to be quick, or she'd lose her courage. She had brought a small torch from Jade's kitchen drawer, and she switched it on. Better to risk light than to knock something over and make a noise. The thin beam roved over the disarray of chemicals and unwashed coffee cups and spent syringes. Had he been trying to go to the forest alone? No, she mustn't think about that.

It was almost impossible to search without disturbing what was there, and with the walls themselves watching her, with the glassy eyes of the dead monkey on her, Mya felt sure that Mr. Richard would be able to feel her presence. He would know she had been here. She had to be quick, or—

There! A sheet of pale blue paper, barely visible beneath a stack of DVD cases and a jar of powdered naga venom. Mya gently extracted it, wincing when the jar of powder wobbled. When she finally got the paper free, it turned out to be coffee-stained but readable: hotel stationery from Madrid. An English word was underscored at the top, followed by scrawled names and addresses in Western letters.

Mya pressed it to her chest. Now, to get out of here—

But something else caught her eye. In her efforts to extract the paper, Mya had moved the keyboard and exposed another piece of paper. This one contained a child's drawing: a little girl holding the hand of what must be her mother. In the sky was a sun. Flowers grew around them. The drawing stopped Mya cold.

It was like the pictures she had drawn herself, when she first came here. But Mya had not made this one. In fact, it was unfinished, the sky only half-colored. A few crayons lay on the mouse pad.

Her heart was beating fast. Mr. Richard had found another child. A very young child, judging by this drawing. Was this child sleeping in Mya's old bed, in a corner of the hallway outside the kitchen? Had this child already learned to travel to the forest— was that why there were syringes on the counter?

A mixture of fear and guilt and, as ugly as it was, of *rivalry* rose up in Mya.

No, she thought. *Don't think that way. Think of how many he has hurt.*

She would go down there, find the child, and take her into the immortal forest before Mr. Richard could use him or her for evil as he used everyone else. She would do this, because if Mya didn't do it, who would? Who could?

She would do it. As soon as she found the courage. She glanced around the computer room, as if courage were to be found in the jars and bottles—well, it probably was, oddly enough.

'Do you know who this monkey is?'

Mya inhaled a shrill gasp and whirled. Mr. Richard was in the prayer room, one hand on the stuffed monkey's head.

Mya tried to form a prayer to return to the forest, but something held her back. The question he'd asked, it clung to her like a thorny branch, holding her to this earth. She switched off the torch but could just make out his slim figure in the reflected light from the monitor, which now displayed a photo of Mr. Richard planting vegetables with two little boys.

'This little monkey was the first to take me to the other world,' he said in his familiar soft voice. 'I was testing drugs on her— ordinary drugs, from the ordinary world. One day I gave her a drug and she disappeared. She came back with a flower that doesn't exist in this world, and I learned that the legends of the immortal forest are true. So I trained her to fetch plants for me. Some of them were powerful plants, like the night orchid. Eventually she brought me enough of the flowers to enable me to go with her, and in this way our essences were mingled.' He paused, seeming to savor the last few words.

'Just as my essence has been mingled with yours, Mya, time and again as we've travelled. This little monkey was the beginning of everything. When she died, I couldn't bear to be parted from her. So I had her stuffed. Her eyes still watch for me. She is better than any burglar alarm.'

Rain buffeted the roof, the shutters, the walls. Mya shivered. The paper that she clutched to her chest was damp with her sweat.

'You need a teacher, Mya. You are empty of knowledge. The path you walk is without honor or merit.'

Mya knew she should return to the forest without a word. Vanish. It was her one strength, that ability to step sideways into the eternal forest. But Mr. Richard's words gripped her, dragged at her. It was like he was a sea creature reaching out with word-tentacles, trying to reel her in.

She couldn't resist saying, 'Mr. Shea has honor.'

He took this in for a moment and then let out a startled grunt of laughter.

'The boy reporter? Are you serious? Mya, the fool is *dead*. Surely you understand that? His time on earth is over. You see, this is what I'm trying to explain to you. There's so much for you to learn. You're not ready to go out on your own.'

No, she wasn't. She hadn't been ready to leave her family, either. She wasn't ready for any of this. So what?

'You have a new student,' she said softly.

The screensaver now showed Mr. Richard at the Yi Peng festival, putting his lantern on the river to honor the water spirits. It made Mya think of Lek, saved by the water-spirit Naga but doomed to give up his venom so Mr. Richard could exploit the spirit world. Mr. Richard disgraced the meaning of the word merit.

'Even if you leave, you and I are already together,' he whispered. 'The space between us is only an illusion.'

'It is said that all of reality is an illusion.'

'You are only at the beginning of your powers.' Mr Richard didn't take a step, but somehow he was closer to her now. She could see the edges of his body beginning to drift a little, to smudge.

'I don't know what you mean, Mr. Richard.'

'You have a specific fate. I know this because our fates are entwined.'

She didn't want to hear this.

'I have made a long study of fate. I chose you because you can tap into time. You don't know how you do it, but you will. Once we are in unity, we both will know.'

She froze, inside. If only she could stop up her ears. If only she could go back in time one single minute, and not hear Mr. Richard say these things. She was not afraid of Kala Sriha or the other immortals, not like she was afraid of this *unity* he proposed. She was not afraid of the ghosts in trees.

Mindreading, he said, 'Also you begin to unfold the forest. You carry the forest within you and open it like a book.'

'How do you know this?' she whispered.

'I know everything that happens to you, my dear.' His face stretched in a wrinkled smile that was not like her grandfather's smile. It was hungry.

He seemed to be closer to her now. Almost, he could reach out and touch her. A blurry smoke came off him, as if his cells were radiating something towards her. Her skin might not feel its touch, but this nameless intention would penetrate deep, seeking out the electric branches of her brain. Looking for a home.

She took a step back and threw open the shutters. A diagonal slash of rain slapped her skin, the wood floor, the flat-screen monitor.

'Go ahead.' Mr. Richard smiled. 'Call the forest. When you can feel the roots in your muscles and the leaves in your skin, you'll be wide open to me. When you can hear the ghosts in your teeth, you'll be ready. And I'll walk in and we'll be one, Mya. That's how I planned it all along.'

Then he reached for her, and as she fled into the forest a finger of the smoke that floated around him came after her. She ran from it, and even after the smoke dissolved the sound of Mr. Richard's soft laughter followed after her.

Let's Get Stupid

NOTHING LIKE LIEUTENANT Perez on the end of the phone to kill a girl's libido.

'My friend?' I moved into Malu's darkened bedroom. The fish were swimming in and out of an illuminated treasure chest in the big aquarium. I sprinkled some food for them.

'You know who I mean,' Perez said. 'Mr. Bean. Put him on the line.'

That was unfair. Shea is hot. Mr. Bean is just tall.

'I have no idea what you're talking about. He hasn't even called me.' That was technically true.

'Don't bullshit me, Jade. If I come over there and he's with you, you can forget all about your trip to Las Vegas.'

'Lieutenant, I'm not even home. I'm at the laundromat, OK? Shea hasn't called me. Why should he, anyway? I told you guys, we were doing an interview the other night. That's all I know about him. He's a reporter for some newspaper.'

I waited for Perez to say *No, he isn't*. But all he said was, 'You know the guy in the drain pipe? He wasn't killed by a firearm. He was ripped up, same as the victim we found down the street from your house. Like somebody took a machete to him.'

'I don't know what you found at the scene, Lieutenant, but at my house there were no machetes. For real. That's not the kind of thing you overlook, you know what I'm saying?'

There was a pause. I braced myself for something bad, but what he said next hit me out of left field.

'I do know what you're saying, and here's what I'm saying.

The men who have been killed are not the kind of characters you want to mess with, Jade.'

With massive effort, I bit back a sarcastic remark.

'The body from the tunnel is private security, ex-SEALS turned bad, not some low-level scum but a real enforcer and known to the FBI. Now I'm telling you this and I want you to open up your angry little ears and really listen, OK? Shea may seem like a nice guy, but he's got enemies—quiet, Jade, I'm talking.'

'I didn't say nothing.'

'I can feel you getting ready to make a wisecrack. Don't interrupt. You listening for real?'

'I'm listening.' I sat down on the bed and ran one finger down my shinbone, feeling for lumps. There were several.

'Shea pissed off somebody powerful. I don't know any more than that and I don't want to know. But you and me go back a long way. You always were an OK kid. I want you to stay away from this Shea. No matter what he says. No matter what he looks like or how *nice* he seems. I've met nice guys who stacked grannies in their deep-freeze, you know what I'm saying? So take it from me. Don't touch him. You'll end up in the crossfire.'

'OK,' I said meekly. I opened Malu's bedside table and took out a package of condoms. *Hmm.* 'But... if that's the situation, how come you don't have him? Did he escape from custody?'

'You think this is funny? I told you, we're not charging your friend. I wanted to take him in for his own protection but I got told no. Between you and me, somebody wants him dead.'

Somebody wanted him dead? Well. Impressive.

Perez said, 'So here's the deal. When I let him go I told him to go home and see the Queen. But I don't think he will. You see him, you tell him I said if he comes near you I'll make some excuse to pick him up. I can do that easy. I can put Homeland Security on him in a heartbeat. So you don't talk to him, you don't hang out with him. Understand?'

'Yeah. I understand.'

I hung up and dug around in the freezer until I finally found some chicken. How hot was Shea now, in my mind? Perez telling me to stay away from him—shit, now I was wanting him really bad. *What is the matter with me?*

Malu wasn't here to interrupt the fuckup series.

The shower was still running. I started to put chicken in the stir fry. Then I remembered Shea saying he was a vegetarian. L-O-frigging-L.

I was looking for Malu's supply of tofu when Shea came out, towelling his hair dry. His bruises had faded, and his skin sort of glowed with moisture and heat. He had dark circles under his eyes, which made them look deeper-set and sort of mysterious and shit. There was an intensity about him that made me think of a hunted animal.

'Do you need a place to stay?' I heard myself say.

He shook his head. 'I'll sort something out. Don't worry about me. I just... I wanted to see you.'

I got busy with the stir fry.

'Well, you're seeing me.'

He leaned against the fridge and watched me. I'm not much of a cook, and Shea was making me nervous with all the watching my every move, and plus? I couldn't find anything. The kitchen is normally messy, but usually it's the kind of mess where I know where everything is. Now there were *holes* in the mess, empty places where food used to be.

'Excuse me, I got to get in the fridge.' I bent and rummaged in the salad drawer for the peppers I'd just bought. *Nada*. 'Damn, where is everything?'

'Never mind the food. Jade, I need to ask you something.'

I straightened up and shut the door with my foot. 'That makes two of us.'

'Do you want me to do the stir fry?' he said. 'Why don't you sit down? You look... perturbed.'

I handed him the spatula and stood aside.

'OK, here's what's gonna happen,' I said. 'We're gonna eat and talk. I'm too hungry to interrogate you on an empty stomach, and I got a flight to Las Vegas tomorrow so no matter what happens, after tonight we're out of each other's lives. Right?'

'Is that how you want it, then? Out of each other's lives? Do you have any rice? Instant noodles sort of thing?'

'All this talking in code is killing me,' I said. 'Can we just talk to each other straight?'

'I am talking straight. Some form of carbohydrate with this meal would be helpful, especially considering the lack of... well, vegetables.'

I dumped some rice into a bowl and added water. 'So you can rip people to pieces and escape police custody and be relatively cool about it, but you're a vegetarian.'

'I never used to be,' he said defensively. 'Recently I've just... gone off meat.'

Except for human meat, right? I snorted and switched on the microwave. Then I said, 'What's with the girl in the red dress?'

There. I didn't imagine that. His eyes had just shifted to the right, really fast. His nostrils had flared. You didn't have to be a CIA investigator to tell I'd caught him off guard there.

'Sorry?' he said, too innocently. 'Girl?'

'You heard me. She was on the bus the other day. I think she's Thai.'

He closed his eyes and took a deep breath.

'What did she say to you?'

'Just answer the question, Shea.'

'See, now that plays into the very question I was going to ask you, actually. Namely, did I say something when I was... you know...'

'No, I don't know. When you were what?'

'At the diner. When I was... not myself. Did I say something about... er... anything odd?'

'You don't remember what you said? Do you remember what you *did*?'

He swallowed visibly. 'Not entirely all of it.'

'I think you better tell me everything you know. Because I have to be in Las Vegas tomorrow and ever since I met you there's all kinds of shit in my life and I think for once it's not my shit.'

The oil was smoking and I went to open a window before the alarm went off.

'It's your shit, Shea. So just, you know...' I waved my arms, both to disperse the smoke and to encourage him to get on with it. 'Just spill, already.'

He took the food off the heat and leaned back against the half-open window.

'You've no idea how much I want to tell you what's happened to me. But it would sound crazy. You'll think... you'll think... Jade, I can't go there. Let's just not say anything to one another, and I'll be on my way and you go to Las Vegas, like you said. I shouldn't have even come here. I don't know why I keep coming back to you. At first it was because of the investigation but now...'

He had thrown his head back and I found myself looking at the lines of his neck and the set of his collarbone and then the way his body was put together. A pornographic slideshow was flashing through my mind. What was the matter with me? Wrenching my mind out of the gutter was like dragging my dad's pit bull off the UPS man.

'About the girl,' I said. 'I think she sneaks in through the window and steals food. I saw her.'

'Oh, god.' He ran his hands through his hair, looking up and around, anywhere but at me. 'I'm sorry, Jade. I'm sorry. I thought... I've been trying to find a connection with your gym and Thailand, you see, and I owe her because she saved my life... it's so bloody complicated.'

'But who is she? Where are her parents? Where is she now?'

Shea swallowed.

'Mya is one of Fuller's victims.'

'Victims? You mean...?' I felt my face scrunch up in disgust. I didn't want to imagine it.

'I don't know the details of their... relationship. But she was with him, and she ran away, and she found me. The thing is, I think he must have drugged us both, or drugged me, anyway. I haven't been the same since Thailand. There's something... wrong with my mind, my memory. I keep thinking I should be dead.'

I snorted. 'I'm surprised you're not. I didn't think you were coming out of that tunnel alive.'

'Er... I'm not sure how either of us ended up in this country,' Shea said, clumsily changing the subject. 'Richard Fuller is a chemist. Not just an ordinary chemist, but a designer of drugs that have highly unusual effects. I've suffered vivid hallucinations since his people captured me, and all I can piece together is that somehow Mya and I were drugged and brought into the country secretly.'

'Whoa,' I said. But I was thinking about the girl on my bath mat vanishing into thin air.

'The phone that you found when you came back from Thailand? It's mine.'

'Yours. Did you set those thugs on us?'

'Of course not! Johnny, the man who worked for Richard Fuller, he took the phone off me when he caught me spying. Then Mya gave it back to me. How you got it is a mystery.'

'And Mr. B?'

'Your manager has bluffed his way through with me and he behaves as if he really believes I'm writing a story about fighters. But he must *know*. And every time I come close to getting caught by Fuller's hired thugs, something with this drug he's given me kicks in, and I don't remember anything about what I do or how I get away.'

'You don't remember anything?'

He shook his head.

'Do you wake up with blood all over you?'

His face closed down. 'No. I don't. What did the police tell you?'

'The police didn't have to tell me anything. I saw you go into that tunnel like a rabbit, unarmed and running scared. And I saw you come out dragging a dead man. There was black smoke around you. I couldn't really see you clearly. You were all shadowy. I thought I was losing it, but Shea, I'm not somebody who loses it. My dad is a violent guy. One of his best friends was a dealer, and I've been around convicts since I was little. I know what those guys are like and you're not it. Nothing fits.'

'I know.'

I squinted at him. I was remembering the quivering wreck he'd turned into right after killing that guy.

'You think it's a drug? Could Fuller have drugged you with something that sets off... I don't know... psychosis?'

He shifted his weight from side to side. The tension was racking up in his body.

'Like temporary insanity. Is that what you mean?'

I shrugged. 'You're telling me you don't remember going on an airplane and your passport didn't get stamped. That right there is weirder than anything. And what about Mya? Shea, the girl disappeared before my eyes and I'm not taking any drugs.' He said nothing.

'Where does she go when she's not here?'

'She says she goes to Himmapan.'

'Hippodrome? What's that all about?'

Shea sighed. 'Maybe you should Google. Seriously. It's a forest where the immortals live, according to Thai legend. But that's all it is. Magic. I don't believe in any of it.'

He looked deflated, exhausted. I touched his arm.

'Hey,' I said. 'You OK? What's the matter?'

'I can't reconcile myself with what's happening to my body. It doesn't make sense. And I have this feeling all the time, it's like there's another one of me, a shadow...'

He looked just miserable. I hate it when people are miserable. I said, 'There's a shadow over me, too. All my life. So what? Everyone has a dark side. Life is for living. If I wait until everything's perfect to do what I want to do, I'll be dead. You have to just go for it, Shea.'

He was staring at me. It was distracting.

We sat down on the sofa to eat. I was thinking about what he'd said. Out of the corner of my eye I was checking him out. I mean, OK, he was too skinny for me, and guys who are smarter than me always make me uncomfortable. I'd rather be the smart one. But... maybe Shea was different. This is going to sound stupid, but he smelled nice. He had a way about him. The way he talked to me made me feel good about myself; he made me sound like somebody I wasn't, but somebody who I would like to be. The me he saw was better than the real me.

And he killed an ex-SEALS private security agent and then got away from the police. That is *hot*.

'What are you thinking?' he asked. 'You're expecting me to do something, aren't you? The man is supposed to be in control, right? That's what women like. A man in control, mastering himself...'

I narrowed my eyes. 'What the hell are you talking about?'

'Oh, I was just comparing myself to your mate Khari. I mean, I don't really have a chance with you compared to somebody like that, do I?'

My face was getting hot.

'You'd have a better chance if you were honest with me.'

He sighed. 'I'm trying. It's not that easy.'

Here we go again with the dark and smoldering eyes, goddamnit.

'The way you look at me is freaking me out,' I said.

'How so?'

I shrugged. 'See, the guys I've known? They treat a woman like a car. They look at you and they're trying to figure out, is she a V-4 or a V-8? Does she go off-road? How does she corner?'

He laughed. 'I honestly wasn't thinking that.'

'No. You weren't. And that's what's weird.'

'I was thinking how I wish you weren't scared of me.'

I laughed and slapped my knee. 'I'm not scared of you!'

He was right, I was a little scared of him. But I'd be damned if I'd admit it.

He flushed. 'I forget, you're not like other girls.'

I snorted. 'Oh, thanks a lot.'

After all, if you're a tomboy like me you always think, well, maybe I'm not a real girl after all because real girls care about shoes. And—in my rich inner fantasy life—I was still hoping somehow that a hot guy who got me would come along. But guys usually go for the obvious stuff. T&A and lip gloss. When they pick me they're usually keeping their options open for something better. I've had fantasies where Khari suddenly sees me, I mean really sees me, and says, 'Jade, I don't know how to tell you this but them ring girls got nothing on you.'

And then they read the Lotto numbers and I find out I won eighteen million dollars. You know. *Fantasies.*

Now Shea said, 'I felt it about you from the first. I was drawn to you. It's almost like a… smell.'

'So now I smell?' I was really laughing. We both were. I put my plate on the floor. We were sitting facing each other on the sofa now, not quite touching.

'Tell me I'm way off base and I'll go. Tell me I'm wrong.'

I was twisting the end of a braid around my finger, smiling all stupid and looking down. What is up with that? I never twist my hair.

'You're not wrong,' I said. 'There is something.'

I kissed him. He was surprised, but then he was into it. His lips were soft, and when I opened my mouth against his I felt him molding against me. His tongue filled my mouth, pushing into me suggestively. Like advertising what else he could do. I pulled away.

'That's what I was trying to get at,' he murmured. He drew me against him and slid his hands up my back under my shirt. Skin on skin. It was amazing how fast I was into it. I'd be all over him in a second and there would be no stopping.

I guess it had been a while for me. Too long. I mean, I had a few boyfriends in my mid-teens but after Dmitri went down for stealing cars and I picked up a misdemeanor, I just quit. Speaking of cars? I got tired of being the dirt bike that got left in the ditch when some Dodge Viper came along. And I mean, I knew I'd have a boyfriend again someday. I just wasn't going to settle for anybody.

Shea wasn't just anybody.

I pulled back.

'Shea, do you have any idea how hard it is for me to stay out of trouble? Just me by myself, without any help from... from... the so-called Thai Mafia or whoever it is you're dealing with?'

He sighed and closed his eyes.

'I know. I'm sorry. You have a competition next weekend. And I'm being... intrusive, and, and...'

Oh, intrude again.

'Maybe you should just go back to London until this blows over,' I said. I loved saying that: *go back to London*. It made me feel like a Bond girl.

'I can't.'

'Why not?'

He seemed to realize he'd said something he shouldn't have said, because he started freaking. He shot to his feet.

'You're right. I shouldn't even be here. It's dishonorable to even think about you that way, given my circumstances. You're going to regret this, and hate me for doing it, and... I'm going to go.'

'Where?' I said, standing up with him.

'What?'

'Where will you go? I hear there's a price on your head.'

He gave an uneasy laugh.God, he was nervous. I just knew he was hiding a lot of stuff from me and instead of being repelled by it, I liked it. What is wrong with me?

'How did you get out of jail?'

He laughed. 'You make it sound like I broke out. Perez came and told me to go back to London. He said somebody above him in the chain of command didn't want me in the system.'

'Why not?'

'I presume Fuller gave an order. That's how he works. Jade, this man has influences everywhere. If I talked to the F.B.I. about him he could have a real problem, so he made sure the police let me go.' I felt cold. He was being so stupid.

'Shea, don't you get what that means? It means you're going to be killed.'

'Oh, I get it,' he said. 'It's down to whether I can get the evidence I need on Fuller before his people can get to me. And that's why I'm going to go. I've put you in enough danger already.'

'I'm not exactly an innocent child,' I told him. ' I can handle it. You can sleep here if you want. But you can't stay here long term. Perez already thinks we're involved.'

'Are we?'

We looked at each other.

I said, 'This is the weirdest situation I've ever been in. And that is saying something.'

He ran his hands through his hair, tugging at it like he expected to pull some understanding out of his skull. 'Yeah. I can't... I can't get over how you dealt with those guys. You knocked an armed man out cold.'

'With a little help from a big 'ole wrench,' I laughed. 'Wish I was going to have one of those in the ring on Saturday night. And if I could sneak up on Gretchen from behind it would be a piece of cake.'

'But I mean... how many people would have done that? You saved my life, Jade.'

I felt myself going hot. But I wasn't going to be distracted by flattery.

'Are you sure?' I questioned. 'Because you killed that guy in the tunnel. You did—no, don't close your eyes and pretend it didn't happen. You killed him, Shea. What did you have, a knife? How did you keep from getting shot yourself?'

He looked down at me and he seemed lost. He put his hands on my shoulders and leaned his forehead against mine.

'I don't know. I honestly don't know. I realize it's an inadequate answer, but it's all I've got for the moment.'

I know one thing. There are very few people in this world who I can be myself with. Truly myself, not the wisecracking, angry, armored-up version. Just me. I think that's why I like animals so much. They don't mess you around like people do.

Me and Shea were understanding each other on some physical level. Underneath words, underneath logic, underneath everything that I was supposed to be thinking about, I was getting into some kind of rhythm with him. He was right: it was like a smell, or a song you remember from long, long ago. There was something about him I just couldn't resist. Didn't want to. I wanted to be where he was.

Our foreheads were touching and his hands were heavy on my shoulders. We were breathing the same air.

I said, 'Let's go in my room.'

I heard him take a long inhale. Then he shifted his hands south and picked my ass right up off the ground. I wrapped my legs around him and he carried me from there.

And I'm not going to talk any more details. I'm not the type to brag. Let's just say, it was good enough that even when it was happening, I knew it had to be a mistake. Some things are too good to be true.

I guess that means I should regret it. Because of the crazy shit that went down after. But I don't.

Oh, no, I don't regret one second of it.

Can you Hear the Schadenfreude Angels Singing?

THERE WAS AN engine rumbling in my ear. Was it a motorcycle? A Maserati? The sound was a deep, throbbing, sexy sound—but when I tried to turn and see where it was coming from, I found I'd rolled over in bed and wrapped my arms around something big and warm.

Then last night all came back to me. Last night with Shea. He might not know who he was, but he knew his way around a girl's body, and that was more than could have been said for my last boyfriend. But now I was waking up to the sound of a Maserati in my bedroom. And a face full of soft, nicely fragrant—where had I smelled that smell before?—this wasn't skin, or hair... this was fur.

Fur? Shea hadn't been wearing fur. There was no fur in our apartment. Malu was a member of PETA. We're talking fur-free zone.

I came fully awake. My eyes opened, crustily. I disengaged my arms from the warm, furry, breathing bulk of something big, and as my vision started to focus I saw a jet black blur in the shape of a body that was bigger than a man. This thing was as big as a horse. It was surprising the bed hadn't collapsed.

I jerked back.

Holy fucking Batman there's a panther in my bed.

I fell out of bed backwards with a thud, scrambled away in a crab-walk, then remembered the handgun I keep in my closet. Perez's guys had confiscated it when they searched the place... shit, was the thing looking at me?

No. It was still asleep, its head on the pillow looking very dignified, its eyes closed. It had stirred a little and sighed in its sleep, that was all.

I pushed myself to my feet, naked, breathing very fast.

It wasn't a panther, for one thing. It was a lot bigger than that. It had a long, luxuriant mane and paws the size of dinner plates, and it was taking up most of my double bed.

Had it eaten Shea? Should I try to find him?

Or should I just leave?

I had to pee.

What day was it?

Where had I left my phone?

If this was the thing that killed Pierce, what chance did I have?

It opened its eyes and raised its head.

'I'm only a morsel,' I heard myself whisper. 'Don't even bother, 'k, 'cos I'm stringy. But I'll go to the deli for you. I'll go get you a side of beef, or—'

Suddenly it hit me that this lion looked exactly like Waldo, only much, much, much, *much* bigger.

'I'm going to get you pizza,' I said. The big cat didn't stir. 'I'll be right back. Don't move.'

I started to edge towards the door, bending down to pick up my clothes as I went. I don't know why; somewhere in my mind I didn't want the headlines to show that a naked body had been found gobbled up in this apartment, didn't want the hot sex I'd been having with Shea to be fodder for the *National Enquirer*, although if I'd thought about it at the time I'd have realized that if the lion killed me and ate me there would be nothing to find but disgusting traces—DNA evidence and red smears, no more. Still, I got my cut-offs on.

In one bound, the lion was up and past me, blocking the door. It lunged at me, playfully almost, like a puppy bouncing from side to side. Or a goalkeeper. That took up most of the room.

'OK, OK, we'll stay in,' I said. 'Uh...'

And without really thinking, I threw myself at the window,

which was halfway open. I fully expected to be grabbed by the leg and made into cat chow at any moment, but that didn't happen. I didn't jump out, I quickly climbed to stand on the window frame, then hoisted myself on to the roof. Scraped my ribs in the process, too, because I was still topless and the edges of the shingles were rough.

I looked down. The lion was staring up at me with great big yellow eyes. It stretched its mouth wide and let out a huge yawn. Then it turned and I saw it hop back into the bed. From here I couldn't see the whole bed, but I could see the black tail with the fuzzy tuft at the end, drooping over the edge of the bed like a bell pull. I listened.

The Maserati purring started up again. I swallowed a hysterical laugh. I was now conscious of being up on the roof of my building at eight o'clock on a weekday morning. Well, I'm guessing it was around eight, by the light and by the traffic I could hear on Anderson Ave., behind me. It was still cool, but you could feel that the day was going to get hot. Pigeons strutted across the roof, like they were amused by me.

The sound of Don Ho singing 'Tiny Bubbles in the Wine' drifted up from the pocket of my shorts.

I had a text from Khari. 'U home? Got2talk.'

Oh, man. A whole chorus of chickens was in my head, all going 'fuck fuck fuck' at once. If I knew Khari, he was texting me from his car and he was probably about three blocks away. If Eva was with him I didn't know what I'd do. Where's one of those portable manholes like the Road Runner has when you really need one? I'd drop the manhole, jump down it, and then pull it down after myself so there'd be no trace of my existence.

Right. Got to get off the roof. I was topless in broad daylight. Lucky what I got is small, and I could pretty much cover them with one hand and a forearm while I scuttled across the roof until I was just above the hallway over the stairs, at the back of the building. There's a window there that opens on to the landing.

It's always locked, but...

I hung over the edge of the roof and leaned over to try to prise the edge of the window open but couldn't reach it, so I leaned further. I got my finger in the gap and if I could just stretch a little further...

I fell. Landed in the privet hedge below.

Need I saw ow? I'm talking lacerations-style ow. I rolled out of the hedge and on to a strip of lawn belonging to the next door neighbours, bleeding, still topless, and of course barefoot. *Buenos dias*, Jade. Getting laid always has its price.

I darted through the neighbours' yard without anybody seeing me, hit the sidewalk and then caught some unwelcome attention from a passing car full of *boys from my school*. Oh frig. I flipped them the bird with my free hand and ran around to the front of the building. I would just have to buzz Irene and tell her I'd locked myself out. She would give me a hard time, but at least she'd have to let me in. We do pay rent.

I got up to the intercom and was about to press Irene's button when the door buzzed all by itself. I grabbed it and dashed in. Nobody was around, so I didn't know who let me in. I was still locked out of my own apartment, and I still had no clothes... I ran down to the basement. The laundry room was empty, but both machines were going full blast. I jerked open the dryer door and a bunch of kids' clothes flew out as the machine stopped tumbling; I grabbed a Furby tank top that probably belonged to Irene's eight-year-old and pulled it on. Then I shoved all the laundry back in, started the machine again, and went upstairs.

'Oh, shit!' I yelled loudly. 'I locked myself out, how the hell did I manage to do that?'

I thundered loudly down the stairs and knocked on Irene's door. The muffled sound of Aaliyah's 'Try Again' came through the door. I knocked again, louder. The music was turned down a little, and Irene came to the door on the phone as usual. She nodded as I blurted my request for access, and said, 'Honey, that's because the man is a dog, you understand me?' into the phone. While she grabbed her pass key I saw two heads appear around the corner from her living room. Her younger kids; I prayed the eight-year-old was still asleep. Crossed my arms over my chest. 'Can I use your bathroom for just a second?' I whispered. 'Emergency!'

She was paying more attention to her phone than to me, so I ducked into her bathroom, moved aside a Nickelodeon magazine, and gratefully peed.

When I came out, Irene wasn't there.

'Where's your mom?' I said to the kids. The little girl pointed upstairs.

'She went to open your door, silly,' she said.

'Oh, shh—ugar!' I cried. 'You kids, stay right there and do not leave this apartment. OK? Don't come outside.'

I shut Irene's door behind me and pelted up the stairs composing in my mind what I'd say to 911. Irene had unlocked the door but luckily for her, she hadn't actually opened it. Now she was on her way back. 'You gotta show him who's boss, girl,' she said into the phone. 'And you know what else? That gets worse after the kids, so you have to confront it now.'

'Thank you!' I said breathlessly, and she took the phone away from her ear long enough to say, 'Where'd you get that shirt?'

I gave her my blank look. I'm a terrible liar, but I can do a blank look and sometimes it's enough. People assume you're stupid or don't speak English.

The buzzer rang at the front door downstairs.

Irene leaned to one side and looked down into the lobby. 'That's for you,' she said. 'Your friend who drives the Corvette? He's parked illegally.'

I laughed nervously and Irene returned to her apartment saying, 'And if you gain weight, forget about it because he'll use that as a excuse—' her door shut.

The buzzer went again. I could see Khari, and it seemed he could see me, too. At least, he could see my feet.

I went down and let him in.

'Hey,' he said. 'Like your shirt.'

'Uh huh, so what's up? I got your text.'

'Let's go up. I gotta talk to you in private.'

He started up the stairs, taking the whole *me casa es yo casa* thing a little too literally right now.

'Uh, don't go in there, Khari,' I called. 'I got a little problem. Why don't we go for a drive and talk.'

'No, I can't drive,' he said. 'I already done about seven shots of tequila and I shouldn't of drove here. I'm gonna just take a cab home.'

He handed me the Corvette keys.

'What happened? You never drink.'

'Ah, I'm just pissed off. Come on, let's go in. I need your advice on something. What's the problem? You spraying for bugs or what?'

I ran after him, but he'd already opened the door and stepped in.

'No! Yes! Well, it *is* a wildlife issue!' I called after him. 'Khari, don't—'

I almost ran into his back. He was taking up most of my hallway, and he'd stopped in his tracks.

'Careful,' I squeaked. 'It's—'

'How you doin', man?' Khari stepped forward, extending his right hand. I couldn't see past him because he's so big, but I recognized Shea's voice all right.

'Morning, Khari, good to see you.'

They were shaking hands.

'Excuse me,' I squeaked. 'Gotta pee.'

I stood in the bathroom clutching my head in my hands, pulling the hair back from my face so that I looked like I was in freefall on a rollercoaster, which was pretty much how I felt.

While I was pretending to be peeing I could hear them talking in the next room. It all sounded normal and fine—both of them were totally OK. I was the one freaking. I wanted to just stay in there, but I had to find out what happened to the friggin' lion.

If there was a lion.

Could Shea have drugged me? Maybe I'd been hallucinating again. Shit happened, you know. I mean, a man-sized black lion? I don't think so. Not on this planet. Maybe my dreams got mixed up with Malu's stray cat and somehow... magnified it. In my twisted mind. Maybe?

Maybe I should just stay in here forever.

'I'll just go see what's keeping her,' Shea said, his voice getting closer. He was talking like he was the host, like he lived here or something.

I opened the door.

He smiled and kissed me. Mmm...

'It's fine,' he said. 'Go on out, it's all fine.'

I must have been some shade of purple when I got into the living room. Khari was sprawled in his usual seat, flicking between stations.

'This is messed up,' I said.

'OK, it's cool, it's cool,' Khari says. 'Sorry I didn't call first, I just assumed... you know. I didn't mean to walk in on nothing.'

I heard myself laughing in a really high voice. 'That's OK. You want coffee?'

'It's all covered,' Shea said. 'The tea is brewing.'

I stifled a laugh. I bit back a remark about crumpets.

'Tea, man, that's good,' Khari said. 'Tea is cool, tea is cool. Listen, Jade, I got to talk to you but I can see I'm interrupting something here, so how 'bout if we just hook up later when you're free?'

'Oh, don't mind me,' Shea sang. He sounded so very... British and uptight and proper, and he came out of the kitchen with Malu's *Futurama* mug full of milky tea and handed it to Khari. 'I was just leaving.'

'Seriously, man,' Khari said.

'No, seriously. I've got lots of paperwork to do, and Jade... Jade, I'll call you later.'

I widened my eyes at him. *Call me later? You and Simba, you mean?*

I thought it, but all I said was, 'OK, tiger,' and punched him playfully on the arm.

His eyebrows went up at that, but he left, rubbing his arm. I felt myself going hot in the cheeks and went into the kitchen to grab some tea myself. When I came out, Khari was dumping his tea into Malu's aloe plant. Then he started pacing up and down.

'So last week she tells me she's going to Miami to work, but when I call her at night I can hear a guy in the background, and she's like, "No I ain't playing you" and I'm like who is he and she's like he's just a photographer and I'm like what kind of pictures are these and she gets real mad and hangs up. So I got a friend in Miami, Vince, he's like tight with an outfit over there you know what I'm saying, and I call him up and I'm like can you check on my girlfriend and Vince goes over to the hotel and she's shacked up with some Arabian guy in his twenty thousand dollar a night suite.'

'Holy shit,' I said when he paused for breath.

'Yeah, right, and so when she got back she comes over all hi, I missed you, sorry about the other day and I told her I know she's a ho and get out of my face, I don't want nothing to do with her.'

'That sounds... smart,' I said carefully. I mean, why was he telling me this? I didn't want to know this.

'So that's over,' he said, spreading his hands.

'Sounds like it,' I said. As Malu would say, *Can you hear the schadenfreude angels singing?*

'I don't get it, Jade,' he said. 'I thought she was different. This shit has happened to me before, but I really thought she was different. We were supposed to be exclusive.'

So I told him my car theory. 'Your problem is you think women are like cars. Well, you wanted a Maserati, and you got one,' I said. 'Car like that needs a lot of attention, and a lot of money.'

'She's all into her career, though. She can make money doing what she does. Why she want to go with some Sheik Abdul maybe got HIV and... shit, Jade.'

'Shit, yeah. You been tested lately?'

He swallowed. 'I don't believe this. I was faithful to her. I could have played around, but I never did. I'm not like that. That's not right, man. It's not right.'

'I don't know, Khari. Maybe you need somebody more real.'

'What do you mean, more real? Eva's real.'

'No, Eva is a fantasy. She dresses up in high heels and parades around for y'all, and she watches you work out and brings you a towel and she's always there on the other end of the phone when you want to talk about your next fight, and you think it's cute that she's a model but you're always worried who else is looking at her, and it makes you crazy. So now she's gone and done the thing you were most afraid of her doing. You don't even know her. Did you know her and Monika want to open a bakery? Did you know they want to live next door to each other and have a bunch of babies? She tell you about that, *pana*?'

'Well, she said some stuff, but that's Monika's idea. Eva wants a show business career. You don't turn down the money she's making to open a bakery and make cupcakes, you know what I'm saying.'

'You might if you got Sheik Whatever giving you big tips. Come on Khari, get real. You weren't going to stay with her. You were just having a good time, so what's the big deal? You can get another Eva any time.'

'I don't want another Eva.'

I never would have spoken to him like this if I hadn't just spent last night with Shea like I did. Shea had made me feel like a goddess. My confidence was at an all-time high, and suddenly Khari for all his looks and muscles, he just seemed like a child.

'Well, what do you want, then?'

He stared at me. Really stared, like it was something he hadn't thought about before and he thought I was a genius for asking it. God, how could I not have noticed before what a dufus Khari can be? Blinded by his pecs, I guess.

'I don't know, Jade. I really don't know. I think I could be done with women.'

I let out a shriek of laughter.

'No seriously, I mean, I'm a fighter. I can't be getting distracted by relationships. I'm not good with women. I don't want to go shopping, I don't want to meet their friends and their parents. I just want a girlfriend I can—'

'Go all night with,' I interjected.

'I was going to say talk to about the stuff that I'm into. Someone to share what I do,' he said, sounding hurt.

'As long as she's five foot nine 36-24-36 with perfect skin, perfect hair, perfect face, Brazilian wax, plucked eyebrows, can walk in heels...'

'OK, OK, I get it. Remember, Eva asked me out.'

'So do a lot of girls,' I said. 'I see it all, remember? Your girlfriends talk to me.'

'What do you mean they talk to you? What do they say?'

'They say you train all the time and you never want to do nothing fun. They say you tell them to measure your junk so they can see for themselves it's 11 inches, but it's really only ten and three quarters.'

Khari shot to his feet. 'Who told you that?'

I laughed. 'It don't matter.'

Khari rubbed the back of his neck, looked at the floor. 'See, a woman like Eva, it's just that she's beautiful and you got to understand how a beautiful woman can turn a man's head. When I walked into a club with her, every guy in the room was looking at me and thinking he wished he had what I had. Everybody would look at us.'

'Wow,' I said. 'Great basis for a relationship.'

'OK, a'ight, take it easy. I come over here for a little understanding and you give me tough love on a stick.'

'You need it, Khari. When you gonna wake up? You want sex, you can get that anytime, you're lucky, you don't even have to pay for it. I see how it goes with you. You don't got to do nothing. Women just seem to fall out of the sky and land on your rhythm stick.'

'You don't got to go getting all rude.' But he looked flattered.

'You want a relationship, you have to compromise something. Maybe you don't want that.'

I stared him down. I don't know where my usual X-rated mental movies with Khari had went to but I wasn't thinking nothing sexy about him.

'Maybe you're right,' he said. 'I guess I got to think about it.'

'Yeah, and get yourself tested,' I added as I showed him out.

When he was gone I burst into an attack of the giggles. I couldn't believe that just happened. Any of it.

I knew if Malu were here, she'd be cheering. I missed her, but how could I talk to her when now we had a resident fucking lion?

Literally.

Truth and the Single Girl

AFTER I SHUT the door I heard a muffled crash from the kitchen. I went in there and Girl in a Red Dress had her hand in the cookie jar. For real.

She saw me and froze. Her expression didn't change. There was something just too calm about this kid. She pulled her hand away slowly and turned to face me. But I couldn't meet her eye, because I was staring at the *giant snake* that lay in coils on my kitchen floor.

Did I say *giant snake*? Sorry, correction. I meant *giant snake with a baby's face*.

The thing filled most of the kitchen and its chubby face stared up at me with an open, curious expression. The baby part of it looked about a year old, if a one-year-old baby could have a head the size of a basketball.

The girl's eyes turned toward the plant on the windowsill and I could tell she was going to disappear again.

'Wait!' I blurted, and grabbed a stale bagel from the counter. I started to offer it to the baby-faced snake and then wondered if babies were allowed to eat bagels, or whether this one had teeth... too late, the creature had opened its big pink mouth and swallowed the whole bagel like it was a Lifesaver. Then it turned, slithered into Malu's spider plant, and was gone.

Oh, man. We need a cuckoo clock to go with all the other stuff goes on in this apartment.

The girl turned towards the spider plant, too.

I fumbled for Thai words and came up with the equivalent of 'Wait up!' The girl didn't move. Her eyes watched me steadily. Just looking at her made me more aware of my own anxiety.

'Wait, *please*,' I said again. I reached for my phone. The hint of an emotion flickered across her expression, just for a second; then she was back to being unreadable again.

Thank god, Shea picked up on the first ring.

'Really sorry about before—'

'Get over here. Now. I'm not kidding.'

'I—'

'The girl is here. Red dress? Vanishes into thin air?'

'Oh, you mean Mya. All right, well then, I suppose—'

I hung up.

'Mya? Your name Mya? I Jade. Stay, OK?' I gestured to the food. 'Please you eat?'

She shook her head.

'Thank you, I'm not hungry,' she said softly, but she looked worried now.

Why was she stealing food, then?

The buzzer went off. It was Shea. He took the stairs three at a time.

'That was fast. Were you lurking around in the bushes?' I said.

'Er... is Mya still here?'

I ushered him in. Mya even smiled a little, which made me feel jealous—not of her, but of him. Mya trusted him. Who would trust *Shea*?

And for the record, sleeping with someone and trusting them are two completely different things, OK?

I took Mya to my room and showed her my posters and the fight program from my match at Lumpinee. She didn't seem to get it, so then I pulled out my camera and showed her pictures and video from Coat's gym. There was a picture of me and Waldo. She pointed at the cat and said, 'Kala Sriha.'

Then she looked at Shea. So did I.

'Never mind that,' Shea said. He started talking to Mya about me, how I was a friend. I ran her a bath and brought her a stack of clean clothes. She could wear my shorts and t-shirts. They'd be too big, but at least they were clean. I showed her the shampoo and towels and gave her a toothbrush. Then I left her to do her thing.

I had no idea how to deal with this.

I found Shea sitting on the floor drinking straight out of the wine bottle we'd opened last night. I leaned against the wall and folded my arms. He didn't look at me. We could both hear sounds of splashing from the bathroom.

'I'm sorry,' he said. 'I wish there were some sort of blanket apology I could make. To cover everything I've done wrong.'

'Whoa, hold up. Before you start in with the I'm sorry stuff, maybe you want to tell me exactly what happened. Like, I think I know how you got in the country without a passport, *Waldo*.'

He took another swig, and when he lowered the bottle I reached down and took it off him.

'That's enough of that,' I said. 'We don't want you turning into anything furry.'

He shuddered.

'I did have my reasons for everything I did. Mya said I needed human experiences, and I felt so drawn to you that I may have let myself forget how much younger than me you are.'

I snorted. 'Now you're annoying me. As if age difference means anything compared to, like, *species* difference.'

'And of course there was the phone. I couldn't let Fuller's men take the phone back to him. I had to try to do something.'

'You were up on the roof that night. You, or... something to do with you. That thing is too big to be a panther. It's more like a lion.'

'Mya says I belong to Kala Sriha, who is a sort of god that lives in the legendary forest of Himmapan... go on, Google it, I'll wait.'

'I can Google later. Tell me.'

'Kala Sriha is a... black lion. Actually, a black vegetarian lion, which would explain...'

'... why the only meat you eat is people's arms and stuff.'

'Something like that. Well, bear in mind I didn't actually swallow.'

He paused for me to laugh at his pathetic joke. I didn't. He said, 'I think, Jade, that we need to not get sidetracked by the supernatural things that are going on here, and focus on what really matters. Like the evidence in the phone. There is footage of two murders on there, and I think we can link Johnny Cook, the guy who committed them, to a number of violent crimes. But it's Richard Fuller I want to bring down. Cook worked for him, but Fuller's got everybody convinced he's some kind of pure-hearted philanthropist.'

'Medicines do it,' Mya said softly from the doorway. Her hair was wet. She was dressed in the clothes I'd given her, and she held a crumpled piece of pale blue paper in her hand. 'Make him seem immortal. Powerful. He can convince you of anything when his medicine is working.'

Shea looked at her sharply, and I saw pain pass across his face. Then he turned back to me.

'There's a link between Richard Fuller and the gym, so there's a link to you.'

He might as well have slapped me across the mouth.

'So what am I, some kind of suspect? What was that last night, softening me up or something?'

I could still feel him in my body, I had his sweat in my pores. My heart went cold.

'There's no need to be like that,' Shea said. 'All I meant was that when the phone came to you, Fuller's attention fell on you. And I involved you again the other night at the diner. You're as much of a target now as I am.'

'Could he be drugging all of us? This Richard Fuller character? Making me hallucinate wild animals, or making you turn psycho?'

'No,' said Mya sharply. 'Not imagination. Mr. Shea is *dead* without Kala Sriha. Sorry, but true.'

She was way too young to know all of this. It kind of broke my heart.

'I saw you in Mr. B's office, Mya. On CCTV. You gave a package to someone. Do you know the name of the person?'

She shook her head.

Mr. B, I thought. *What the hell?* I couldn't turn a blind eye. Drugs. Human trafficking, too, according to Shea. I had to walk away from both of them. I went into Malu's room and looked at the fish tank. I could smell Malu's perfume, and I looked at her shelf of books organized by subject and her stack of notebooks and her desk with its cubbies and four different colored highlighters. Malu was the most organized person I knew. What would Malu do in this situation?

Don't panic. Gather information.

I could almost hear her say it.

Yes. Malu wouldn't go in with guns blazing. She would find out as much as she could and then make a calm, rational decision.

My hands were clenched into fists unconsciously; now I put a fist to each temple and pressed my skull as if I could squeeze my brain into understanding this better.

Deep breaths.

Taking a deep breath just made me want to hit something.

I went back into the living room and found Shea and Mya sitting on the sofa, talking quietly in Thai.

'Don't you think you could have said all this last night?' I said. 'What were you thinking, getting close to me knowing what could happen? I'm lucky to be alive, right? I woke up next to a man-eating lion. Do you have any idea how insane that is?'

Shea hung his head.

'So why did you pick me?' I said to him.

'I'm sorry? What do you mean?'

'In Bangkok. You were the only friend I had. You found me and you… you attached yourself to me. I thought I was a mule, but now I'm starting to think Waldo was just using me to get entry to the United States.'

Shea ran a hand through his hair and looked at the ceiling.

Then he looked me in the eye. He was angry.

'I'm a human being, Jade,' he said. 'Whatever is happening when... when I'm not myself? I can't be responsible for it.'

'Nice,' I said. 'I'm starting to see Perez's point.'

'What point?' Shea's nostrils flared.

Mya made a small sound.

'You got something to say?' I snapped at her, and she flinched away from my tone. Damn. All my *jai yen* out the friggin' window.

'Maybe it's your destiny,' she said. 'Kala Sriha knows why he picked you. Shea doesn't.'

'Kala Sriha my ass,' I said, and immediately regretted it. There had been something else in Shea's eyes last night, something more to him than just a nice-looking boy—and let's face it, that *something* was what I had gone for.

'Kala Sriha wouldn't harm you,' Mya said softly. 'Kala Sriha saved Shea because of his true heart and the merit of his mission. Trust him. Help him. Please.'

'Oh, *Madre de Dios*,' I cried, rolling my eyes. It's funny how when things get crazy I start to act like Nana. Now Nana is dying and I feel like an imposter.

I went back into Malu's room, like I was fighting and Malu's bed was my corner. This time Mya followed me. She went to the Norfolk pine and touched its needles.

'Jade,' she said softly in English. 'I am sorry for stealing your food. I will repair, I promise.'

'Sorry for stealing—? Mya, you can have as much food as you want. Don't even worry about it for one second.'

I wanted to laugh, to run, to hide—to do *anything* that would get me out of this position—but there was something about the kid that stopped me in my tracks. What must she have been through? If she could deal with it, then I could, too.

Mya handed me the paper she was holding.

'What's this?' I scowled at the handwritten list of names and addresses on a piece of expensive stationery. They were all different countries.

'It's a list of the people Mr. Richard deals with.'

My heart thumped faster. The addresses were all over the world. Combat Sports Emporium was not on the list.

Shea stuck his head around the door frame.

'I've got to be in New York,' he said in a tight voice. 'I have an appointment at the Consulate.'

'Yeah? Well I have to be in Las Vegas.' It was an exaggeration because my flight didn't leave until the afternoon.

'You don't need to worry about Mya,' Shea said. 'She can come and go on her own steam. Don't ask me how. I'm probably losing my mind anyway.'

'Yeah,' I said, making my voice hard. 'That explains all this. It's all about you.'

Right? Because what other reason would Shea have to be interested in me, except to help *himself*? It's the same old story. This. Is. Why. I. *Don't have a boyfriend*. It always ends up being about him. Drama all the time, and always his drama.

Take control, Malu said from my mental corner.

'Right,' I said. 'Here you go, Shea. Mya just gave me this. I believe it's evidence.'

Color rushed into Shea's face when he read the list. 'What... how...?' he stammered. I interrupted him.

'Here's the plan. We're going to take you to the Consulate to get your passport. Shea, you're going back to Thailand to talk to the police and do what you have to do. I got a fight tomorrow, and even if Mr. B turns out to be the dirtiest mofo in the history of the sport, I'm not backing out of this one. That's my damn decision.'

I picked up Khari's Corvette keys.

'Oh, look!' I broke out laughing. 'Fast car. Icing on the cake.'

Crunch Time

I NEVER CRY. I just hit things. On the drive to the East Side in Khari's Corvette I packed all my emotions into my angry bones, saving them for tomorrow's fight. At the George Washington Bridge toll booths Shea leaned across to my side of the car and murmured, 'Are you OK?'

I just grinned and said, 'Stupid question.'

It was probably for the best that this thing with Shea wasn't working out. Because to fight I had to stay sharp, and I needed rage in my system. Not endorphins and cuddly shit. Gretchen was the one who'd need a boyfriend to put ice packs on her boo-boos, after I was through with her. Me, I'd stay hard.

Nobody said nothing during the trip. Mya slumped under her seat belt looking small in the back, and she stared out the window, taking everything in but not making a sound. As we got closer to the British Consulate we passed through one of the richest neighborhoods in New York, and I dealt with my nerves by making a little game of counting women with handbag-sized dogs on the sidewalk. I got up to five, and then we were there. I pulled over in a no-standing zone.

Shea turned to Mya in the back seat and they exchanged a flurry of quick reassurances to each other. I heard her wish him luck. Then he turned to me.

'Thanks for the lift. And good luck in the fight. I'll call you.'

I knew he wouldn't kiss me in front of Mya, so I just nodded and waved with no real feeling. It had to be obvious I was pissed off, but Shea didn't have the nerve to talk to me about it. Like the big bag of wimp he is, he just shut the door and loped across the street to the Consulate.

I turned to Mya. 'Want to ride up front?'

The gecko started itching as I drove north on Third Avenue. I'd been planning to go right the way up to 125th Street and then cut across town, but I trusted the gecko, so I turned off at East 60th. A black Town Car pulled in right behind me, too clean to be a gypsy cab, too aggressive to be a limo. It tried to pass, coming right alongside like a shark. Snarling, I turned down Lex. The Town Car didn't follow. I took another left on East 56th, and as I crossed the lights at 2nd Avenue a florist's delivery van cut in front of me. I had to brake hard.

'This city is full of assholes,' I muttered. I restrained myself from a bigger display because Mya was just a kid. The gecko was still itching. I crossed First Avenue.

The black car swings in behind me.

Fuck.

I know what this is. This is a hit.

We're now going through this canyon of big delivery vehicles parked on both sides of the street, and I can see the black Town Car behind us and I'm shitting myself, calculating where the nearest subway stations are in relation to here, wondering how fast Mya can run, or whether she'll even listen to me and do what I say.

The van in front of me brakes for no reason and all of a sudden I'm out of time. This is it.

Here's the thing about me. I may be crap at relationships and talking and expressing my feelings, but when it's crunch time and you need somebody to think fast, I'm your girl. I could see what was going down like it was a math problem: a) van cuts me off, b) guy on my tail—well, c) is pretty obvious, right? They had us sandwiched between the van and the black car, so they'd probably grab Mya and throw her in the van or maybe grab us both, or maybe shoot us both. Simple, inescapable. We were fucked. I might not know the exact variation on the theme, but my money was on grab us and throw us in the van because otherwise, why have a van?

Before I'd even stepped on the brake I knew what had to be done.

The car was still jerking to a stop as I reached over and snapped Mya's seatbelt off. Looked her straight in the eye, talked to her like she was one of my dad's pit bulls:

'Mya! Come!'

I ripped the keys out of the ignition and gripped them in my left hand, dragging Mya out of the car after me with my right. With my left eye I clocked Dark Suit One getting out of the Town Car as I ran along the length of the florist's van. Under the suit he'd be rock-hard from kettlebells and creatine, and behind the dark glasses he was probably psychotic. Flower Delivery Guy was scrawny by comparison. He had opened his door and was climbing out of the van. I couldn't see his left hand—it was on the seat of the car as he faced backward to confront me. He had to be going for a gun.

I was at full charge, Mya stumbling behind me. I let her go just long enough to transfer the keys into my right hand, where they would make my fist good and hard. Then, skipping half a step to close the gap, I threw the overhand right at his cheekbone and felt his head spin as I followed through. Goodnight, moon. He staggered and went to sleep on his way down.

I might have broken my hand, but that's a small price to pay for being alive.

Bending, I turned to get hold of Mya again and a bullet whined as it passed over my head. I heard glass shatter. The engine of the van was still running—of course, because they'd planned to peel out of here with us in the back. Only now, we were in the front. I bundled Mya into the van and put it in gear, stepping on the accelerator even as Dark Suit One came running, shooting, and the door was flapping because Flower Delivery Guy had wrenched it fully open when he crashed. Dark Suit One shot the glass out of the driver's window before I got the door shut and accelerated away from him. In my side mirror I could see Dark

Suit Two also running after us. I saw the flash from his gun, and then the van lurched as the right rear tire blew.

I kept up a continuous stream of bad words as I drove on the rim. I turned onto Third Avenue and they weren't following me anymore. They would go back to their car, but Khari's Corvette would be blocking them. I'd bought us some time.

'This could end badly,' I said. Mya was huddled on the floor of the passenger side beside a potted office plant. 'I'll try to outdrive them, but if they have us on GPS they'll just follow wherever we go.'

I turned south on Sutton Place and then west on 56th. Then we picked up a silver BMW, tailgating like an angry hornet.

'This can't be for real.'

Did Richard Fuller have an infinite supply of mercenaries in dark suits? Did he have them on tap? Was he flying them in from somewhere, or were they appearing like just-add-water cartoon Martians?

My gecko tattoo was itching like never before.

'Mya, you can really disappear?' I said in Thai. 'Maybe you can disappear *now*.'

But she stayed where she was, and at least her head was down out of range of bullets. There were green leaves in her hair. Her eyes were closed and her lips moved.

That was when I noticed a blurriness on the edges of my vision. The buildings on either side of me seemed to be shifting position in my peripheral vision.

I saw the road, the lights, the pedestrians, the headlights of the BMW right up in my wing mirror first on one side, then on the other; the driver was weaving to pass me or run me off the road. I couldn't pay attention to anything else, even when trees started breaking out of buildings, when walls turned to air, when concrete and girders gave way to the movement of living creatures.

Then came the smell, just like the smell in my apartment. The inside of the van already smelled like flowers but now there was something else, a sharp tang of earth and wood. A green tongue of flickering motion slithered across the dashboard. Something alive; something fast. I reached behind me for the gun but Mya grabbed my arm.

'No, Jade!' she cried. 'Don't hurt the gecko!'

'Gecko?'

But there was no time to think about the gecko. Instead I had to worry about the tree.

It was a tree just like the bodhi tree near Chiang Mai, where the bus had stopped. This one rose right out of the road ahead, too big to go around, much too close. The thing was huge, a Grandmama of a tree, decked out with ribbons and brightly colored offerings like a roadside memorial. Except it wasn't by the roadside, it was smack in the middle of the road.

I flashed that already-too-late sensation that usually only happens in nightmares. Mya and I were about to become the kind of crash victims that these memorials are supposed to honor.

Everything went sharp and clear.

It was as if my brain was so hungry to stay conscious that it was trying to grab as many impressions as it could before the end.

The air was green, wet, and clean in a way New York can never be. It was full of insects in clouds and swirls. There was a gecko hanging from the van's rear-view mirror like a Bangkok taxi-driver's talisman, its eyes making tiny ultrafast movements as it took in the sight of me.

I came off the brakes. The muscles in my arms clenched hard as I tried to swerve the delivery van around the tree, turning the wheel with little jerks like my old boyfriend taught me to use when we were joyriding.

I almost made it. The van's nose passed the obstacle, and the parked cars to the left simply vanished so that instead of hitting them we plunged into soft undergrowth. There was a bone-jarring jolt as the spinning rear end of the van sideswiped the tree. The gecko went flying out the window. With a crunch, the rear side panel collapsed, the chassis buckled, and the shock shattered the windscreen, sending a torrent of tiny pieces of glass falling on Mya and me. I shut my eyes.

When I opened them I didn't know if I was alive or dead.

The Bodhi Tree

I COULD HEAR Mya breathing fast and shallow. We were both covered with flecks of glass. She was unfolding from the floor of the delivery van as if in slow motion, bits of glass dripping off her like dewdrops. She held the potted plant in her arms like a teddy bear.

We were in the woods. The enormous tree had let go of leaves on impact, and they now drifted down through the broken windscreen, afterthoughts.

The engine had died. The noise of the city was gone, leaving a kind of stillness that wasn't silence. There were pale sounds, diffused though the air like the smell of toast fills a house. Ambient insect noises, high-pitched bird calls, faint and soft. The movement of leaves.

My heart was the loudest noise.

I opened my door and stepped out, shaking the glass off myself. The front of the van was all right. The middle of the vehicle had collided with the tree, and the impact had wrenched the back axle out of alignment. I walked around the back and opened Mya's door. She stepped down into the ferns without looking at me.

'Are you hurt?'

She swallowed and slowly shook her head. She was looking into the woods, and I followed the line of her gaze to a pine tree. The gecko was clinging to the side of it, perfectly at home.

I started to laugh. I couldn't help it. Mya flinched and moved away from me a little, so I pulled myself together for her sake.

Why I was worried about her, I don't know.

'You did this,' I said. 'I told you to escape and you... did this. Where are we?'

Mya went around to the tree we had hit. She stood looking at it silently. I slapped at mosquitoes and looked, too.

It wasn't the same tree that had popped up in the middle of the road in midtown. Well, obviously this wasn't midtown. But also, it wasn't the same tree. The image of the tree I'd swerved around was imprinted on my memory like a photograph. Or I thought it was. The night my father threw my mother across the room and broke her neck I had an image of her in shorts and a stripy tank top, flying across the room like a doll. But the clothes they showed Aunt Jennifer at the hospital had been Mom's nurse's uniform. They'd had to cut it to pieces to get it off her. When I told Aunt Jennifer what I remembered seeing, she said, 'The mind plays tricks under stress, *chika*. It's a neurological thing.'

Was I experiencing a 'neurological thing' right now? I'd seen the vines twisting around the enormous trunk. I'd seen the light green leaves. And I'd seen the ribbons tied around the trunk, the little gifts and stick figures offered to the ghosts who lived in the tree. Just like in Thailand.

For those moments when I tried not to smash into the tree, somewhere in my mind I'd been thinking Mya had brought a piece of Thailand here. Or brought us there. Like the smell in my house when she was around, like the strange creatures that came with her and ate my trail mix. It had seemed so real.

Now we were standing at the base of a big pine tree. Or maybe a fir. (I can never tell them apart. Like I said: I hate the woods.) There were no ribbons. No offerings. It wasn't even as big as I remembered it.

I started to cry.

I don't even know what happened.

One minute I was looking at the stupid tree feeling pissed off at the way everything was slipping and sliding underneath me. Like the world was some unsolvable puzzle that I'd had enough of. I just wanted to throw it across the room. Like you throw a woman you say you love. Like you throw your opponent. Like you throw your chances in life, if you're not careful.

Then I was on my knees at the roots of the tree, my hands covering my face, crying like a baby.

I wanted my mother. I wanted Nana to not be dying. I wanted the world to be solid. And it isn't.

It really isn't.

After a little while I felt Mya's hand on the back of my head. As if it had a will of its own, the crying stopped.

She said, 'I can't take you to the forest without the night orchid drug. Only myself. I tried, but we came here instead.'

I stood up and wiped my face with the end of my t-shirt. Beyond the van there was a shallow hillside, and I could see a trail of crushed underbrush and battered saplings where the van had crashed through. The forest floor was torn up by the skid. At the top of the slope I could see light, a break in the woods.

I ran up there. It was a country road, and we'd driven off it. Trees everywhere, in all directions. Great.

I took out my phone. There were seven texts and two messages from Malu.

Oops.

I hit 'Call.'

'Tell me you're at least alive,' she said.

'Of course I'm alive. Malu, you know that app our parents use to trace our phones? Like, when they want to find out if we are where we say we are?'

'You mean the app I used on you to see if you were really at Mr. B's and you were at the apartment?'

She was mad.

'I'm sorry, Malu. I had to lie. There were good reasons. You didn't tell Mr. B, did you?'

'Where the hell are you now?'

'Well... I was sort of hoping you could tell me that.'

'This is a joke, right?'

'I'm not sure where I am. I had an accident. Can you come get me?'

'Can I...? Jade, I have no words for you right now.' This was a whole new level of mad for Malu.

There was a pause. I could hear her clicking and tapping on her phone. Then she said. 'What the hell are you doing in the Pine Barrens? Don't tell me somebody threw you in a sack and dumped you there.'

'Malu, please. I'm supposed to be on a plane in three hours. Please...' My voice broke. I really was about to lose it and not get it back.

'Stay where you are. Sit your ass down and wait. I'll call you when I get closer. Under no circumstances are you to hitchhike. Got it?'

I hung up.

'I don't know how she turned out so bossy,' I said to Mya, turning.

The back of the van was open, revealing heaps of flowers wrapped in cellophane and several gourmet gift baskets. Mya had grabbed as many of these as she could carry, with their wedges of cheese and expensive jams and chocolate-covered pretzels.

I stared.

'You're thinking about food *now?*' I marvelled.

'I have to go, Jade,' she said. After listening to Malu bellow at me over the phone, Mya's Thai sounded even softer than usual. Like soothing music. 'We will see each other again. Tell Shea good luck.'

'But—'

She was way ahead of me. By the time I got out the word '*but*' she was fading away into the green, leaving the door of the van swinging open and a red Mylar balloon drifting up into the trees with its message: *Welcome Home.*

Beast

I GOT TO the weigh-in late but they hadn't started yet. The room was full of twitchy fighters in silk robes advertising their sponsors, surrounded by endless handlers. Mr. B's contingent had Khari surrounded. There he was, showing it all off for the cameras, talking to his nutritionist and his yoga teacher and the rep from the supplement company who make all the shakes and pills and potions he takes. You could barely see him with all the people he had around.

Holding my event ID out in front of me, I slid into the room and sat down next to a water cooler. I hate all this bullshit, and I didn't even want to talk to Mr. B or I'd just end up accusing him of being a slave trader or worse.

My mother left me in this dude's custody, and here he was doing business with perverts and psychos.

Tommy Z swept in with his girlfriend Jemima Stone of *Circus Freak* fame. The cameras all turned to the TV beauty and the action star, clearing one side of the room. Across the empty space, Khari looked up and noticed me. While Tommy was making a little speech Khari swaggered over, smiling.

'You in so much trouble,' he said out of the side of his mouth. 'Why you ignoring my messages? Where my car at?'

'Oh, long story.'

'You look like hell. What you do to your hand?'

The fist I'd used to take down the Florist Van dude was bruised pretty bad. I'd iced it and loaded it with arnica, but it still looked blue-black. Khari said:

'You got problems with that English dude?'

I shook my head.

'Yeah, I get it, you don't want to talk. You go on and weigh in ahead of me and then get out of here and up to your room ASAP. Tell you what, everybody want to interview you. They billing your fight as Beauty and the Beast. Don't play into it. No head-butting the media, got it?'

Over Khari's shoulder I could see Mr. B making a point of ignoring me. Was it because I was late and blowing off his messages, or was it because he was in on the Richard Fuller child trafficking thing and he knew I knew?

Everybody was looking like an enemy to me now.

I weighed in four pounds lighter than I'd planned. Ignoring the questions about why I was so skinny and would it hurt me in the fight, I kept my head down and my mind still. Reporters taunted me and tried to get me to 'show my beast fangs'.

'I'm saving my fangs for Gretchen.' I got out of there before they could make me take pictures beside Gretchen.

I tried to eat my room service dinner, but my guts were reacting to the nerves and it was just like Thailand all over again, except with softer toilet paper. For hours I prowled up and down the room, stopping only to twitch the curtains aside and look out into the neon. Looking for trouble, because I had a feeling it would be looking for me. My mother called. Then Malu. I let them both go to voice mail. I didn't trust myself not to break down if I had to talk to family. Malu would squeeze me for the truth, and the truth was crazy.

I didn't sleep. In my mind, the fight had already begun. Everything between now and that starting bell was meaningless.

The Las Vegas venue was nothing like Lumpinee. No more ancient traditions; no more stained old canvas. No *wai kru*, no musicians to spur on the fighters. We were into full-sized American bigbucks, complete with giant screens and Dolby stereo. Big crowd, spotlights, cheesy dry ice, sound effects.

Khari was third on the card. They'd matched him with a former submission champion who should have been an easy knockout, but Khari walked into a guillotine in the third round and lost control of the fight. Afterward he shook off everybody's efforts to console him, and I think Mr. B was afraid to say much in case Khari started tearing down the locker room. Khari hates losing.

But Khari surprised me. Before my fight he came over and asked me if I was ready.

'You'll do great,' he told me. Our gazes met. He didn't have to say anything; we could read each other. He knew I was scared. He didn't know everything about the shit with Mr. B and the gym, but he could put some of it together. 'I got your back,' he said.

'Thanks, baby.' I hugged him. 'Now I have to go throw up.'

'Man, that's harsh, Jade.'

'Nothing personal,' I gulped, and ran for the bathroom.

Here's the strange thing about the fight. When I got in the cage I wasn't nervous about Gretchen. I was scared of a world that could crack open, where ghosts could walk out of trees and stuff like that. I was scared of the forest coming *here*. My skills meant nothing in that place. It's not like you can punch a ghost.

Up in that cage, the whole gladiator thing was unreal. The dazzle of the lights and the energy of the crowd made it feel like my whole body was plugged into a socket. I jogged up and down in place, shadow-fighting a little bit and working the kinks out of my neck. I could see myself on a giant screen, scowling and twitchy. The red mouthguard made it look like my mouth was full of blood. I quickly turned away from that view and found myself with my eyes locked on Mr. B. He was wearing a rhinestone suit so loud it could only belong in Las Vegas, but I didn't find him amusing. He looked very, very serious, and he was talking even faster than usual to Cake and Khari in my corner. When he saw me watching, he thumped his fist to his heart and then punched it at me.

I felt hollow.

Focus, Jade. Better late than never. Come on.

Celebrity announcer Max 'the Axe' Hartman was in the ring, reading our names in that blaring, exaggerated voice. *Focus, Jade.* Now the ref was giving us our instructions, I had my eyes fixed on Gretchen's blonde head and she was tonguing her mouth guard and flexing, staring daggers at me with them blue-blue eyes, but it still didn't seem really real. We were touching gloves... and the bell rang.

Now it was real.

Gretchen came at me like a tank, gunning for my head. I never had nobody charge across the ring at me so fast and nasty. Rights and lefts coming in hard and furious. She drove me back and within seconds I felt the cage behind me. I covered up so all she could hit was elbows and shoulders, but she was still landing shots.

I had two immediate impressions about Gretchen: a) she was bigger up close, and b) she had total contempt for me. She was thinking of me like an obstacle to be knocked down and stepped on. She wasn't afraid of me one little bit. She was the predator and she had me down as prey.

I could hear the distinct thump of each punch as it knocked against my skull. The cage was bouncing against my back and the crowd were screaming for my blood.

But you know what? I was OK. I was still standing, upper body curled, guts sucked in tight, head down against the storm. She could batter me but she wasn't going to knock me out like this. Every time she gave me the slightest opening, I hit back for two, three, four shots, until she shut me down again. I didn't really land anything, but I wasn't going to just crouch there like a victim. I hit when I could and waited for her to wear herself out. I could hear her grunting with the effort of hitting me, and it gave me some satisfaction to know that whatever she did, it wasn't enough.

I broke out and came back at her, bang-bang-bang, but I ended up eating a left and covering up again. Blood in my mouth. I hate fighting southpaws. Those left hand shots come out of nowhere. I locked her up in the clinch for a second but then she nailed me with a series of uppercuts before sliding away out of range. I grabbed a breath and started to pull away from the cage, but it turned out she'd only let up with the hitting long enough to step back so she could charge in with a flying knee. It took me right off the mat.

I guess this was supposed to crumple me up, but I rode it. I'd taken plenty of them from Pook and Gold. Then I got hold of her and clinched her. I glimpsed Gretchen's face. She was frustrated. She'd given me everything she had. I was supposed to be smeared all over the mat by now, but I wasn't.

My heart filled.

I hadn't planned on going to the ground, but it was getting pretty obvious that the only way to get my back off the cage would be to shoot on her. So I took her down and went for the mount, but they don't call her 'Greased Lightning Gretchen' for nothing. With all that BJJ in her background, Gretchen's guard was an automatic response to the takedown, and I found myself right where she wanted me to be. She had her legs wrapped around me like she'd strategized the whole thing; I was in her sweet spot now.

When she went for an overhook I knew I was in trouble. She had outpowered me on the feet and now she was outclassing me on the ground, and that didn't leave much for me to do other than survive and hate her with a burning hate deep in my angry bones.

I was fighting out of the bottom of my belly now. This wasn't about prize money or contracts or career anymore, it was my life, it was Mya's life, it was a fight for the next breath and the next moment of being on this planet. Not to be snuffed out. Not to give in.

All those holds they do in MMA were making me angry. I just

wanted to hit her. So I kept stacking her, pressing her hips higher and higher until she lost the overhook. Stacking, stacking, moving my weight up against her and pushing her knees towards her head so she couldn't get any room to work. I wanted to mount her but she wasn't going to let me do that, and I was tired already. Two minutes into the fight and we were both struggling for breath.

I got high enough on her body to use my head to turn her head away from me, grinding my skull against the side of her face to give her pain and compromise her neck. All those neck exercises in Thailand were paying off. I used my head like a drill. I started working her toward the cage, moving her along the floor inch by inch. Put in my shots where I could. I knew if I could just survive, I'd figure her out, find a way to beat her. But Gretchen was planning on ending this thing in the first round. I'd have to figure fast.

She was starting to angle herself into position for the rubber guard. If that happened, I was screwed. Delayed pain messages from the first minute of the fight were coming in now from pretty much everywhere. I was swallowing blood. I shut down on it. Not important.

She went for the rubber guard.

There just aren't enough swear words in English or Spanish or Thai to cover how I feel about getting caught in that sucker. Not going to happen; not if it kills me. As soon as I felt her starting the move I reacted explosively.

Miraculously, she gave. I broke out.

She was on her back with her head against the cage now, and there was a scramble. I lost my gum shield, she pushed me away with a kick to the belly, then sprang to her feet and the ground phase was over. The crowd screamed. She was in a hurry to get away from that cage wall, but before I could capitalize, the ref stepped in and called a time out.

He took me to the side, where Cake handed me a clean gum shield and said, 'Circle left.'

We faced off and I saw Tommy Zhang standing up in his seat. He was leaning forward, his eyes on fire. When I looked past Gretchen at him, he glanced away, but I'd have to be an idiot not to know how to interpret the expression on his face when he looked at me.

Hate. I know it when I see it. He hadn't forgiven me. So why was I here?

Gretchen and I moved around each other. I had to knock her out before she took me down. I was watching her head, but out of the corner of my eye I sensed Tommy. Talk about staring daggers. Something wasn't right here. There was something I was missing. A hole in my awareness.

The next thing I knew, Gretchen's left round kick had come out of freaking nowhere and was slamming into the side of my head. I was going down.

Out of nowhere.

The crowd went nuts. I was falling, and there was a split second where I was not all there—but then I came back, and even falling, even stunned, I resisted the blow. I wouldn't give up consciousness. She moved in. The ref must have been over us, watching every move, getting ready to stop the fight. But I didn't see him, just saw Gretchen's pale feet moving across the mat in my line of vision and then felt the weight of her landing on me.

No. No. I wasn't thinking no more. I was riding the blow and turning over to get back up even as I hit the mat. I must have been stunned, but I didn't know I was stunned and so I was fighting on anyhow. Probably the crowd and the ref and the coaches thought the fight was over. Gretchen sure thought it was. And here she was, literally getting on my back and trying to exert control.

The fight was not over. She did not have control, because I was pure chaos. Never mind Old Jade. There's an older Old Jade, older than anybody, older than this lifetime. There's an ancestor Jade who remembers how to survive, down in the bones. Beast? There's a part of me that's a fucking cavewoman. I could hear myself grunting and snarling and I could smell Gretchen's sweat and feel the shape of her skeleton where she tried to exert leverage on me and I twisted and thrashed like a rabid animal and shook her off. Got up to my knees still hand-fighting her.

Then we were on our feet, locked together, my back arching and every scrap of style got stripped from my performance. I must have looked like a mental patient, because I saw her face as I drove her back.

She was scared.

And she broke away from me. A tactical decision, maybe—but I think she just didn't like what she saw.

Let's face it: it's like those old horror movies where the bad guy is supposed to be dead but he keeps coming back, even with a knife between his ribs, even with an axe through his head: you can't kill him. I'm that guy. And now I was moving flat-footed and my muscles were full of lactic acid and I was sluggish, but so was she.

Then her corner screamed encouragement—she was winning the fight, after all. She only had to finish me off. How hard could it be? I must have looked half-dead already.

She came again. And again her onslaught drove me across the mat and put my back to the cage.

The bell rang.

Round One over. Longest three minutes of my life.

I crashed onto my stool and spat out my mouthguard. Water on my face, in my mouth, Cake shoving sticks of cotton up my nose to stop the bleeding.

'You got to circle left,' he kept saying. 'She get you again with round kick, so circle left, circle left.'

Sometimes I am a little slow, but I get there in the end. The kick had come out of nowhere because she was a southpaw and I'd moved right into her powerful side.

Gretchen's coaches huddled around her. They were fussing with her gloves. The ref went over and talked to the coach while

Gretchen switched gloves. My gecko started itching like crazy. I slapped my ass to make it stop itching.

It's not like I don't know I'm in trouble, gecko, buddy. Tell me something I don't know.

Round Two.

Circle left. Gretchen wasn't quite so much of a slugger now. She was saving her energy, doing little range-finder thingies with her right hand, testing me out. Trying to set me up for that left round kick again, but I kept stepping around left like Cake said, so she couldn't get the kick off.

Gretchen was confident. She knew she had the skills. She had muscles that made me look like an old chicken. She had sparks in her eyes, too. What did she see when she looked at me? A substandard opponent who had gotten lucky so far and who was only here on freak appeal. A scrappy little nobody. A nuisance.

But I was still here. She could not put me away with punches, I'd survived her guard, and now I had her big round kick figured out. I was moving around the ring freely and she couldn't get me now.

So then she tried the left round kick against my left leg. Wanted to take out my knee or maybe just hurt me, slow me down, but my right hand reached down and caught the kick instinctively, while I moved in with my left arm across her body and threw my head down, dumping her.

No surprises—she put me in guard again. In fact, she stuck me in a low guard with my head against her belly and her legs wrapped around my upper back, which meant she'd be setting me up for an arm bar or maybe even a triangle choke.

Except I wasn't scared of her guard anymore. I wasn't scared of her BJJ. I was going to hit her. Just like before I started stacking, forcing those legs back toward her head, forcing her to curl up, and at the same time I stopped her arms by reaching over my head, grabbing her biceps and pushing her arms away from me while I drove with all the strength in my legs. I could hear myself roaring as I drove into her. I wanted to hit her.

Like a swimmer coming up for air, I lifted my head for a second, drew back my right hand and brought it swinging in with a big overhand to her face; then head down and bicep control locked on again, still driving and stacking her until her head and neck were against the fence. I broke off and hit again. And again.

I was starting to get through.

She was covering up with her right hand, no longer trying any ties, just defending. So I swung with the left, and the right again, big blind swinging hits, until I'd made myself enough space to really get to work. Then she was mine. I was rearing over her with both fists going like pistons. The ref was there and his hands were between us and he was stopping the fight.

Gretchen Van Der Hoef lay beneath me, bleeding. Defeated.

Victory

THE CROWD CHANTED 'Beast, Beast, Beast!' There was a haze of light around me. After a little pause Gretchen pulled herself together. Her corner huddled around her. Then both of us came to the middle of the cage. Max the Axe read out the results and threw my arm in the air. Gretchen leaned over and gave me a perfunctory losers' hug. My gecko itched and itched, but I was too high to care.

I ran up the side of the cage like a monkey and sat on the top bar, waving back to the crowd.

There was a stabbing pain in my left eye. Then, very suddenly, I was not feeling too good at all. My eye must have swelled up where I got hit, because that side of my vision was going black.

I swung my leg over the side of the cage to climb back into the ring, but I couldn't seem to control any of my muscles.

I fell off the cage and hit the mat. Rolled. There were knives stabbing into my body. My eye was burning. My vision was messed up. But I could see Tommy Zhang looking at me. I could see Gretchen's trainer dragging her gloves off her hands and shoving them out of sight, looking right at me as he did it.

They done something bad to me. A chorus of geckos sounded in my ears and I heard a sound like wind in the trees.

'Jade! Jade, what's wrong?'

Mr. B was beside me, his face down on my level. He looked scared. I was on my hands and knees on the mat, and there was foam coming out of my mouth. It felt like my skin had cracked across my face and the cracks were spreading and all along the fault lines my nerves were screaming at the invasion. It felt like razors were scoring me, and acid poured into the cuts. Knives bit deep into my skull, across my back, down my legs, into my stomach, under my nails. I tried to stay still, thinking it would pass. It would have to pass. No pain ever went on so long.

But it just got worse. And I couldn't pass out. No escape.

There were feet and legs around me. The ref was waving his hands in my face and shouting at me, one latex-gloved hand on my shoulder. The medic was kneeling beside me, talking to me. Asking me questions.

A shock went through me. I screamed and jumped up. Threw my head back. If I could have jumped out of my body, I would've. Would have jumped right through the roof of the hall.

Then Khari got hold of me. All those times I'd fantasized about being in Khari's arms. His strength, god the smooth ripple of his six pack, the way his shoulders made a v-shape, his brown skin as smooth as a baby's on the inside of his arms, with those biceps... oh, yeah, I used to think about him a lot.

Now I didn't notice none of that good stuff as he scooped me up and carried me away from the scene, shoving away a medic and two of Tommy's people with his knees and shoulders as he walked.

I couldn't even relax into it; I was stiff as an ironing board in his arms, and I clawed at him in panic. There was foam and vomit on my face and then on his t-shirt, and I smelled the forest again.

'Mya!' I choked.

The crowd parted and the noise subsided as he brought me back to the dressing room.

'Just take it easy, Jade. Let the doctor check you out.'

The doctor stuck a needle in my arm. He peeled back an eyelid and shone a light in my eye. I jerked away from him. In my peripheral vision I could see vines. I smelled flowers.

The doctor was talking but it was like he was on an international line with a bad connection.

'Jade! Jade, stay with me. Jade, are you allergic to anything?'

I tried to answer but I couldn't get the air. My whole body was on fire. I writhed in his arms, trying to get away from the heat. Khari's deep voice was in my ear and faraway, like the sea in a conch shell. He said, 'Mr. B got all the water bottles, he's checking everything to see if somebody mess with you. This is so fucked up. The ambulance is outside.'

I looked up at him. It made sense now. Tommy Zhang had brought me back from Thailand to kill me. What a hater.

'I'm dying,' I said. Then the convulsions started.

They tried to roll me into the recovery position. I kept kicking over onto my back, and the fluorescent lights above me stretched and blurred.

I could hear Khari saying stuff like, 'No, you ain't gonna die. The ambulance is right outside. You stay right here with me, Jade. Everything's gonna be—'

Photograph

I WAS IN another place. World of pain doesn't begin to describe it. The pain was like an entity that only knew how to hate. It dragged me in and out of consciousness. Then it broke into beats that hammered on me one at a time, each blow jerking my whole body. The beats slowed. Finally they stopped.

I was gone. It wasn't just that the pain had left. I couldn't feel my body at all. But I could see.

I was in the woods. I seemed to be lying on my back, and there were fluorescent flowers all around me, flowers the size of hats and umbrellas. Looking down on me were animals: a deer, a huge bird, a dog—real animals, but in bright, Crayola colors. They looked down at me like I was the zoo and they bought the tickets.

'She will be one of us soon,' said the voice. 'She has been poisoned with the night orchid.' There was no language barrier. I understood perfectly.

One of us? I wondered if Khari had tried the kiss of life on me yet. With all that foam and vomit, I really hoped not.

'Jade!' Mya was there. She fell on her knees beside me. Her pupils were wide with fear and her tone was urgent. 'Jade, this is bad. You are in trouble!'

I felt sorry for her, having to see me like this.

'How did you know?'

'I hid at Combat Sports. Everyone watched the fight on TV. As soon as you collapsed, I knew something was wrong. The animals helped me find you.' Mya touched the skin near my eye. 'Gretchen had night orchid on the glove,' she said. 'It must have gone into your eye.'

A boy's ghost bent over me. 'Night orchid. It's way Mr. Richard always kills people.'

This had to mean Mr. B was in on it. The feeling of betrayal was horrible. But I had to face it: Richard Fuller's poisons... the CCTV footage showing Mya stumbling into the gym... the poison introduced to my system during the fight. There was no other interpretation. Richard Fuller and Mr. B had been in it together all along. I'd been betrayed by my own trainer.

Mya was talking to me urgently. 'The drug in your body. In small amounts, it lets your body and spirit travel here. If you have a guide, like me, and if you have the antidote, you can come here and return alive. If not, you die here.'

'No, that can't be right,' I muttered. 'This is just a dream.'

'It's a very old trick,' said the ghost cheerfully. 'You would not be the first.'

'I can't take you back,' Mya continued. 'Your body is poisoned. The drug holds you here.'

'She is doomed,' said the ghost.

Mya closed her eyes. 'I know where Mr. Richard keeps the antidote. Stay with her, Luck.'

'Don't leave me here!' I called. It was only when I tried to raise the volume of my voice that I noticed I wasn't making any sound. I tried to get up, and something really funny happened. I seemed to peel away from my body, like a sticker from a kid's sticker book, leaving only the outline of myself behind. I looked down at my body. Sweat still gleamed on my muscles, and my eyes were rolled back.

I didn't want to see that.

I started following Mya, but my feet didn't seem to touch the ground. Without my body I was all soft and flexible. You know those old cartoons where Bugs Bunny or Sylvester smells something delicious and they go drifting along all soft and stretched out, swimming in the air and following the smell? That was what it felt like. It was like I was all lips and eyes, following

Mya while a smoky outline of my body trailed away uselessly behind me.

She closed her eyes and held her hands in front of her chest to pray. Then she stepped through some underbrush and climbed down into a dark room.

It turned out to be more of a covered porch than a room, a wooden expanse of floor covered by a slanting roof and open to the forest on three sides. It was night here, and there was a wide open door leading into a house lit only by the faint blue light of a computer monitor in the adjoining room. The light passed through a bead curtain, glimmering, and caught on a display of carvings of Thai deities that decorated the outside wall of the house. By the doorway there was a Western apothecary table with a pathetic-looking stuffed monkey on it, standing guard.

I tried not to think about what was happening to my real body in the forest. It was easier just to float. I couldn't see myself. I seemed to be everywhere and nowhere. When I turned my attention back toward the forest I couldn't see it anymore. We were in the 'real' world, on the upper floor of a house that stood on stilts surrounded by jungle.

'We must hurry,' Mya whispered, slipping into the computer room. 'That monkey sees everything.'

On the other side of the bead curtain Mya started going through drawers and rummaging among bottles. There was equipment that looked like a still or something to do with chemistry. There was also a desk. I drifted over there, scanning for something I could use, some way I could help Mya. The computer was running. A video chat service was onscreen with the userpic of Fuller himself, I guess—a freckly old goatee-wearing dork with a weak chin. His contact list was huge and international. I saw the names of politicians and celebrities, one after another. Shea hadn't been kidding when he'd said Fuller was an adviser to the stars.

Then I saw the video contact, **'VShea.Independent.'**

Of course. Shea had helped his boss interview Fuller about the orphanage. Fuller had saved Shea's contact information.

If only I could type! But it seemed that although I could look anywhere I wanted, from any angle, I couldn't act.

I had to reach Shea. If I could just move the mouse, just a little, and click on his number...

'Mya!' Even though my words didn't sound in the air, Mya understood me. She turned.

I pointed to the mouse with my ghostly hand. She came over and clicked.

Please let Shea not be in Bangkok. Please let him be close. Please let him be... human.

'Hello?' he said over the speakers.

'Shea, it's me. Jade. I'm at his house. You know, Richard Fuller. Can you get here fast?'

'Hello?'

'Shea? Can you hear me?' Of course he couldn't hear me. I wasn't even really here. I was in a forest beyond the world, half-dead. Mya backed away from the screen. Her mouth clamped shut. She put a finger to her lips, looking again at the stuffed monkey.

'I don't know,' I heard Shea say to someone on his end. 'I can't hear anything. Guess it's a wrong number.'

'Better turn the phone off,' A woman's tinkling voice said in Thai. 'No interruptions.'

I want to say I felt like I'd been kicked in the stomach, but the fact is I've been kicked in the stomach plenty of times and it was nothing compared to this.

Well, I thought. *Looks like I'll die here. And Shea's already got female company.*

I wondered if she knew about his 'problem.'

Mya set about ransacking the drawers of the apothecary chest. Pills and powders and syringes came out of the drawers. Bottles. Bags of fluid. Ugh. Then Mya gave a little cry. She held up a bag in her hand. Except for a few specks of blue powder, it was empty.

A soft voice said, 'A good thief never burgles the same house twice.'

Richard Fuller was standing in the doorway that led to the rest of the house. He held up a second bag, this one full of a blue powder.

'Fortunately, you will not be a thief the second time. I have saved you from that.'

Mya's face had become a mask. She must have been terrified, but she showed no expression at all.

Richard Fuller was gawky-looking. Harmless and soft-spoken. His physique was waxy and weak, but his voice had a quality of persuasion.

'You try to do good, but everything goes wrong for you. When you steal food and bring it to the animals in the forest, you only prolong their suffering.'

He paused, but Mya did not move. She knelt by the apothecary table, as still as a statue.

Mr. Richard shook his head sadly as he moved out to the porch. 'This is foolishness, Mya. You are a child. You have misunderstood everything, and your actions have lost merit for your family.'

Mya's body was shaking but her face gave nothing away.

'When we are together, then you will understand. My wisdom will guide you and you won't make all these tragic mistakes. It is time for us to be joined as a single being, to move through all the worlds as one.'

At last Mya moved. She shook her head slowly from side to side.

'Go back, Mya,' I told her. 'Run away. Don't listen to him. He's a scumbag.'

She didn't look my way. I wondered if she could still hear me. I wondered if I was already dead and this was how it was going to be, like in movies where ghosts talk and can't get through to the living.

Then the video application chimed from the computer, announcing a call. Mya jumped. I felt a surge of hope—could it be Shea?

It was Tommy Zhang.

Richard Fuller ducked through the bead curtain and glanced at the screen. Shea's contact information was still up there. His eyes narrowed as he took this in, but he just clicked on 'answer' and Tommy's voice filled the room.

'I did what you asked,' Tommy Zhang said. I wasn't even sure whether he was speaking English or Thai. It didn't seem to matter anymore. 'She disappeared. Like magic. Was that supposed to happen?'

'It is all part of the plan,' Fuller said. 'Play along, pretend she has left of her own free will. Hint that she may have staged some kind of stunt to escape the police, because she has had some trouble with the law back in New Jersey. But don't make any open accusations, and be sure you show every concern for her safety.'

'Yeah, uh, that's what I wanted to ask you. There's a problem with her insurance. They're asking me if the show will pay for her treatment. My lawyer says the show is not liable. So do I pay or not?'

'You pay for the best doctors,' Fuller intoned gently. 'Don't be foolish about details. Act as though you're dreadfully worried about her and say you will pay.'

'They talking about flying in a specialist from Chicago. How much is this gonna cost me?'

'Don't be a bloody cheapskate, Tommy.' Mr. Richard's voice went from mellow to biting. He rifled through the papers on his desk as though looking for something. 'They don't even have a body. How can a specialist charge for a patient he never sees?'

Tommy said, 'Richard, I don't like this. It's not what we agreed.

You are landing me in the middle of—'

His voice cut off. Fuller had come up with a large color photograph, which he now showed to the webcam.

Tommy said, 'No, wait, I thought—'

'It's not your job to think, Tommy. Never has been. You do what I say. Sort it out, or this image and others like it will be all over the internet in a matter of minutes.'

'OK, OK, calm down, I—'

'Shut up, Tommy. It's too late to change your mind. Jade Barrera is dead. Deal with it.'

Fuller cut the line.

His words rang in my mind, over and over.

Jade Barrera is dead?

A Family Way

THE ONLY THING that could distract me from the news of my own death was the fact that I recognized the photograph Richard Fuller had shown Tommy. The same picture Shea had showed me at the diner. The old white guy was Fuller, pictured with a tall Asian beauty.

When Shea showed me this picture in the diner, I'd thought the beautiful girl looked familiar. At the time I assumed she was a model, somebody I'd seen on a magazine or in a shampoo ad. I'd missed the truth entirely.

I'd seen 'her' before, all right. She'd put on muscle since then, and she was was older. And she didn't dress as a 'she' anymore. In fact, 'she' had been on the cover of men's magazines, displaying 'her' abs.

I had beaten her up in defense of a cat named Quinton.

'She' was Tommy Zhang.

It all made sense now. Richard Fuller knew he had control of Tommy. The old man wanted Mya back, and he knew Mya would come for the antidote to save me, so he set Tommy up to put the poison on Gretchen's gloves. Fuller must have been behind Tommy's fake change of heart towards me, too.

I can't even describe how I felt. Tommy Zhang had set me up. When it came to my murder, he seemed more worried about the effect on his wallet than on his karma. I should hate him, right?

But I felt uneasy. I remembered the ladyboys that visited Coat's gym. I remembered Nong Toom and her courage in fighting Muay Thai in lipstick. I knew ladyboys were a normal part of life in Thailand, but people in the US wouldn't get that when this picture was splashed all over the tabloids. They'd see Tommy's past as shameful and hilarious—especially his beer-swilling, monster-truck-driving fan base.

Maybe that was why Tommy acted so macho and aggro—to compensate for the reality of his situation. Or maybe Richard Fuller had pushed him into it. To get his career in Hollywood Tommy had beefed up and swallowed charisma drugs and spin-kicked his way into the ultra-macho world of action movies. Now he had fanboys all over the world who worshipped him as a Real Man.

Tommy used to annoy the hell out of me because he posed as a fighter without being the real thing. He's an acrobat, a model, an actor, yes. But a fighter? No way. The deception pissed me off because the risks I take in the ring are real, not CGI.

Still, if I'd known Tommy was hiding a bigger secret, maybe I wouldn't have been so quick to relocate his nose. I felt a weird pang of sympathy. Faking your martial arts is one thing, but having to hide who you really are? That has to eat away at you.

My head was ringing and flashing like a pachinko machine.

I thought about the video contact list and Richard Fuller's stationery with its international names. I pictured the nasty old dude with his invisible tentacles spreading across the world, manipulating power-hungry rich people.

And now he wanted to possess Mya. It was sick.

'Give back the phone that you stole.'

The phone held murder evidence. What would the old guy do when he found out Mya had set Shea free with the phone?

Mya didn't move. She needed protection, and here I was disembodied, powerless to protect her. Some bodyguard. My blood was boiling. OK, my blood would have been boiling if I'd had any blood. All I had were thoughts.

Somebody had to stop this evil piece of shit.

'Mya, you better get out of here,' I said. 'Forget the antidote. Get out of here before he does something bad to you.'

'I can't,' she whispered. The old man's gaze followed her glance to me, but he couldn't see me. I guess he wasn't so magical after all.

'Have you been talking to ghosts? I warned you about that.'

He turned his back on Mya. He returned to the prayer room and dumped the blue powder into a metal bowl.

'Last chance to change your mind, Mya. It is your fault she is poisoned, and her death will count against your karma.'

'What about your karma, bucko?' I shouted noiselessly. I tried to grab him but he was completely unaware of me.

He lit a match.

'Wait!' Mya lunged toward him. Fuller held the match, poised, above the powder. That was my life, in that bowl.

'Wait,' she said again. 'I don't have the phone. But I can get it.'

Richard Fuller dropped the match in the powder and my last chance went up in green and white flames. A smell like burning hair filled the room.

'You're lying,' he said in a distinct, measured tone. 'I'm not a violent man. You know that I practice compassion for all beings. I eat no meat. I kill no insects. I've helped countless young people escape desperate circumstances. But you. You test my patience.'

Mya had been backing away as he spoke, until she literally had her back to the wall. She slithered sideways, toward the computer, jerking when she passed the stuffed monkey.

'Get the photographs and go,' I told her. 'They're right behind you.'

She groped behind her back and took the sheaf of them, easy as pie. Her grace under pressure was amazing.

'Did Tommy send you?' Fuller seethed. 'The two of you are ungrateful children. Tommy owes me his career, and you owe me your life. And your family's lives. All of them would be dead if I hadn't sent for you. Think what I will do to them if you betray me.'

'Mya,' I cried. 'Run! Go to the forest. He has no power over you.

Don't listen to him. Run!'

But she didn't. She was too young, and the way he used her family to control her, it was sick. He had her believing he was the powerful one when all along it had been Mya who could do the business.

Everything about it was wrong.

She made herself small. I saw her looking into the branches of the trees that grew close to the house. The wind tossed droplets from their branches on to the porch.

'Your family live or die by my command.'

Her face went completely still.

'Goddamn it!' I shouted. 'In and out of my kitchen like it's Grand Central Station but now she stays put? Mya, get out of here!'

Mya's lips moved in prayer. She called the forest, and it came. The house was built on stilts ten feet above the ground, but now the other forest was outside with its floor right here on her level. All she had to do was step out of the porch and she would be free. She lifted one leg over the railing.

Richard Fuller grabbed her by the shoulders. He jerked her back into his world.

'You dishonor your family, your ancestors, your nation,' Fuller whispered against her neck. And she was buying it. I could see the drug haze around him, the aura of the medicines he took that made people so gullible around him. It was like actual visible bullshit pouring into her ears and eyes and nose. Poison. Mya's whole being seemed to compress in fear and dread.

'Mya, he's a fake. He has no power. He can't go to the forest. He can't even hear *me*, right now. He's just a scuzzy blackmailer. He's not a wizard, he's a child abuser. He's not fit to be in the same room with you. Dust him, already.'

The old man was all up in her face, and his fingers flexed on the fabric of the t-shirt I'd given her. Visions of his violent death passed through my mind, but I couldn't do jackshit.

A yellow smile seeped from between his lips.

'You are becoming strong, Mya. A superior vessel for my power. That is why I let you go. You didn't think you escaped on your own, did you?'

In my disembodied state, I could feel Mya's pulse as if it were my own. Her heart skipped a beat when he said that. Of course she had escaped on her own... but now he was making her doubt herself.

I'd seen my father do it to my mother. They call it gaslighting. The abuser makes the other person think they're crazy. Erodes their confidence in their own powers, so the abuser can control them. Mya was only twelve years old. He had her in the palm of his hand.

Mya looked away from him, toward me. Her gaze fixed on something behind me and her body gave a jerk.

'Mya!' I called. 'Don't listen to him. Get out of here!'

What was she waiting for?

'I wish I could have saved you, Jade,' she said. 'He is too powerful. I can't leave her.'

Leave her? Leave who?

'Just *leave!*' I said. 'Just—'

Then I saw the new kid. She must have come from inside the house and now stood beside the computer. She looked like a younger version of Mya, and for a second I thought Richard Fuller had somehow dialled her up from out of the past... but her face was a little different. And she had none of Mya's ability to control her emotions. Her mouth was half-open and her eyes were wide.

'Mya!' the girl breathed. 'My sister!'

The Fight in the Dog

THE OLD MAN told Mya, 'If you go, I will join myself to her instead. But you won't go, will you?'

Mya's face went blank as a mask. Her eyes turned inward. She didn't even seem to see her little sister, who bit her lip and stood uncertainly, waiting for a response.

'If you let her go home I will stay,' Mya whispered.

He smiled.

All my life I been getting angry. All my life I been acting out. I've made a career of it. Put somebody I don't like in front of me, and I will hit them until they bleed or pass out or beg for mercy. And I'll be happy about it. Because it's a fucked-up world and the power to fight is the one thing I got.

Until now. Now the fight in me had nowhere to go. My spirit was moving through some other plane of reality, where ghosts and animals and gods and mortals are all mixed up, and the trees move and the flowers are too bright and the light is never the same as the light on Earth. A place beyond the world. And I was plugged into everything: dirt, sky, trees, worms, elephants. I was in everything.

I was mad as hell but I couldn't do Fuck All.

That's when this weird fogginess came over my vision. I was so angry that at first I thought I couldn't see straight, but it wasn't that. The room was distorting, just like that time in New York when the buildings changed to trees. In my peripheral vision the masks and statues began to shift a little. To breathe. The other forest was close by. Flowers, vines, bark. I could feel the rain and the Himalayan snows and the bottom of the river where nagas swam. I could feel it just as if the forest was inside of *me*.

Richard Fuller opened a cupboard and took out a bottle and something that looked like a Bunsen burner from high school. He moved into the middle of the covered porch, moving slowly and with an air of great concentration.

'I have completed my work on the medicine,' he told her. 'We will do this tonight. I will enter you as a smoke. All of my knowledge will be yours. All of my ambitions. We will join forces. I will lead you high in the world. You need never fear for your family, not after this. Together, you and I will be powerful and untraceable.'

I saw her eyes. I couldn't read her. Did she believe him?

'I am not afraid,' he said softly. 'My life as I know it will end. My body will die—and I will escape any investigation that would put me in prison. But you, Mya. You will gain immeasurably.'

He said he wasn't afraid, but his hand shook as he struck a light.

'Stay back, Thiri,' Mya said to the other girl.

Mr. Richard began mixing his medicines. He heated a liquid over a flame, and it began to smoke. With my altered eyes I could see his body beginning to break down like a digital image. Where the smoke touched him, he was pixillating, turning into light...

'Mya, don't do this. Take your sister and run for it!'

She ignored me. Her eyes were closed. Her lips didn't move, but she held her hands in the pose for meditation, or prayer. I hoped she was praying for the same thing I was.

The trees were full of life. The night moved.

I could feel it. The forest was here, and it was bringing its own consciousness. Eyes like jewels formed tiny windows looking out from the jungle. Ghosts.

Richard Fuller's spirit body surrounded him like a rainbow. It began to drift towards Mya, a hungry cloud. She kept her eyes shut.

'Mya, please...'

'Jade, you must have *jai yen*,' she whispered.

Jai yen, my ass. I needed some kind of weapon. Where was Kala Sriha now?

Mr. Richard's spirit surrounded Mya now. Light coruscated off her as though the surface of her were made of moving water. His body sagged, his eyes flickering white as they rolled up in his head. I could see the outlines of his bones.

'Kala Sriha,' I prayed. 'We got this far together. I'm asking you, please don't abandon Mya now.'

A living thing was coming out of the forest. The creature was forming out of light and shadow that solidified as it passed out of the forest and into the porch. Trailing vines and moths, the shadow took the shape of a dog. I could see its bottleglass green eyes and I could feel its ribs move as it barked. When it entered the porch its head burst open, turning inside out like a piece of popcorn until it had changed into an elephant's head before our eyes.

Richard Fuller saw the dog-elephant and let out a startled yelp. The old dude's concentration was broken, and the rainbow light around Mya began to disperse. The dog had changed fully into an elephant and took up most of the porch. Other animals were coming now, shifting forms as they arrived.

'Now, children,' he said to the strange creatures, licking his lips. 'You know you are not permitted to come to this world.'

Yeah, right. Like he could do anything about it. More creatures burst out of the forest. A winged snake wound down from the branches above. I saw its head become a unicorn's head; then it seemed to change its mind and went back to being something like a dragon with no legs.

The animals were all familiar from paintings and statues I'd seen in Thailand—creatures that were a mix of parts of different animals. It never occurred to me until now that the artwork might not be meant to show an elephant-headed dog, but instead a dog that could become an elephant. Or vice versa.

Because that's what I was seeing now. Animals that could become other animals. And when they changed shape, I could feel their freedom like blood running in my veins all over again.

I looked up and saw that the ceiling was gone. Trees stretched into sky.

The animals crowded around Richard Fuller, driving him back across the polished wood floor. He gripped Mya by the hair, holding her up in front of him so that she was between his body and the immortal animals. They forced him back toward the house until he bumped into the apothecary table and knocked over the stuffed monkey. In mid-fall the monkey came to life. It leaped screaming at Fuller's face, scratching and drawing blood.

That made him let go of Mya, and she scrambled away between legs and under wings. The old man began to gabble and bark in fear. Words failed him as claws came out and teeth glittered. Mya waved her sister back into the house, but Mya herself crouched in the doorway, fascinated and horrified.

Richard Fuller was about to become a snack for the wild things. He fully deserved it, too. I hoped they ripped his head off. I hoped...

Whoa, Jade. Slow down.

Through the brightly-colored, wild bodies of the immortals I could see something else. I could see another side of them, flickering like an old movie reel. Under the feathers and fur, slipped into the half-beats between moments, I could see *children*.

There were human beings mixed in with these divine animals. Their human potential was still there. It hadn't been destroyed. Now I understood why Mya had been feeding them—they had a chance to come back, *if* they could remember the human world.

I thought about Shea and how he'd been willing to sacrifice his life to expose Richard Fuller's involvement in human trade. My life was already over, but theirs could be just beginning. They had a second chance. They could eat human food, learn human ways again. They could return with their spirits intact, kept alive all these years by the animal guardians of the great forest. That was the way to defeat Richard Fuller.

Not by killing him, but by the children reclaiming their stolen lives. And they were about to throw that potential away.

The wild ones had knocked Fuller to the ground. They were all around him, standing on him, growling. Hungry.

'No!' I cried suddenly. 'Stop!'

And for a second, they did. They stopped and turned their attention to me. Fuller took advantage of the break in the action to reach back and grab Mya by the hair, still holding the smoking vial of medicine in one hand.

'Listen, you guys,' I said. 'I'm dead now. I can't beat up this scuzzbag or believe me, there's nothing I'd like more. But it doesn't take a genius to see that if you gobble him up, he'll be inside you. That's how eating works. The old man is poison. Walk away.'

I know, it's rich coming from me, right? I don't usually do *noble*. But I'd been wrong about my moment. My moment hadn't happened in the cage against Gretchen. It was happening *now*. I was gonna find a way of taking care of this situation without fighting. I had no choice.

'Come on, Mya,' I said. 'You have a chance for another life. You don't have to stay with him. And violence ain't gonna solve it.'

My social worker would have peed herself laughing if she could hear me say that. But I didn't care. Mya's sister was listening.

'You must run, Thiri,' Mya said. 'Go now. As long as you are here, Mr. Richard has power. That's because the power is *you*.'

Fuller held Mya's hand with one hand and the other was preoccupied with the vial of medicine. He couldn't stop the younger child escaping.

After she was gone he set the vial down and wrapped both arms tightly around Mya. Shaking with fear, he took in the snarling mouths of the animals that surrounded him.

'Ploy!' he called in a loud voice. 'Come up here, please, and bring a sedative for the child.'

Below, there was a noise of people moving in the house. Someone was coming up the stairs.

'You give me no choice,' the old man said in Mya's ear. 'Ploy will give you an injection. When you wake, you will be mine and there will be no more of this nonsense.'

I found that I had drifted up into the trees without meaning to. There was an invisible current pulling me away from the earth and towards the sky. Below, animal eyes gleamed and tails lashed. I could see the flanks of the immortal creatures moving as they breathed. They were still hungry.

It was a terrible feeling. I knew how they felt. No forgiveness was possible, and they'd choke on Fuller's flesh even if it meant they doomed themselves. I'd have done the same thing in their position. I couldn't pretend otherwise.

As one, they converged on Richard Fuller to tear him limb from limb.

Darkness was taking my sight.

I couldn't feel my heart beat, and I wasn't breathing. I was removed from all the usual things my body would have done at a time like this. I was diffused through both worlds, like I had this giant consciousness.

Darkness was coming.

It moved through the forest, and as it came I was starting to break down. I could feel a presence in the rainy trees, in the spaces between the leaves and under the roots. The presence of some unseeable being came rising up through holes in the world like black ink into a sponge. As it grew more, I grew less, until my own consciousness was more of a rumor than a reality.

I heard the bead curtain move and a woman said, 'It's all right, Mya. It will be over soon.'

Mya screamed.

Then the bead curtain chattered again as it parted, and somebody crashed into the room.

'Jade!' Shea shouted. 'Jade, where are you?'

My sight came swimming back to me. From above, I saw the animals scatter as if Shea were some huge threat, dangerous far beyond the powers of his pacifist bean-sprout-eating frame. Although, I have to say, he was doing a pretty good job of putting the pacifism to one side.

Shea scanned the room and fixated on Richard Fuller. In two strides he was on Fuller and pushing him up against the wall that had so recently been forest. Ploy scurried back into the house and collided with another woman; then the two of them disappeared down the stairs. Mya darted under the shadow of the forest where it met the edge of the porch.

'What a joke,' gasped Fuller as Shea collided with him. 'Not you again. Should have killed you. So ungrateful. Leave before I get tough on you.'

In my abstracted, presumed-dead state I couldn't help noticing what an absurd attacker Shea made. He was taller than Fuller, but he'd obviously never been anywhere near a fight in his life. The way he moved was hilarious. Strangely, I found this endearing. Even though he was a total geek, he was prepared to try.

'Leave you?' Shea snorted, attempting to pin Fuller to a wall. 'You've got to be joking, mate. The police are here.'

'Let them come,' Fuller panted, jamming an elbow into Shea's gut. 'I own the police.'

'Not this time,' Shea said. 'Where is Jade? She called me from here. I'm sure it was her.'

So I *had* gotten through to him! My dead heart tried to leap.

Fuller had wriggled along the wall pursued by Shea until he was jammed into a corner, his back up to the wall.

I sensed what Fuller was up to before he did it. With one hand behind his back, Richard Fuller was reaching inside a drawer. He was pulling out a syringe. I screamed at Shea, but I couldn't get through to him.

'What have you done to them?' Shea grunted with the effort of holding Fuller in place, but he didn't do anything to control Fuller's left hand. 'So help me, if they've been harmed I'll kill you myself, you—'

The needle went into Shea's neck. Shea's eyes rolled back. His body went rigid. He hit the floor with an awful sound, eyes open.

It was the worst thing I'd ever seen.

Richard Fuller was shaking like a crackhead as he stepped away from Shea's body. He wiped spit from the corner of his mouth.

'I don't know how you got out of the forest, but you can't come back from this. You're a dead man.'

Fuller looked at the syringe like it was his best friend. Then, with an effort, he rolled Shea's body across the floor. The roots of otherworldly trees stretched across the porch.

A lion-shaped shadow loomed beyond Shea. Kala Sriha was there, a heavy darkness just beyond the realm of sight.

Shea couldn't be dead. He couldn't. Why had he taken on Fuller as a wimpy journalist? Why hadn't he turned into the lion? Kala Sriha was *right here*. It wasn't fair. Everything was wrong.

Weird cries came from the jungle. They were high-pitched, repetitive, and also somehow familiar. Too mechanical to be animals. Lights flashed in my eyes, very bright. The windows lit up blue and red. I thought it was my brain shutting down, but the old man reacted, too.

Sirens. Police.

Voices sounded from the stairwell. Fuller looked down at his dishevelled clothes and brushed feebly at himself, like he was preparing to entertain guests.

This time when the bead curtain parted, it admitted four police officers in riot gear. One of them was a slim, middle-aged woman.

'Shea? Are you there?' she called, peering into the shadowy forest as if sensing something strange was going on. Shea's body was wreathed in leaf-shadow on the edge of the porch.

'Has there been a misunderstanding?' Fuller said in Thai. 'I didn't call the police. I—'

'Don't talk,' one of the other officers said. 'Down on the floor!'

Weak and miserable, the old man complied.

I looked down on the scene from above. The female officer knelt down by Shea. She was half in the forest but didn't seem to notice. She picked up Shea's hand and felt for a pulse.

'Call the coroner,' she said.

No Goodbye

I HUNG AROUND Shea, frustrated and sad. I was disoriented. Everything looked green and complicated, but I couldn't tell up from down. His body still lay in the leaf litter, eyes open. Then his spirit form rose up and his ghost caught sight of me. We stared at each other in shock.

'I was an idiot,' he said. 'Mya tried to tell me.'

'Are you sure? I was kind of hoping none of this was real,' I said.

'Jade. You don't belong here.'

'I could say the same to you.'

We stared into each other's unearthly eyes. It was happening again. Just like that night we'd spent together. I'd seen through the surface of him and glimpsed something on the other side of Shea. Something that I knew, something that knew me.

I was looking at that Shea now. It was a beautiful feeling, the best feeling ever. And for a second I felt like myself again. The old Jade. The real me, just for a moment.

Just long enough for my heart to break.

Below, the great black lion prowled. It was huge, even bigger than it had been that morning I'd woken up with it in my bed. As big as a horse, at least. It had long legs and huge paws, and an elegant tail with a tuft at the end. Its eyes blinked slowly. It sniffed Shea's body. Oh, no. No, no, no...

'You got my call?' I said, trying to lighten things up. I wanted to cry but it's hard to cry without a body. It was getting harder to hold on to myself. Parts of my smoky cartoon self were starting to drift away and blend with the trees.

He tilted his head and his brown eyes softened. 'I just got here. Parawat, my contact in the police, has been watching the house. Nothing seemed to be happening, but when I got that call I just knew. She told me to wait until she could put together her team, but I didn't listen to her. Guess I cocked it up, eh?'

He touched the pinprick mark in his neck where the needle had gone in.

'You came just in time,' I said. 'If you had waited even a minute longer, it would have been too late. But how did you convince the police?'

'I gave them the information Mya gave me, about the safe. They'll be going through that evidence right now.'

'So can they prosecute him, or not?'

'Because it's international, it's complicated. He's part of a larger ring. They have evidence for kidnapping of children, but they can't get him for murder when they have no bodies.'

His frown lifted as he thought of something.

'Of course, there's my murder now, I suppose...'

Like that was supposed to be a good thing.

'Jade, listen. Mya needs help,' Shea said. 'You have to look out for her and her sister.'

I didn't even know where Mya was. The police hadn't spotted her. The strangest thing about this scene was how the police were talking on their radios and securing the building even as Shea and I hovered in the trees. The woman called Ploy had come in the room and was now berating the handcuffed old man, accusing him of perversity and drug use and bribery and cheating on his taxes.

'You have to go back, Jade,' Shea said.

'We both have to go back.' But even as I said it I knew I was too feeble to go anywhere. I saw Kala Sriha lie down beside Shea's body. More police were here. They were taking photographs and writing down notes while Shea lay there, not breathing.

This couldn't be happening, but it was. The darkness was coming at me like the end of time.

I heard Mya's voice. Where had she gone? The sound was very faint.

'Jade! Jade, where are you? Come back!'

I watched as Kala Sriha covered Shea's body entirely in shadow.

'How am I supposed to help Mya? She isn't like a regular kid. Shea, tell Kala Sriha to help her.'

His image smiled a little in that dry British way.

'Kala Sriha is a god, Jade. I don't give orders to Kala Sriha.'

'But Shea... what's happening? Where are you going?'

He was starting to fade. He was slipping back to his body, into the great blackness of Kala Sriha with his golden cat eyes, and I could hear an ominous rumbling sound. Purring.

'I'm supposed to be here now,' Shea whispered. I couldn't see him, but I could feel his breath in my ear. 'Kala Sriha saved me the first time for a reason. Mya was the reason. I have to go now.'

'Shea, wait! Kala Sriha has to make you live! Because I can't hold on, and without you and me she's alone.'

I couldn't see him anymore.

'Jade? Jade!' Mya was calling me. 'Jade, come back to your body now.'

No. It was too far to travel. Shea's ghost was gone, and Kala Sriha's great warm shadow moved away from his corpse. The corpse was empty, but now the lion's black pelt sparkled with the light of a thousand stars.

My thinking was starting to melt, like when you fall asleep. Everything was running together making its own kind of untraceable sense, as if I were breaking into pieces and drifting away from myself. And if I'd been hoping for a real goodbye—some final moment to bring closure to my life—it didn't happen. I couldn't even hear Mya's voice anymore. I was disintegrating and there could be no going back. The sky was pulling me up and away.

Where is the Love?

SOMETHING HAD BITTEN me in the stomach. No, stung me. A needle as long as a screwdriver had gone in and stayed there much too long. Then came the burn as venom slid into my blood.

My body convulsed. The pain was back, wringing and grinding and pulling at me no matter how I moved or didn't move. I writhed uncontrollably and that made it worse. I tried to lie still and every breath felt like getting hit by a bus.

But I was breathing.

My eyes were open.

The locker room got bigger and smaller. I was lying on a physical therapy table in one of the side rooms.

Mya was holding my hand. The forest was there, in the smell and the flowers and the green light, and my bed seemed to be tilting downhill. I glimpsed the giant baby face of Lek; then the huge naga's body was sliding past me like a moving wall.

Mya whispered something in Thai to me, and it was no longer easy to understand her. I struggled.

I think she said, 'Don't tell them it hurts or they'll give you the wrong drugs.'

Or maybe she said, 'They put handcuffs on Mr. Richard and he couldn't stop them.'

Or maybe, 'There's a naga under your bed.'

Then the room seemed to expand to become a vast, green hall, and Baby Lek slid under the massage table and vanished into a large tree. The room snapped back to normal and I heard the guttural noise of Khari screaming and yelling. He vaulted over the bottom of the table and stood on a bench, pointing at the floor.

Spit flew as he gabbled, 'Snake! Snakes! Snakes on a plane!'

I licked my lips. Wanted to speak. Hurt to breathe, to blink, to squeeze blood through the heart, but these had to be done. Mustn't show pain. Needed to know I was alive.

Closed my eyes. Little rest. Please. Just a tiny one.

A doctor came in with Mr Big and Tommy Zhang. The doctor asked Khari to climb down off the bench and Mr. Big confirmed that there was no snake under the massage table.

Khari's voice was ragged. 'But Jade... she disappeared... how did she get here? And who's the kid?'

I half-opened my eyes, saw Mr Big pat Khari gently on the shoulder.

'It's OK, it's OK,' said Mr. B. 'You got confused, I know, you're fond of Jade. It's OK, man.'

'No, she was gone, like not there,' Khari was saying as Mr. B led him away.

Then the doctor broke out his stethoscope and I felt cold metal on my chest. Why do they have to make them things so cold?

'Am I alive?' My words didn't sound, but I must have done something because I felt Mya's hand squeeze mine.

'Jade?' the doctor said urgently. 'Jade, can you hear me?'

He was shining a light in my eyes. I started blinking, squeezing Mya's hand. Pretty soon there were a whole bunch of people around me. I grabbed the doctor's flashlight and shoved it away violently. Then I shut my eyes.

'We think you had some kind of rare allergic reaction to the synthetic material in your opponent's gloves,' the doctor said. 'The ambulance is waiting.'

'Shea...? Mya, where's Shea?'

Mya held my hand in both of hers. 'He is gone,' she whispered in Thai.

I shook my head.

'He can't be.'

'I'm sorry, Jade.'

She slipped a brown envelope into my hand. 'It's the photographs. Don't let anyone take them. I must go now.'

The doctor spoke right over Mya as if she wasn't there. Maybe she wasn't.

'Are you in pain now, Jade?'

Yeah, pain would be one word to describe it, but the word 'pain' wouldn't be painful enough. Then I remembered me what Mya had said about the drugs.

'It don't hurt,' I whispered, though it hurt worse than any person could ever hurt me. 'Don't give me no drugs, 'cos it don't hurt at all.'

I HAD A private room in the hospital, but it wasn't private for long. Tommy Zhang came sailing in, literally smelling like success. He was probably still using Fuller's charisma drugs.

'What the hell happened to you?' he said. 'I thought you were gone.'

'I know you did,' I whispered. 'I know everything.'

His face hardened. Defensive, he talked even faster than usual.

'You disappeared. The doctor tried to help you but you were gone. You weren't even really sick. You faked everything.'

'I didn't fake beating Gretchen,' I retorted.

He bent down close and in my ear he said,

'You got nothing on me, Jade. I made sure. You got nothing.'

Then he straightened, but when I looked at him all I could see was scared. Scared, scared, scared.

Man, I was so tired of having to always fight. I didn't want to hate Tommy. Too many bad things had happened. When I thought of Shea I felt like someone had reached inside me and scooped out all the good feelings forever. I thought: where is the love?

I reached over to the bedside cabinet and passed him the brown envelope. Scowling, he opened it. When he saw the photographs inside his eyes widened. He seriously looked like he was going to shit himself.

'Richard Fuller is in police custody,' I blurted. 'As far as I know, those are the only copies. They're yours.'

He stiffened.

'What do you want?'

I shook my head. 'It's not like that. Tommy, I had no idea what you were going through. And just so we're clear: I didn't know about that video Eva took of, you know, the thing that happened behind the gym.'

Tommy wasn't the greatest actor in the world, but he had a mobile face and I could see the nuances of emotion passing across his perfect features as he took in the news. I realized all of a sudden that not only was he scared now, but he'd been scared before, too. For years, maybe for all his life, he'd been scared. His whole persona was a front.

It had to be, didn't it? What choice did he have?

'He gave me medicines,' Tommy said softly. 'To get me parts. I don't mean physical beauty. I already had that.' And he tossed his head a little, like a diva. 'The medicine made people love me, admire me. But it was always at a price. I had to do what he wanted. And I'm not a violent person. I think you know that.'

'I don't see why you couldn't be a ladyboy *and* an action star,' I said. 'But that's coming from me. You know: *the Beast*.'

He shook his head. 'You don't understand.'

'OK. Maybe I don't. Your past is your business. Bottom line? Richard Fuller is going to jail. He can't do jack to you.'

Suddenly I was feeling much stronger than usual. I added, 'Sorry I lost it and smashed up your face. I guess I over-reacted. I got a little bit of a temper.'

Tommy laughed at my understatement but his eyes were filling with tears. Now I could see the girl in him, the delicate beauty that must have been even more stunning fifteen years ago when all this started.

He whispered, 'For real, Mr. Richard is going to prison?'

I nodded. 'The police came for him. The international media are on to him. The evidence is there. He's going down for a long, long time.'

Tommy sniffed and blotted his eyes with the back of his sleeve.

'Good,' he said, and stood up. He twitched a little in his own skin, like he was shaking something off. Then he said,

'Gretchen said it was a good fight, she hopes you are OK. She didn't know nothing, so don't blame her. The TV crew is still waiting to interview you.'

I didn't say nothing, so he kept talking. 'You'll be eighteen in a few months. You can turn pro. I want you to come fight on my circuit, Jade. What do you say?'

A lot had changed since the day Tommy's bodyguards didn't want to let me in my own gym. I must be moving up in the world. I remembered the roar of the crowd. I remembered sitting up on that cage, arms over my head.

It would be such a feeling of power to tell him no. Screw you. And I could. With TV crews outside it was clear I had other options.

But sometimes fate works through us. And there was this thought running around in my mind like a gecko on energy juice. About Mya. About her animal friends. About Pook.

I could feel my ass getting ready to make a speech.

I painted on a smile and said, 'It kind of depends on how you want to play things from here on out.'

He tilted his head, puzzled.

'Richard Fuller may be in jail, but there are children he left behind. They're only half in this world.'

Tommy nodded. 'Richard's estranged wife has already stepped in and taken over the orphanage. She's trying to work with the police to make amends.'

'It's not the orphanage I was thinking of,' I said. 'I want you to get behind a relative of Mr. B's so she can start a boxing camp in the North. She has the land. She just needs help getting it off the ground. It would be right up your street. In the long term you'd be investing in legitimate fighters.'

He looked confused. 'Most fighters ask for a car when they sign with me! Why do you want this?'

'For the kids he stole. The farm is close to the forest. They are… you know. Half-animal.'

Tommy closed his eyes.

'I don't want to talk about the forest, Jade. I'm not ever going there.'

'Nobody's asking you to. But if you want me to fight for you, here's my condition. If I can arrange it with Pook, then I want you to help her get started.'

He let out a sigh and nodded. I folded my hands to *wai* to him, and he moved to shake my hand at the same time. There was an awkward in-between moment of hesitation. Then we shook hands. And we *wai*'d. We laughed nervously.

Both of us were taking a big fat chance.

Mystery Ringtone

THIRI PICKED UP Pook's phone on the ninth ring. Pook was outside talking to the builders about the way she wanted the dormitories for the fighters to be constructed, but she had left her phone in the kitchen. Mya and Thiri were chopping up vegetables. Mya froze when she heard the ringtone. It was the same strange tune that Shea's smartphone had played when the woman who sounded like Mya's mother had called. This was a different phone, but the sound of that music was unmistakable. Mya trembled, not daring to pick up.

So Thiri grabbed the phone and answered.

'It's for you,' she said, passing the phone over.

Mya held the phone for a moment, hesitating. She had never told Thiri about the call that had sent her running into the forest, the call she had been so certain had come from their mother.

'Go on,' Thiri urged. 'Find out what they want!'

'*It's me,*' said the voice. '*If you're not sure who I am right now, it doesn't matter. You'll work it out in time.*'

The voice did sound like their mother's voice, but this time the woman was speaking Thai, not Burmese.

'Why do you sound like my mother?'

'*All the women in our family have similar voices. Do you get it?*'

'No.'

Laughter. '*It's OK. You will. Time doesn't always flow in a straight line. Mya, the future isn't how you think it is. You'll find out. I know it's hard right now because you have abilities but no teacher. I can't do anything to interfere, but I can strengthen your heart. You will learn how to see along the river of time just as you already know how to move between the worlds.'*

'The river of time? Are you... calling me from the future?'

'I am with you always, Mya. Trust that you do have a place in the world. You will find it. Have faith.'

The connection cut.

'Who was that?' Thiri asked.

Mya lowered the phone, stunned.

'I think it was me,' she said.

New Jade

I CAN'T REALLY say whether coming so close to death changed me. It sure seemed like there was a lot of death in my life at once. Nana passed in September, a week after I beat Gretchen in Las Vegas. That hurt, but at least I knew her battle was over. As much as I missed her, I knew that by the end of her illness she had been ready to go.

It was good to have my mom home. I never thought I'd want to be fussed over and protected, but after what happened? I didn't mind so much.

Waldo had been waiting for me when I got back from Las Vegas. I cried all over him, but he never changed into Shea. Or a lion. He was just a beautiful cat, a good friend with a passion for fig cookies and pineapple yogurt. He still disappeared from time to time, but only in the way all cats do.

Shea's body was never found. I exchanged e-mails with Parawat, and she couldn't explain what happened. She told me she was going to focus on making sure Richard Fuller stayed in prison for the rest of his life. She said that Shea had understood the risks when he became involved.

'The rest is down to fate,' she wrote.

That didn't help me. I was in pain.

I didn't know what to think about fate.

I WAS IN my dressing room warming up and trying to decide if I had to puke yet when the door burst open and Malu came in.

'Atlantic City is so tacky,' she said. 'It's all crusty old white people with orthopedic shoes. Why can't you go down to Rio to fight?'

'Maybe next year,' I said. 'Let me get through this one first.'

It was December and I'd just turned eighteen. If I could beat Keisha Grant tonight, I'd win my first title.

If. Keisha's not exactly made of strawberry jam.

'How's my mom?'

'I talked her out of coming back here. She doesn't want to break your concentration, but she'll be in Mr. B's box, cheering for you.'

I started working the kinks out of my neck, but I could sense Malu giving me the Malu-eye.

'What?' I said.

'Cake asked me to give you this. From Mya.'

She held out a letter. I unfolded the thin airmail paper and a photo fell out. The letter was written in Thai, with Cake's English translation pencilled in between the lines.

Dear Jade,

I hope you are healthy, my friend. Thank you for the toys. Baby Lek enjoys the cars. Pook is getting used to nagas and is not freaked out anymore. She is a kind grandmother to us.

Pook asked me to stay on the farm and not go to the forest for a while. She says I must be an example to the others so they won't be animals. Maybe I will change my mind about this! I will come through your spider plant and surprise you! I am kidding. Maybe I'm not kidding!

Soon we will have internet at the camp and we can talk face to face. Until then I am keeping you in my prayers.

Last week I saw Kala Sriha in the jungle, near the farm. He watches. You told me you are sad about Shea. I understand, Jade. Thiri and I still miss our parents. Pook cannot find them yet, but we won't give up.

I believe we live many lives. I hope you will be happy in this life. The future is very large. You wouldn't believe me if I told you how big it is.

Mya

P.S. Can you send Eva's recipe for pączki? Everyone here wants to eat them.

I looked at the photo. Pook was in the middle with one arm around Mya and the other around Mya's sister Thiri. I'd never seen Mya really smile before. The effect was dazzling.

I wiped away a couple tears. Shea hadn't died for nothing.

'Oh no, none of that,' Malu said, whisking the letter away before I could drip on it. 'You got to stay hard for this fight. Keisha's probably over there in her dressing room chewing on some raw steak or something.'

I laughed. 'Khari said almost the exact same thing.'

'Did he?' Malu made a hmmph sound. 'I saw him hanging around outside like a big giant puppy. What's going on with the two of you?'

'Nothing,' I said, and she snorted.

I could see myself in the dressing room mirror. I hadn't even thought about Khari that way, not lately. And I used to want him so bad.

Could I be the same girl who had been so intimidated by Eva that I'd gone outside to visit Quinton instead of standing up for myself? Was I the same Old Jade who had lost my shit all over Tommy Zhang and accidentally set in motion this whole chain of events that had ended up with Richard Fuller in jail, Mya on Pook's farm, and Shea dead?

I don't know. They say you can't put your foot in the same river twice. Maybe I was still the same river, but there was a lot of water gone downstream since that day I'd woken up with a black eye and a bad attitude.

'Khari and me are just friends,' I said. 'I had my chance, but I decided to take a different path. That's how it's meant to be.'

Malu looked surprised. Maybe I even surprised myself. My ass says all kinds of things I don't expect.

AFTER SHE LEFT me alone in the dressing room, I started going through my pre-fight rituals. First, I puked. Then I brushed my teeth and did a little shadowboxing. I was probably outmatched by Keisha Grant, and I didn't really care.

I picked up my rope, did some skipping in the dressing room, thinking of the kids in Bangkok training hard every day. I imagined Pook setting up her camp—if she wasn't afraid of nagas, why should I be afraid to be happy? Maybe I just had to accept that the things that make me happy are the things that make most people run the other way.

'Jade? You ready?' Mr B. was tapping on the door.

Limping a little, I followed him down the hall to the open doorway where I could see my team waiting for me. The lights and the noise and the music hit me like a wave. It was everything I ever wanted.

'I'm ready,' I said.

Acknowledgements

I started working on *Shadowboxer* in 2008, which is a long time ago now! A lot of people have helped me; if I've overlooked anyone, I hope they will forgive me.

For their thoughtful and encouraging readings of various drafts I would like to thank Stephanie Burgis, Kim Raimann Harnett, Justina Robson, Renée Sweet, Nicky Browne, Farah Mendlesohn and Alis Rasmussen. For professional advice I'm grateful to Karen Mahoney, Patrick Ness and Mic Cheetham.

When it comes to writing across cultures, I tried to follow the guidance in *Writing the Other* by Nisi Shawl and Cynthia Ward. I did as much research as I could, and I ran the book by people who know the cultures. No doubt I will have made mistakes here, but I have done my sincere best. I'm grateful to Lee Ferguson for telling me about life in a Muay Thai camp in Bangkok. I thank Rochita Loenen-Ruiz and Aliette de Bodard for talking at length with me about the mistakes writers make when working across cultures, and for helping me to recognise when I was making them. Dariya Suebkraisorn was instrumental in advising on cultural detail and I especially value her suggestions for ways to depict Thailand without continually falling back on stereotypes. I am indebted to Azyaded Huerta for her kind assistance with details of Latino culture in the New York City area. I thank Marianne de Pierres, Caroline Holley, Tori Truslow, and Samuel Cerritos for offering valuable contacts.

Huge thanks to my partner Steve Morris for explaining so much about MMA and for technical advice on fights and training.

My agent Alex Adsett believed in this project even in the times when I lost faith. Thanks, Alex. I'm grateful to Erik Mohr for applying so much talent and effort to the cover art. I would like to thank my editor Jon Oliver as well as Ben Smith, Michael Molcher, Simon Parr, David Moore, and everyone else at Ravenstone. Working with you guys has been such a pleasure.

Finally, a big shout-out to my kids: Tyrone, Rhiannon, and Sean, who are the motivation behind everything I do.